Like a jaguar, Ethan slipped from her favorite chair and stopped an inch from her face. His warm breath singed her lips as he pinned her to the spot with his gaze. Her palms grew sweaty and her knees weakened. Somehow she forgot to breathe with those sea-gray irises holding her in place.

"I'm going to find out the truth, Audrey." His silky voice conflicted with the dagger-like words. Just as the desire in his eyes conflicted with the very purpose of his presence. "When I do, you'll want to spill everything to me then."

His lips parted and his gaze moved to her mouth. The inch between them became a millimeter. If only her mind wouldn't let her care anymore, she'd let her body loose. Explore every wild thought in her mind.

"If you find out the whole truth, I won't have to spill anything. To anyone."

Praise for Susan Sheehey

AUDREY'S PROMISE was a finalist in
the NTRWA 2013 Great Expectation Writing Contest
Single Title Category

Audrey's Promise

by

Susan Sheehey

Audrey's Promise

Cover Art by *Angela Anderson*

The Wild Rose Press, Inc.
PO Box 708
Adams Basin, NY 14410-0708
Visit us at www.thewildrosepress.com

Publishing History
First Champagne Rose Edition, 2013
Print ISBN 978-1-61217-929-2
Digital ISBN 978-1-61217-930-8

Published in the United States of America

Dedication

To My Son—Dreams Come True
To My Family—For Your Love
To all my critique partners, who helped me grow,
this is the start of something wonderful

Chapter One

Audrey Allen squirmed under the dozen cameras and bright lights glaring on her face. Sitting in the sofa chair across from the TV anchor might as well have been a police interrogation. *What am I doing here in front of these bloodsucking media fiends?*

"And we're back in five, four..." the producer counted from behind the shadows of the camera.

Because I have a sick need to constantly punish myself.

An even brighter light switched on and burned into Audrey's retinas. Her normal motto of keeping her distance from reporters had to be sacrificed like a Mayan virgin to cruel gods, if only for three minutes. Every nerve ending in her body compelled her to stand and walk out. She pulled the collar of her sapphire blouse closer to her neck and forced a smile instead.

Breathe. Smile, Audrey. You agreed to this.

"Welcome back, folks. I'm Cathy Claise here with Texas State Senate candidate, Audrey Allen."

Could this woman's hair be any more bleached? Sandra Dee meets televangelist Jan Crouch in her mid-forties, desperate to look a decade fresher. But viewers had no idea she looked this fake up close. The magic of TV.

"Audrey has captured the political field by storm, stunning all of Dallas's second district as the one candidate to take on Wyatt Williams in this surprising runoff election. Audrey, how have you managed to earn votes from both liberals and conservatives? Some conservatives criticize that you refuse to answer questions on family and religion to hide your deep-set liberal views."

I knew this was a bad idea. Fire fused to Audrey's throat and spread up her jawbone. Even with the oncoming heartburn, she knew this question was bound to come up. Journalists latched onto any pinprick of weakness and blasted it into a gaping wound, turning what was nothing into a hemorrhage of lies and misinterpretations. Despite her heart rate thumping against her sternum, Audrey kept smiling.

As she opened her mouth to answer, she threw a glance over Cathy's shoulder to her campaign manager, Miranda Gates, who'd stopped guzzling coffee and stared back at her.

"Cathy, I'm glad you brought that up." *That way I can quash your attempt to sideswipe me.* "First of all, I'm happy my message has reached both conservatives and liberals on the independent ticket. After all, if elected I'll be serving both parties equally. However, the only thing liberal about me is the high-def powder on my face from the make-up crew here."

Audrey continued through the muffled snickers from behind the cameras, "Just because I don't talk about my family or religious views doesn't mean I don't have them. I'm proud of my family. I'm the person I am today because of them." *Even though they may not be proud of me.*

"My focus right now is my campaign and the people I intend to help with my platforms. Not marriage. So many women in my district need help and a safe place to seek support. The Women's Crisis Center I'm sponsoring will provide that refuge."

Way to plug in the WCC, Aud. She could almost hear Miranda's cheers, silenced by guzzling more coffee. She watched Cathy open her mouth to jab another potential zinger, but Audrey's fire was up.

"And Cathy, my personal faith has nothing to do with my ability to be an effective state senator. My experience in Texas politics has taught me that an ability to work with others and keep a level head is the best way to help everyone, without losing your sanity in the process."

Cathy's laugh-on-command was more a nervous cackle, devoid of genuine emotion. It bubbled under Audrey's skin like hydrogen peroxide. *This desperate TV anchor was more fake than half the plastic-surgery-addicted women of mid-town.* But also the most watched by that demographic.

"Austin has its way of piling on the body count at the Capitol steps," Cathy quipped. "You seem more than ready to take on Wyatt Williams next week. Though the other senators from around the state might be less forgiving."

Audrey bit the side of her tongue to keep from rolling her eyes.

"This Women's Crisis Center has a fundraising event coming up, is that correct?" Cathy added.

Finally, something worth talking about.

"Saturday night at the W Hotel in Dallas. We'll be auctioning some valuable gifts for this incredible charity."

"Don't you think this event on Thanksgiving

weekend is bad timing? Won't many people have spent all their money on Black Friday?"

She never quits. "On the contrary, Cathy. This is the season of being thankful for your blessings and there's never a better time to give back to those who need a little help and compassion."

"Well spoken, from The Peacemaker of the Second District." Cathy flashed her veneers at Audrey until her cheeks cracked. A final turn to the camera let Audrey breathe. Cathy peered into the camera. "Thank you, Ms. Allen, for joining us here today. Stick around, viewers. We'll be right back with the perfect trimming for that Thanksgiving turkey."

The producer with a massive headset held up his fingers to count down. "And we're clear."

The microphone clipped to her silk blouse was the first to come off, followed by the bulky battery in her back pocket. As she fumbled with the wire, Cathy did as well with her words, fake yet again. "Thanks so much for coming today. And sorry for that last round of questioning. My boss would have fired me if I hadn't asked them." Fluffing her bleached bob, Cathy motioned for her make-up assistant. But trusty Miranda stopped her.

"Just how many times will you face termination before you'll practice ethics?"

Amazing how her fake smile dissipated so quickly into a Nancy Grace scowl. *She must practice that in the mirror.* "Politics is a brutal game, and our viewers expect us to ask the important questions."

"I think viewers are more interested in the truth, not sleight-of-hand tactics. Good luck getting us to visit your show again in the future." Miranda bit with a half-smile. Her hazel eyes pierced Cathy's plastic exterior. Audrey loved Miranda's passion and unwavering loyalty, and even more loved watching her take the graceful kill. But the election was seven days away. As much as Audrey hated to do it, they needed to give the media a sliver of mercy.

"Cathy, thank you for having me on the show today." The gracious tone was a lot easier to muster than Audrey expected, now that she'd handed back the microphone to the adolescent-looking sound tech. "And have a wonderful Thanksgiving."

Ten years of interning in the political quagmire as her mentor's aide and eventual protégé had taught Audrey that cooler heads always prevailed on the senate floor. But no amount of time or turmoil would ever dampen her dislike of the media. Stepping off of the artificial living room in the small studio, away from the intruding cameras, the nagging necessity of the media grew with every ding of Miranda's phone.

"I need a Diet, Mandy." Tension pulled at the muscles in her neck. Maybe it was the weight of the extra make-up they made her wear, or the weight of the election taking its toll. Soon enough it would all be over, and hopefully Audrey could make the impact that her district desperately needed.

Without taking her eyes off her phone and lightning-fast thumb, Miranda reached into her massive purse and pulled out a silver can.

"You're scary sometimes. But I love you." Audrey opened the can and sipped the delectable bubbles, letting it run across her taste buds.

"Pampering you is what I do best."

"More like handling. Have you heard back from

the investors yet?" Audrey asked between gulps. "We need their support for that building, otherwise the Crisis Center won't get off the ground."

"Relax, Aud. They'll come through." Miranda shoved her phone in her pocket and readjusted her purse. "Besides, I need you to put your Peacemaker hat back on, because there's someone you need to meet."

"Who?" Another gulp of Diet.

"Ethan Tanner. He's standing in the corner waiting for an interview with you."

Soda went up her nose, burning every inch of the way up.

"I thought I said I didn't want to talk to him," she managed to say as she grabbed a tissue from Miranda's purse.

"Audrey, we need his interview to help us in the polls. This runoff election is getting brutal. With as much attention as his columns get and his series on every candidate, we can't afford to pass this up." The distance was closing between them and the corner as Miranda prodded her along, where a shadowy figure loomed against the wall.

"I do *not* want to give an interview to the *Dallas Morning Journal*'s most ruthless investigative journalist, just so he can write one of his infamous exposés. He's a glorified dirt digger." With each word Audrey lowered her voice.

Though hidden in shadows, Audrey could see the figure smile, or more precisely the cheeks rise, in a mocking grin. He wasn't tall, maybe an inch higher than her, but something about his air that screamed "dare me."

"Shh. Peacemaker face," Miranda whispered back

just as they approached the dreaded figure.

Audrey took a deep breath, forcing her diplomatic smile once again and braced herself for another onslaught. Ethan finally pushed himself away from the wall and stepped out from the shadows.

Every impression Audrey had of male journalists consisted of pushy individuals in casual and baggy clothing, often appearing as if they had just rolled out of bed and grabbed their bags from a city dumpster. Ethan's wrinkled sports jacket and cargo pants certainly fit the stereotype, but everything else about this journalist shook her resolve.

Damn, it has to be illegal to have a smile that charming. The way it spread across his shaven jaw line and cheeks and up to the corners of his light gray eyes stunned her. The color matched his sports coat and glimmered under the studio lights as he reached out to shake hands. *Strong hands, hmm.* Smooth chin, wide shoulders, and short mahogany hair that curled at the ends. Now Audrey knew how he'd managed to dig up so much dirt in his career. He'd wooed it out of his sources with his slick style.

All his charm and momentum vanished the second he opened his mouth. "Audrey Allen, pleasure to meet you, but I only dig up dirt on the weekends. The rest of the time I just watch the stories unravel themselves."

"And you just happen to be watching from a shaded corner every time?" Audrey pulled away from his soft hand, amazed by his strong grip. Its warmth countered his cold words.

"That's what makes me good at my job. Speaking of which, I'd love to catch you in a corner…for a quick chat." The glimmer in his eye was hard to miss.

Slippery and full of…something. A wannabe Casanova. Another check in the journalist stereotype. If Audrey wasn't so occupied with trying to dislike him, she might feel sorry for him.

"I'm sure you would," Audrey murmured, hiding a smirk.

"We're interested to see how your columns for this runoff election will play out. What will you focus on for these pieces?" Miranda chucked her empty cup in a nearby trashcan and flung her ponytail off her shoulder. Hard as nails when she needed to be, and Audrey needed it for this one.

"Well, I like more casual conversations. Fireside chats, so to speak." He winked his long lashes at Audrey.

What was he searching for, an interview or a date? "Do you plan on asking the same questions with Wyatt Williams? The same fireside chat?" Audrey let her smirk rise to the surface. The more this guy got on her nerves, the more she liked throwing a curve ball at him.

"I'm equally fair with all my interviews."

"And equally brutal." Audrey wanted it to sound like an insult, but why did this feel like flirting? She never bantered with media. *What are you doing?*

"I'll be up front, Audrey." Ethan pulled out a hand recorder. "What ghosts do you have in your closet?" The wink he threw at her didn't disguise the seriousness of his intent, despite the playful tone.

"Don't you mean skeletons?" Miranda interrupted.

"Nope, ghosts."

"What's the difference?" Miranda eyed the recorder.

"Skeletons are only scary. Ghosts from your past

can truly haunt you."

"Aren't you a little old to believe in ghosts?" Audrey asked with an infectious smile.

"No. They make my job the most entertaining." The light flashed in Ethan's eyes and his grin became wicked. Audrey's heart thudded against her sternum. It wasn't fair to look that enticing.

"Sorry to burst your pubescent bubble, but Halloween is over." Audrey smiled through Miranda's chuckle. But she couldn't take her eyes off Ethan, assessing his resilience. *Would he push and badger just like every other journalist? Were his cojones as big as he flaunted?*

Almost on cue, his eyes darkened with hunger. He switched off his recorder and placed it back in his pocket. "Then I look forward to an adult conversation. Are you free now, or perhaps this afternoon?"

"This afternoon should be good. Unless you have plans with family for Thanksgiving." Miranda reached into her pocket and pulled out her phone, searching for an open slot in Audrey's schedule.

"No plans for Thanksgiving," Ethan replied without taking his avaricious eyes off of Audrey. Crossing her arms to the sudden feeling of being an open book felt necessary. Ethan's smile grew more playful with every second. "So this afternoon or tomorrow morning if you prefer. Before all the hustle bustle of turkey dinners and football."

"Can't tomorrow morning. I'm driving back home for Thanksgiving, so we'll squeeze him in this afternoon." Pretending to browse her schedule over Miranda's shoulder gave her a brief escape from those probing gray eyes.

"She has a few meetings this afternoon, but we could—" Miranda stopped and cocked her head at Ethan. "You said no plans for Thanksgiving?"

Oh no. Miranda's sideways smile was not a good sign and made the worms crawl up Audrey's spine again.

"Nope," Ethan grinned.

"When is your article deadline?" Miranda spoke faster with every word. Excited about something Audrey wouldn't share in.

"Saturday night, running in the Sunday paper before the election."

"I have a great idea." Miranda turned to Audrey and braced her elbow. "Why don't you join Audrey for Thanksgiving? She's going back home and you can see what her family is like. Get a more in-depth look for your article."

Audrey's sharp breath rocketed through her nerves. *Has she lost her mind? This was her great idea?* The most conniving journalist in Dallas joining her at home was a certain recipe for disaster. Media belonged on the other side of a fifty-foot canyon, not in her hometown, and certainly not in her childhood home. *Just how in-depth was this going to get?*

Audrey's reaction must have sparked a fire in Ethan's mind, as his smile stretched across his cheeks, looking at her like a lamb ready for slaughter. Bringing his satchel forward, he pulled out a small notepad and pen. "Excellent idea! You leave tomorrow? What's the address?"

Audrey grabbed Miranda's arm, but then immediately let it go. She was in front of media; she couldn't look scared or pushy. It would only invite more inquiry. So instead, she faked disappointment. "Sorry, Ethan. There's no room at my family's house for another guest. We'll have to keep the interview to this afternoon."

"I'll stay at a hotel. What time do we leave in the morning?"

The urge to slap a smile off of someone's face had never been stronger than that moment. Until Miranda beamed back at her over this horrible plan.

"Ethan, excuse us for just one moment." Audrey turned and walked away, knowing Miranda would follow. Striding calmly to the break room was harder to pull off, since every muscle wanted her to run, despite wearing her black two-inch heels. She craved something to quench the rumbling in her stomach, and soda wasn't cutting it. The vending machine became her new target.

"What are you thinking?" Audrey spat under a breath. Miranda joined her side instantly, gripping her phone. "That man broke the story of the Dallas county commissioner's embezzling scandal, and you just invited him to join me home for Thanksgiving?"

"Keep your friends close and enemies closer. It's the perfect strategy."

"I haven't been home in ten years, and my first trip back you want me to drag along a scandal seeker?" *More like rabble-rouser.* Audrey was familiar with those. And her hometown's reaction to them. Audrey scanned the vending machine's limited options and settled on animal crackers. She yanked a dollar from her wallet and inserted it into the slot. When it shot back out at her, she snatched it and flipped it over.

"What's there to be nervous about? You have

nothing to hide. Once he sees how wonderful you are and your small town roots, he'll write the piece we need to clinch the election. If he's convinced, everyone else will be, too."

The dollar spit out at her again and Audrey clenched her fists.

"Here." Miranda pulled out change from her pocket and pushed it into the slot.

"You've never met my family," Audrey continued as she waited for the animal crackers to fall. "For all you know, they could be redneck hicks with a billion embarrassing stories about me they'd love to sell to the highest bidder." *Unlikely, since they haven't visited me since I left. But Miranda doesn't need to know that either.*

"Doubtful. They raised you, didn't they? The Peacemaker. And you came out mostly normal for an obsessive control freak."

"Don't call me that. It's a dumb political label from the media." Audrey rolled her eyes and ripped open the bag. The first animal cracker couldn't get down her throat fast enough.

"Dang, hyena! Slow down."

"I didn't have breakfast."

"You were that nervous? We really need to help you get over this aversion to cameras."

"It's not the cameras, Mandy. It's the people behind them. News people. And if they *have* to exist, I'd rather them behind cameras and *not* in my home."

"Audrey." Miranda placed her hand over the bag and caught Audrey's eyes. "We need this. Poll numbers show you're neck and neck with Wyatt, and we need something to bring you over the top. Tanner has the highest read column in Dallas. If you can convince him how great your ideas are, the election is ours."

Miranda was right. Audrey didn't want to say it, since something in her gut roiled again. She expected a little bird to appear on her shoulder and whisper into her ear *you'll regret this*. But there were so many who needed her help. Who'd sat in her office and begged her to make a difference in their lives. The Crisis Center needed her to win the election. There was only one gut-wrenching conclusion. To win, she needed Ethan Tanner, the worst newsman. Audrey grimaced.

Chapter Two

"This is gonna be better than I thought," Ethan laughed into his cell phone. "And when I nail this story, McGevin, you're going to give me the referral I deserve." Ethan shoved a set of socks and boxers in his overnight bag that sat amongst the dirty laundry scattered across his mattress in the studio apartment. He'd have to lug his clothes to the Laundromat when he got back from nailing Audrey Allen to the wall.

Oh, what a scrumptious image. An unlikely one though, once he found the dirt for his article, thereby ruining yet another politician. She had a sweet pair of legs and perfectly rounded ass hidden under her silk suit. Audrey Allen was prettier than most female politicians he'd met, in a woman-in-the-coffee-shop kind of way. Wavy, dark chocolate hair to her shoulders and blueberry eyes accentuated her deep rose lipstick. Those thin lips must have spent most of her life frowning, but when she smiled, even the fake ones lit up her whole face. It took all his energy not to lean in and see if she tasted like raspberries.

At that point, she probably wouldn't be receptive to any kind of night with him.

"You're slicker than hot syrup, Ethan," Bose McGevin replied. "Only you could have pulled off an entire weekend trip with Audrey Allen. Your idea?"

"I'd love to take credit for it, but it was her

campaign manager's idea." Stepping over more dirty towels and clothes, Ethan perused his bathroom shelf and debated which colognes to pack. The shaving kit and toothbrush went next, along with his phone charger and laptop.

"Wow. The brunette with glasses and phone addiction?"

"Yep, Miranda Gates. Talks like a New Yorker without the accent."

"Never would have expected that insane suggestion from her. Must not be as smart as those glasses make her look."

Audrey was the hottest chick in politics. Even though most of her competition was middle-aged women and pudgy good ol' boys, her senator portrait would definitely be worthy of a men's calendar. If he stuck around long enough after the article, he might think of pursuing a two- or three-night stand. Like she'd want one after he killed her election chances. But still, she'd chosen politics and thereby must welcome the scrutiny and brutality of the media.

Holy hell, when did I start thinking like my boss? My mother would shoot me.

Ethan yanked a few buttoned shirts off hangers and rolled them all together before he tossed them in his bag. "Her mistake is my gain. I'm sure she's hoping I'll see the 'family side' of Allen and have nothing negative to report. But there's always dirty laundry in a politician's closet."

Politicians are all the same, just like my father. And he's the dirtiest of them all.

"Easy, Trigger. Gates might not be as smart as we thought, but I guarantee Allen will be tougher. I'd say go for any means to get your story with her, but I don't think she'll let you closer than a pit bull."

"I'll wear her down. It's what I do best. Hell, I've got two hours alone with her on the drive out there."

"Where's her hometown?"

"Mackineer? Some tiny backwoods town just north of Tyler." The drive was the part he was most looking forward to. One on one, no interruptions, completely candid. A person's driving revealed a lot about them, but how they reacted to outsiders in their personal space screamed volumes more. He opened a drawer and pulled out a long strip of condoms. *Hmm...I really* am *thinking like Bose.*

He tossed them in the bag.

"Small towns are prime for juicy stories. This should be walkin' a poodle in the park for you."

Ethan stopped perusing the books on his desk, which was shoved against the wall and littered with magazines and newspaper clippings. It had been months since he'd seen the oak underneath where he'd scratched his name on the surface as a kid. "Bose, I'm serious. When I nail this article, I want your next phone call to be your producer friend in New York. I'm perfect for the job up there and you know it."

The hesitation on the other end of the phone felt like a threat. *Don't you dare, Bose.*

"Bose, your word or I won't give you the Wyatt Williams article I've already written."

"Fine. New York will be my first call. But that Allen article better light up the phone lines and race up the ratings."

"I'm sure it will." He grinned as he tossed his camera in the bag. He'd have to go out for a drink tonight and celebrate the upcoming victory. Jack on the rocks sounded perfect about now, which is why he'd settle for a black coffee, a bowl of peanuts, and the first coed who offered to buy him a shot.

"When do you leave?"

"First thing in the morning. Thanksgiving dinner with the family, tour of the town on Friday, and we come back that night. She has some big charity fundraiser Saturday night here in Dallas that she can't miss. That gives me a full day to write the article of the year."

"Updates twice a day. And don't grow a conscience when you're out there."

Laughter murmured from inside his chest. "Not likely."

Ethan snapped the phone shut and tossed it on the bed.

Finally. Nine years later and I finally have my shot. Screw you, Dad.

Chapter Three

"Screw you, Clayton!"

"You're just an ignorant redneck!"

The two men were held back from each other across the crowded conference room by a dozen arms, including two police officers.

Audrey shook her head, amazed that she and only one other person in the room remained calm among the turmoil. Ethan Tanner leaned against the back wall, a wicked half smile on his lips as he held a recorder in his hand. *What in the hell is he doing here?*

The vicious words between the two men, who were still being dragged apart by police officers, didn't crack Audrey's resolve an inch, but Ethan's tempting physique and debonair stance stirred up her nerves. *Focus, Audrey.*

She stood from the center chair in the front of the room and whistled, loud and piercing. The room silenced as both men finally stopped and glared at her. "Violence will not be tolerated," she spoke firmly.

Her poker face consisted of calm and stern eye contact; no emotion. Unlike the two red-faced men who slowly took their seats. The relief on the cops' faces rippled across the room. "I don't think either of you want to spend this evening in jail away from your families. This is a passionate topic for many, but name-calling doesn't solve anything."

"They only care about their bottom line and whether or not they'll have enough for Christmas bonuses!" Tommy shouted, blotch-faced and stiff necked. If the bald man had any hair, it would have been white.

"Tommy, we are so close to a solution. With the concessions both sides have already made, do you really want throw all that work away over just ten grand?"

With a shake of his head, Tommy clamped his mouth shut and leaned back in his chair.

This was what Audrey loved best. Everyone's eyes focused on the solution. One everyone could live with. If they'd just let go of their egos and open their ears.

If only one man didn't keep looking at her like his own personal holiday feast.

"The ranching industry is booming in this area, and we want to keep those jobs here. If it weren't booming, we'd have a different problem on keeping people from the unemployment line. So arguments like this are a *good* thing."

Reluctant murmurs of approval filtered throughout the room. A quick glance to the other side of the room and Audrey received the head-nod from Miranda, coupled with a knowing smile.

"From where I sit, you both need each other to keep this industry successful. Ranchers need Clayton's distribution company for your product. And distributors don't exist without the ranchers. So you help yourselves by helping each other. Calling your customer an ignorant redneck isn't the best way to ensure repeat business."

Clayton's lips pursed and he crossed his arms.

"Telling your distributor to screw himself only makes him less willing to help you in the future." Her admonished stare to Tommy brought the same response.

"Folks, ten grand is the only thing keeping everyone from getting paid and having a great Thanksgiving with their families. Which Clayton concedes his company can spread across the five-year contract." When her eyes met the plump man on her left, he nodded. "Tommy, I've seen that old tractor sitting out behind your barn for the last seven years. The one you've meant to sell but never got around to. Driving around these parts as much as I have, I've noticed almost all of you ranchers have some piece of unused equipment." A dozen more nods around the room made Audrey smile. "Something that you can either sell or donate and get the tax write-off. Things you already planned to do anyway. All of which can go toward this gap. Combine that, I bet you'll have more than enough to cover this. Maybe enough to give you all that unexpected Christmas bonus."

More nods and approving murmurs. Miranda gave her a discreet thumbs-up while Ethan jotted down a few notes on his notepad, juggled in the same hand as his recorder. *Damn, that smile of his was distracting.*

"Now, who wants to call this a done deal, leave the beef business alone and go home to fat Thanksgiving turkeys?"

When the papers were signed and the room cleared, Audrey brushed her hair from her face and gathered her briefcase. A heartbeat later, Miranda patted her on the back. "Damn, you're good. Your former boss couldn't get this dispute off his desk for six months, and you solve it in one meeting."

"It wasn't that hard to fix." They strolled out of the room. "Think of how more productive they'd be if they spent the same passion in their jobs as they did bickering."

Miranda handed Audrey another soda from her tote. "After you helped arrange the agreement for the homeless shelter, I told Mason you should take this one off his hands and he could retire in peace."

"Congressman Nichols has earned it. Meanwhile, Texas has lost an incredible asset in the Senate."

"Only to gain an even better one," Miranda smiled and gave her another pat on the shoulder. "One that will stick around for a long time to come."

"God willing." Audrey cracked open the soda and sipped. She had to cut this habit, but long hours of campaigning and still performing her duties as a Congressman's aid threw her New Year's resolution off the priority list.

"What was Ethan Tanner doing here?" She asked after she recovered from the fizzing bubbles.

"I invited him. Wanted to show him how good you are at what you do best."

"I couldn't concentrate. And I doubt this negotiation will be highlighted in the article he's trying to twist against me."

"I think he's sweet on you."

Audrey snorted. "Like a snake on a mouse."

"You're sexier than a mouse. And twice as smart."

"Audrey Allen." Clayton waddled across the lobby. "Brilliant work in there."

"Thanks, Clayton." She shook his outstretched hand and sausage-like fingers. "Amazing how much one can accomplish if you remember where your paycheck comes from: your customers."

"Too true," he replied with a laugh, his belly shaking like a Jell-O mold behind his thick, southern drawl. "I'll be telling my bosses about your work here. If you're ever interested in the corporate world, you let me know."

"Tempting offer," Audrey smiled, not missing Ethan's raised eyebrow from across the lobby. "But I have a great job already."

"Well, in the meantime you've got my vote."

"And mine." Tommy, the bulky rancher, shook Audrey's hand. "All us ranchers have your back, Miss Allen."

"Thanks, Tommy. Tell Cora I'll miss her delicious corn casserole this Thanksgiving."

"Maybe she'll save some for you," Tommy laughed and pushed through the double doors. A cold blast of air burst through the lobby. When Clayton moved to follow, Miranda caught up with him.

"If you're free this Saturday, there's a fundraiser for the Crisis Center that we're sponsoring…"

Miranda's campaigning drifted outside, leaving Audrey a moment of panic in the lobby with Ethan Tanner. Alone.

The man was lean, yet toned, even under that frumpy jacket. Evidently good at more than just writing articles and shattering careers. Shattering a woman's senses seemed a natural forte of his.

How long would a guy like that last under the covers?

Whoa! Get it together, Audrey.

"You have a gift, Audrey Allen." His words sizzled

from across the marble floor. His footsteps bounced off the walls at the same rhythm as her heartbeat. The cold air in the lobby was nothing against the urge to unbutton her jacket from the escalating heat from that man's eyes, staring back into hers. "Blinding men by your words and three-button blazers."

His eyes roved over her suit, slowly, lazily. Audrey moved her briefcase in front of her, shifting her weight to one leg. "I'm not surprised you can't tell the difference between blinding someone or making them see reason. You're too busy distorting the truth to make it fit your own need."

"And politicians don't? That's a whore calling a prostitute a slut."

"Excuse me?"

"Just a figure of speech," his lips quirked.

"You're a breath away from losing your interview, Mr. Tanner."

"Lighten up." Ethan adjusted his messenger bag strap on his shoulder. "No implication on you. On the contrary, I think you're one of the most prudish women in politics."

"Prudish?" Audrey couldn't stop her raised inflection.

"Not a hint of cleavage, no skirt above the knee line...I doubt you own a single shirt or blouse that doesn't go all the way up to your neck."

"Perhaps because I'd rather people pay attention to my words than my body."

Ethan's eyes flamed and his entire face lit up. "Not possible."

Why didn't this creep have a dozen sexual harassment claims against him? Is this his idea of a compliment? Bringing him home to meet her family was a big mistake. Trusting the media was already difficult enough for her, but keeping an eye on this media man, as slippery and conniving as he was, would make it unbearable.

"Unlike you, Mr. Tanner, I love making a difference. Simplifying a problem, getting everyone on the same side, winners all around. No problem is impossible to solve. You just have to find the right foundation on which to build. The rest are just details. As long as you're willing to listen and keep your *libido* out of it."

Heat flushed her cheeks as her eyes drifted down and rested on his crotch, however briefly, and caught sight of the bulge against his Dockers. To which she was even more mortified when Ethan shoved his hands in his pockets and caught her wandering stare. He leaned forward, their bodies only a few inches apart. His warm breath smelled like peppermint gum, mingled with his musky cologne.

"I'm looking forward to this weekend, Audrey." He smirked. "Should be a lot of fun." He lingered a moment longer, his mouth parted and waiting. When Audrey couldn't move, he stepped back and opened the door, the wind rushing in and slapping her in the face.

That's what I'm afraid of.

Chapter Four

Audrey shook her head at the press release in the *Dallas Morning Journal* about the fundraiser. The Crisis Center's logo was supposed to be next to the article, but instead the editors published her headshot. Though black and white, she hated that her skin appeared splotchy and her freckles could never be erased, no matter how much makeup they used. But what she hated more was taking attention away from the Crisis Center.

Miranda had told her not to fuss over it. Either way, it was good publicity for both her election and the Crisis Center. Besides, she had a much bigger article to prepare for. Audrey tossed the paper in the trash and grabbed her brush from the bathroom sink. The hot shower hadn't released the tension in her shoulders, so chamomile tea was next. Most of her day had been a whirlwind of interviews and glad-handing voters on her platforms. Relaxing in pajamas alone in her apartment felt like a gift. Elections were only the precursor to life as a senator. *If only.*

After she brushed out the damp strands of hair along her neck, she strolled into the kitchen and poured the steaming water from the stove into a coffee mug. Papers lay scattered across the dining room table behind her, waiting to be reviewed as her tea brewed.

Legislative agendas, letters from campaign

supporters, and cost estimates for the Crisis Center building all blurred together in a white flood of responsibility. Audrey pulled the edges of her purple bathrobe tighter across her chest. She knew how to handle a room. Her internship provided her the perfect means to study what tactics worked best in negotiations, how a simple hand gesture or body movement signaled resistance or defeat on a bill. Getting people to air their hesitations and secret motivations is why the media coined her notable nickname: The Peacemaker.

Audrey never saw it that way. It was all about getting people to find common ground and build from there. Though common ground was harder for politicians, Audrey had a knack for making the greater good come to light. Those ten years with her mentor, Congressman Mason Nichols, taught her everything she needed to know about Texas politics.

Despite her depression.

In the end, it was only about the people. The battered women, the innocent kids clinging to their mothers' arms and the helpless looks on their faces as they held Audrey's hand. She overcame her depression by focusing on the people, depending on her strength to do what was best. If only she could use that strength to let go of her dread about this weekend.

Ethan Tanner would be nothing but trouble. And she'd be hurt all over again. Only this time, splattered across every newspaper in Texas. Audrey turned away from the table and carried her tea to the sofa. Curling up on the cream suede cushion, she grabbed her sketchbook, which always sat on the windowsill behind the couch. Gliding the pencil over the thick paper, she created soft lines of the familiar hill next to a small pond lined with tall grass while the same thought drifted in her mind. This weekend was a mistake.

Home for the first time in ten years. The thought sent shivers through her nerves. The pressure between her shoulders grew, along with the weight. Toting a vicious journalist with her would only make it more difficult. Why hadn't she insisted to Miranda this was a bad idea? She needed to do this alone.

A sip from her tea filtered warmth down her throat, and her mind lingered on Ethan's face. Turning a new page in her sketchbook, her pencil went to work. Ethan's tongue was too sharp to have such clean lines angling his chin and cheekbones. At first glance his face was perfectly symmetrical: eyes, ears, and nothing lopsided about his mouth. But his hairline dipped a sliver lower on the right of his forehead. When he smiled, the dimple on his left was a smidge higher than the right.

If she used colored pencils, she might be able to fill in the exact color of his light pewter eyes, with a touch of cobalt by his pupils. But the pencil would capture the shadows between the layers in his irises. If anyone dared look through her sketchbook, she'd be embarrassed that she thought enough of a newsman to render his face. But it was one of several things Audrey kept hidden, along with a few things in her heart.

Not that there was anything malicious. Privacy was important to her. Everyone had the right to reflect on mistakes in peace. Granted, politics eroded that privacy a bit, but it wasn't just her life she needed to live. It was the lives of all the people who voted for her.

One in particular.

Her fingers caught the cynicism in Ethan's face, almost as if he whispered *liar* from the paper. She closed her sketchbook and placed it back on the sill. *Tea. More tea.*

The mug was empty in less than a minute. Sleep would make things seem better in the morning. *Fresh perspective, fresh start.* Her mother's words echoed in her mind. The bedroom was small, but homey with a few splashes of bold colors in the furniture. Other than the full bed with its lavender comforter, the bookcase against the far wall was the largest item in the room. She ran her fingers across the volumes and chose her favorite, *Emma* by Jane Austen.

Her suitcase had sat at the foot of her bed for the last week, packed and ready for a rough trip. Much like Audrey's emotions. She fought sleep for as long as she could, hoping the light and romantic reading would dissipate the repetitive tortured dreams of the last month. It didn't take long for Audrey to slip off to sleep, the book still open on her lap.

Twisted metal collapsed around her legs and the cold seeped into her bones. Wind scraped along her backside, sending a chill to her toes. The metal vibrated against her skin—am I shivering?—*as a siren rang in her ears. Audrey fought to open her eyes and shrieked in pain from the shards of glass covering her lashes. Red glass. Blood. Hers? Everything hurt, so it could be.*

Turning her head sent scorching spears into her brain. And an incessant pounding. She forced her eyes open again and focused on the image next to her. A chair. Something mangled and twisted lay in the seat. Circular, or it used to be. A steering wheel?

Muffled sounds came up from all around her as the

chill blew stronger at her back. The ringing billowed until she recognized they were voices.

"Help," she whispered.

"There's one over here," a distant voice called.

Audrey waited, expecting someone to come into view or to feel a hand on her arm. Seconds, or hours passed. Nothing.

"Help," she called again. Or maybe it was just her mind.

More minutes passed.

"They're gone. Check that pile."

Freezing streaks trailed down her cheeks. But she couldn't move. The urge to scream could only manifest through more freezing streaks.

Help.

"I got one!" a voice yelled.

More streaks seeped into her skin, numbing her face.

"Hang on, Audrey," the dark voice called over her trembling body. Pain soared through every muscle as her form was lifted from the mangled scraps, her legs twisted as they were pulled from the wreckage.

Her neck dangled over the voice's arm, whose face was covered in shadows, leaving only one image. The remnants of the driver's seat. Besides the steering wheel, it was empty. Who'd been driving?

Red surged into her eyes and the screams drowned out all other noise. Her screams. Hot red flooded her vision as the ice chill seeped through, drifting into darkness.

Chapter Five

"He's late." Audrey vented into the phone, tapping her thumb against the steering wheel.

"Did you call him?" Miranda asked. The yawn on the other side of the phone was contagious.

"I shouldn't have to. He's the one who wants the story." Audrey glanced at the dashboard. Time: 7:12 a.m. Temp: 48 degrees. The first chill of the year infiltrated North Texas with perfect timing. Great football weather for Thanksgiving. Though the color change in the trees of Dallas sucked in comparison to East Texas, a few reds and purples scattered across the yellows and browns in the shrubs by her condo. Audrey adjusted the heater and changed the radio station.

"Give him five more minutes, Aud." A coffee grinder spun in the background.

"When do you leave for Houston?"

"Flight's at noon. I'll be back Friday night to finish the final touches on the fundraiser." Miranda yawned again.

"Tell your family I'm sorry I'm taking up some of your vacation time."

"Oh, you know them. Just send 'em a fruit basket or a ham and they're good. They said to tell you if they lived in your district, you'd have their vote."

A red truck, dented with faded paint, pulled into the space next to her Acura. The windows were fogged, obscuring the driver's face. If it was Ethan, there was another unexpected trait for a journalist. They were supposed to drive eco-friendly two-doors, even though this was Texas.

The door squealed open and Ethan stepped out. Audrey held her breath and watched him. From her angle in the car, Audrey could only see his backside as he reached into the back bed. Dark jeans covered his slim waist and two cheeks worth a slap. Or squeeze.

Audrey whirled in her seat. *Where the hell did that come from? Focus on the radio.*

"He's here, finally." The journalist's round ass made her forget she was even holding a phone.

"Play nice," Miranda warned.

"Shouldn't you be saying that to him? Besides, I bought him coffee. That's as nice as I get at seven a.m."

"Relax. He's probably just as anxious as you are. Call me when you get there."

A knock on the trunk made her jump. Audrey flipped her phone shut and pulled the lever for the trunk. When her car sank with the weight of his luggage—*what did he pack, a box of books?*—she unlocked the doors.

Ethan sank into the passenger seat, put a bag by his feet, and shut the door. He was all grins with perfectly white teeth and an even more perfectly shaven face. "Mornin', sunshine."

Oh crap. He's a morning person. Amazing how sleek and toned he looked in baggy jeans and leather jacket. How could a journalist afford a custom fit coat? And he had way too much energy for Audrey's taste. The coffee was a bad idea.

"I didn't know how you took your coffee, so I

bought you a black." Audrey used her cup to block her frown. The pumpkin spice latte scent wasn't nearly as strong as Ethan's fresh cologne, now overtaking her senses in ways she didn't dare admit. But a quick glare at Ethan's Converse sneakers pulled her attention back to the purpose at hand.

"Aw, honey," Ethan started with a coo. "We're gonna get along great, I can tell." With a wink, he stripped off his black leather coat and tossed it in the back. He pulled out a small notepad from his bag and set it on the dash before he grabbed the coffee. "For future reference, I like my coffee like my women."

Audrey gave him a wary stare, her coffee cup poised in mid-air.

"Hot and sweet." His smile turned playful as he took his first sip.

Great. One of those *guys.* Bad pickup lines and infantile shoes. Audrey turned her head to lock the doors and rolled her eyes. The notorious Ethan Tanner was a wolf in awkward-adolescent-wannabe-player skin. This was going to be a long trip.

"But it's gonna take a lot more than coffee to soften me up just to write a puff piece about your campaign." Ethan clicked on his seatbelt and settled into his seat, absorbing the very air that surrounded her. Audrey plastered on her Peacemaker face and gave him an intent look.

"I'm not interested in glorified advertising."

"Then what *are* you interested in?" Those gray eyes bored straight back into hers with more sincerity than the words themselves. Her breath caught for a second before she spoke.

"The truth. A piece that shows the potential from

my platforms and the good they can do. Something that makes people's lives—"

A snore broke her concentration, and Ethan's head lay against the foggy window, mouth open. Audrey scowled. This guy took nothing seriously. Half of her mind told her to push him out of the car. Instead she threw the gear into Reverse and pulled out.

His snore broke into a chuckle. "Sorry, but you politicians need to lighten up. I asked what *you* were interested in. Not my article. What do you like to do when you're not kissing babies, posing for pictures, and negotiating between a bunch of good ol' boys?"

By the time he finished chuckling at her, Audrey had pulled out of the parking lot and onto the main road. The heat from her cheeks could have warmed the entire car to tropical levels. Despite the patience she had cultivated as The Peacemaker, this guy certainly tested her levels in just sixty seconds.

"Wyatt Williams may have an entire portfolio of glad-handing head shots, but while he's busy saying 'cheese' to anyone with a camera, I've been working in Austin to negotiate settlements on the budget, education, and setting up the Crisis Center. Turning a room full of stubborn politicians may not be as glamorous to your newspaper, but it accomplishes a lot."

Ethan raised his eyebrows and stared at her with a silly half smile.

"What?" she blurted.

"You have pumpkin latte on your upper lip."

Audrey licked her upper lip. *Shit. All of that to prove my seriousness as a politician, and I pull a milk ad.* She grabbed a napkin from the tray and wiped her mouth. "You were going to let me keep pontificating with coffee on my lip, weren't you?"

"Of course. It looked delicious."

Audrey crumpled up the napkin and threw it at him.

"Just tryin' to loosen you up. You've been around donors and voters too much, and I want to get to know the real Audrey Allen."

Her smile faltered and she fought to focus on the road signs as she merged onto the highway. *The real Audrey Allen. If only he knew.* It sounded almost haunting coming from a man who was just looking for scandals.

"This is the real me. No schmoozing or BS-ing."

"Sure," he tossed back, grabbing his notepad from the dash. "Bullshit is the official language of politics. But your dialect is sweeter."

"Why, because I'm a woman?"

"You said it, not me."

"Figures."

"What figures?"

"Throughout history, the media has been more brutal to female candidates than men. You narrow in on them like heat-seeking missiles, and then criticize her cleavage and hair."

"That's bullshit."

Audrey counted off the names on her fingers as she steered the wheel. "Hillary Clinton, Sarah Palin, Michelle Bachman…"

"Oh, come on…they asked for it! Everything they said deserved to be ripped."

"The only politicians that *deserved* that kind of brutality were dictators: Hitler, Stalin, Chavez, Castro.

And they all disbanded the free press."

"Yeah, because none of them had thick skin. Couldn't take the heat."

"And you can?"

"I'm not running for office."

"Or perhaps you fear exposing the skeletons in your closet."

"I welcome the exposure," he laughed. "Every day, if the law would let me."

The sparkle in his eyes unsettled her stomach. Everything about him crawled under her skin, lighting a fire to argue with him. To prove him wrong. To prove he was a rake. Prove she wasn't like every stereotypical candidate and meant what she said. And his gorgeous teeth kept smiling through it. *Prick.*

"What skeletons are in your closet, I wonder—or should I say under your mattress—that makes you so good at uncovering the bones others try to hide?"

"I'm as clean as a virgin's underwear."

Audrey nearly gagged at the imagery.

"You're welcome to check under my mattress yourself," Ethan elaborated. "In fact, while you're at it—"

"Not a chance, Tanner."

"Well, the offer stands, if you're interested."

"I'm interested in what you plan to write."

"Don't know yet. Need to get to know you first."

The thought of a journalist "getting to know her" made her nauseous. Or was that anticipation roiling around in her gut? Something she hadn't felt since...

Miranda was going to get the biggest kick in the butt when she got back. If her campaign wasn't ruined by then.

Bantering with Ethan for the next hour grew exhausting. For every topic he had an opinion, and every one was the opposite of hers. One of the only things she liked about him was that he never got angry. He let any tiny jab roll off his shoulder and threw it back in her face like a water balloon.

Twenty minutes out from Mackineer, the trees grew taller as the colors in the leaves deepened to plum, crimson, and gold. The narrow farm road curved around forest bends and the shoulder disappeared, replaced by a thicker forest and muddy grass. A light mist began to fall on the windshield and Audrey flipped on the defroster.

"Couple things before we get there." Audrey lifted her coffee for another sip, but it was empty.

"Ground rules?"

"Something like that. First, you're staying in the hotel. My parents don't have a spare room or wi-fi, so you'll probably prefer it anyway."

"It's the twenty-first century; who doesn't have wi-fi?"

"Second," Audrey ignored him and continued. "And this is not negotiable. Whatever you plan on writing, it stays on me. I'm the one running for the senate seat, not my parents or siblings. They're small town folks and don't have as thick a skin for the media to stab. You can come at me all you want, but not them."

"You really think I'm out for blood, don't you?"

"You don't write puff pieces or human interest stories. From everything I've read, you specialize in exposures and scandals. By the way, how did you uncover all that dirt on the county commissioner?"

Ethan smiled and shrugged. "Find a weakness and poke around."

"Exactly. I don't want any of my family's weaknesses poked around and plastered across the front page. They have big hearts and an even bigger kitchen and they're the best people I know. I don't want them hurt by anyone. So whatever you're after, leave them out of it. Deal?"

"You have a lot of rules."

"Deal?" she repeated, louder.

Ethan sighed and scribbled on his pad. "Deal."

"Thank you."

"So tell me who I'm about to meet. Start with your siblings." He kept scribbling on his pad and Audrey noticed the way he wrote with his index finger covering his thumb. *He must suffer from hand cramps like crazy. The size of his palm, too...were other areas as proportionate?*

Audrey flipped the defroster to her face and prayed she didn't look as red as she felt.

"Adam is eleven months older than me, but we were in the same grade through school. He went into the Army and did two tours in Afghanistan. Now he's married and a deputy in the Mackineer Sheriff's Department."

"So, blackmailing him for dirty stories is probably a no?"

"Go for it. You'll have a comfy overnight stay in the local holding cell. Save your newspaper the cost of the hotel."

Ethan laughed and scribbled more.

"Addy is sixteen."

"Addy?"

"Adelaide. Real big into pageants. Trying to save her winnings for a powder blue Mustang. And world peace, of course."

"A southern belle." Ethan leaned back in his seat and studied her. "Were you ever into beauty pageants?"

"No. Mom tried, but I was stubborn. Although when Addy was younger, she would have been a headliner on that *Toddlers and Tiaras* show."

"Stubbornness must be genetic then. What does your sister think of your political career?"

Audrey laughed as she exited the highway. "You'll have to ask her that, but she's sixteen. She's more concerned with high school and boys." She threw Ethan a look. "As she should be."

"And Adam?"

Audrey pursed her lips and turned onto a small two-lane road lined with spruces and pines. "Like most law enforcement and military men, he doesn't have a taste for politics. Or liberal media."

"So you're saying he's a hard ass."

"I'm saying don't piss him off."

"Protective type, eh?"

Audrey clenched her jaw, but refused to respond. Her coffee cup had been empty for the last thirty miles and she really needed to wet her throat. Her hand must have unconsciously grabbed her cup again because Ethan reached down and pulled out a bottle of soda from his bag and handed it to her.

"Sorry. I planned to give you this earlier, but you're distracting."

Audrey shifted her eyes from the bottle to Ethan, and then back to the bottle. "Thanks." *A nice gesture. Surprising.*

"It's your favorite, right? Saw you drinking one at the studio."

"Yeah." *He pays more attention than I thought.* "And I'm only as distracting as you let me be. Besides, you must have written the book on diversion. You haven't answered any of *my* questions."

"I didn't say diversion, I said distraction." The way his eyes gleamed from the passenger seat, completely disinterested in everything except who sat in the driver's seat, jacked up her heartbeat. "All you have to do is just sit there to accomplish it."

Audrey snorted.

"Come on. You know you're a brunette Botticelli babe. One smile from you, and you'll have every vote in your district."

"You're the king of diversion. First, you're just trying to butter me up for this article. Second, you'd say that to any female candidate under the age of forty. Third, you still haven't answered my questions."

"Because I'm not as interesting as you are."

Audrey looked straight into his eyes, easing her foot off the accelerator. "You're scared."

Ethan laughed, never taking his gaze off hers. "I told you I don't have any scandals under my mattress."

"Not that. You're afraid to let me in. To let anybody in."

Ethan scoffed, but didn't say anything.

"Prove it. Tell me about your family. You have siblings?"

Ethan chewed on something inside his mouth and glanced out the window.

"Pansy," Audrey muttered.

Ethan took a large breath as the smile dissipated

from his slender face like the rain spots on the windshield. "Nope. Only child, Mom died years ago, and Dad hasn't been in the picture for double that."

Audrey blanched. "Wow. Practiced that one a bit, have you?"

"Nothing interesting there. Which is why I focus on other people's lives."

"Why do I highly doubt that?"

The trees grew thicker alongside the road as they drove, the drizzle subsiding to a glossy sheen on the bright foliage. The car slowed through curves and turns, and the road opened up to Central Avenue, the shops, restaurants, and tiny deserted parking lots.

"So this is where you grew up?"

"Mackineer, Texas. Population 2,412. Home to the sweetest blueberry cobbler in the South."

"Your mom's?"

"Missy's Diner on Pearl Street." Audrey pointed out the restaurant with silver aluminum siding, faded moniker, and empty side lot.

"Must not be that good. Doesn't look like Missy's in business anymore."

Audrey laughed. "This isn't the big city. Everyone's at home cookin' and watching the parade on TV. Missy will be open tomorrow."

Turning another corner they passed a grove of pecan trees where a six-point buck darted across the road and into the brush. Audrey didn't have time to react and cruised slowly down the street while Ethan's eyes followed the trail.

"Incredible."

"Yeah. Sad to think in less than a month he may be dead."

"Why?"

"Hunting season."

Watching Ethan engaged in their surroundings threw her off guard. She expected him to be more aloof, completely focused on digging for dirt. But he seemed genuinely interested in her hometown. Could he really have an honest agenda? She wanted to think better of him. *It'd be nice if someone surprised me.*

More than that. She wanted her heart to match her body's reaction to him. But he was a journalist. How honorable could he be?

By the time they reached Audrey's parents' house, the sun peeked out behind the scattering clouds and cast a light across the sparkling wet lawn. They pulled up the gravel driveway and parked under an oak tree, its branches shading half the two-story house. The tire swing still hung from the lowest branch, but the rope was worn and fraying.

As she unbuckled her seatbelt, Audrey looked up at the center window on the top floor. She'd crawled out of that window and down the porch balcony over a hundred times. Strange, how the drop didn't seem as high now.

"We'll go in and introduce you. I'll drop off my things and then drive you to the hotel to check in."

"I can't get to know you and your family from sitting in hotel room. Well, unless you'd like to keep me company there." He winked at her as he reached into the back seat to grab his coat. *No honest agenda for this playboy.* She really needed to stop thinking the better of people. It only led to disappointment.

"Listen." Audrey gulped and tied her hair back. "It's been a while since I've been home. So, just...take it easy. Don't push them into questions."

His bewildered stare as he paused holding the door handle made her second guess herself.

"This isn't my first interview or meet the parents movie. Get the stick out of your butt and relax. It's Thanksgiving."

When she watched him step out of the vehicle and shut the door, Audrey braced herself on the steering wheel and took a deep breath. *Exactly. It's Thanksgiving.*

With a jerk on the handle, Audrey stepped out, along with her purse and soda bottle. The charming white wooden porch with seat swing and frosted glass door loomed over her like a scalding authority time couldn't diminish. *This has to be done eventually.* Like pulling off a bandage, even if it ripped off half the skin.

They both clomped up the wooden steps, each plank creaking, but strong and sturdy. As always, Mom's flower gardens on either side of the stairs were immaculate, the rose bushes pruned and fertilized for the winter season, flanked by chrysanthemums and tulip bulbs. Audrey took one last sip of her soda and shoved it in her purse. If she lasted through the next five minutes without losing her cool, she'd reward herself with a giant glass of wine. Clenching her fist, she knocked on the door and held her breath.

The door swung open and the familiar scent of apples and cinnamon flooded over her. A giant figure stood on the other side, with a full head of white hair and permanent scowl.

"Hi, Dad."

He merely stared back at her glowering, but his eyes shadowed in disbelief.

Chapter Six

Her father's stunned eyes threw her back into adolescence the way only a parent's face could. The lines on his forehead, cheeks, and around his eyes had deepened, but his brawny arms seemed larger. Apparently ten years couldn't erase disappointment or heal wounds.

"Happy Thanksgiving, Dad." Her voice was strong and sturdy. *Stay positive.*

"Audrey," he replied, low and noncommittal. He could have been addressing the postman with the level of intensity.

"Mr. Allen," Ethan began with his charming smile and pearly teeth, reaching out to shake her father's hand. "I'm Ethan Tanner. Pleasure to meet you."

If a scowl could freeze hell, her father was Jack Frost. He looked as though he might vomit. Audrey cringed, realizing her first big mistake.

Her father stretched out a large, roughly callused hand and squeezed Ethan's. "I'm Paul Biddinger."

Ethan's smile wavered. "Biddinger?"

"That's what I said." He released Ethan's hand and looked him over like a disturbed lion. "You dragged along a boyfriend?"

Audrey opened her mouth to protest with every bone in her body, but Ethan beat her to it.

"No, I'm a journalist with the *Dallas Morning*

Journal." Ethan molded the smile back on his face, as if he'd practiced that line over a million drinks. "Audrey let me join her this weekend to meet you all. I'm writing an article on both candidates."

Paul moved his tongue like he was chewing on tobacco, and hated the taste of it. When his eyes landed on his daughter once again, Audrey felt like running.

"Your government thing, huh? How original."

"Paul, honey, who is it?" The high, flowery voice came from behind the door as Audrey's mother approached. When she saw Audrey standing there, gripping her purse with blue knuckles, her mother's jaw fell to the porch, along with the dishrag in her hand.

"Is that really my Audrey? Sweet pickle, Paul, don't just leave them to mold on the porch. Come inside and get warm." With a light push of her hand, her husband stepped back and allowed the two to come in.

Audrey's heart swelled as her mom grabbed her for a tight hug and waved away the building tears. The lavender-scented lotion she used soothed Audrey's worries, just a touch. "Good to see you, Mom. You've worn that rooster apron every Thanksgiving since I was two."

"If it still fits, I'll wear it. The Macy's parade is almost over, but you can still catch Santa. You know that's Addy's favorite part."

The smell of the turkey roasting in the kitchen filled the house, just like when she was a kid. In ten years, their tradition hadn't changed. Neither had her mother's heartwarming thick East Texan accent.

"And who is this strappin' young man?"

"Ethan Tanner, *Dallas Morning Journal*." Ethan

didn't skip a beat. "This house is so charming. Who is your decorator?"

"Aren't you funny! Myrna Biddinger," her mother almost swooned over him. "So glad to have you. We can always fit another place setting at the table. Especially for someone as handsome as you."

There he goes again, plastering on that schmoozing smile. You'd think he was born with it. But at least he'd won over one person in this house. Dad hadn't changed at all, and neither would have Adam.

As Myrna fussed over taking their coats and bustling them into the family room, Audrey noticed her father retreat to the back of the house. Probably escaping to the den where he'd feast on another beer and the pre-game football show. He didn't even give her a hug. This was going to be a harder weekend than she thought.

Though the house looked exactly the same. Warm, open, country-inviting with a wooden antique dining set on one side of the entry way, and upholstered sofas in the family room. Books everywhere. In the built-in bookshelves, on the coffee table, even stacked on the floor by the red brick fireplace. Books on quilting, flower arrangements, gardening, and a hodge-podge of other do-it-yourself topics.

Ethan grabbed her elbow and lowered his voice when her mother was out of earshot.

"Biddinger? Have something to hide already?"

The heat from his fingers shot up her arm into her brain like an electrical current, even through her long-sleeved shirt. If those eyes would only glitter at her for a different reason. But everything else about his words proved his true intentions about the visit. It made her sick.

"No, Sherlock. I changed my last name years ago to protect them from situations like this."

"So, no secret marriage certificate for me to dig up?"

"If there was, you really think I'd keep the last name? Politics is ugly and I didn't want my opponents—or bloodthirsty reporters—badgering my family."

Ethan's eyes narrowed on her. "That doesn't make any sense."

"Why not?"

"Most politicians depend on their families for support. *Public* support. And you're keeping them from it. Why?"

"Everyone deserves privacy. And they aren't the type for the public circus."

Just as Ethan opened his mouth to fire back, Myrna returned, all smiles, with a tall, blue-eyed blonde bounding behind her. Adelaide's fully figured form and makeup-covered face resembled the tiny, natural rosy-cheeked cherub Audrey remembered. She had the same inextinguishable light in her eyes and perfect smile, but Audrey struggled to accept this woman before her as her sister.

"Audrey!" Addy pushed past her mother and threw her arms around Audrey's neck, nearly squeezing the breath out of her. "You're here! You're actually here!"

"Addy, when did you get so strong?"

"Tae bo keeps me fit for pageants. Look at your hair! So long now, and those posh highlights."

"Addy, dear, step back and let them sit in the family room." Myrna took off her rooster apron and glittered over Ethan. "Can I get either of you a drink?"

"Who is this?" Adelaide stepped back and roved her innocent eyes up and down Ethan's clothes. *Buttering him up, already.* "Is he your boyfriend?"

"Ethan Tanner." The man never missed a beat, or a chance to flash that grin. "I'm a journalist writing an article on your sister. You must be the beauty princess, Adelaide *Biddinger.*" Enunciating the last name sent fires raging through Audrey's veins. He wasn't going to give up on that. The least important part of what she was sure would be plastered in his article.

"A journalist? Then you must know all the TV anchors on NBC. What are they like?"

Audrey laughed. "He writes for the *Dallas Morning Journal*, Addy. He's not that important to know TV anchors." *Score one for the politician.* Audrey threw him a victorious smile, which weakened when he looked back at her with a teasing smirk.

"Drinks, anyone?" Myrna asked again, who eyed Audrey's interaction with Ethan.

"I'd love some coffee, Mom."

"Coffee's good for me, too."

Audrey followed her mother into the kitchen to help, smirking under her skin that Ethan would be left alone in the family room with Adelaide.

The kitchen smelled more glorious than Audrey remembered, with the battling scents of sherry roasted turkey, cinnamon coffee, and stewing apple cider.

Apple cider!

"Wow! I'll have the cider instead."

Myrna started to fill the coffee pot with water. "Yeah, Sally's been craving apples lately."

"Sally?" Audrey paused from reaching for a mug

in the cabinet. "Adam and Sally are here?"

"Yes, they're back in the den with your father. Do you mind fillin' a mug for her, too?"

Audrey unconsciously reached in to the cabinet for another mug and filled both to the brim. The sweet waft of cider numbed her shock—slightly. But she really shouldn't be surprised. Thanksgiving meant family gatherings. It made sense for her brother and his wife to be here. Deep down, it also made sense that he hadn't come to welcome her yet, either.

Lost in thought, Audrey hadn't realized her mother stopped preparing coffee and stared at her from across the kitchen. "How are you?" Her mother's question hung in the air with more concern and love than Audrey had felt in years.

"I'm great," she replied, political smile intact despite the yearning to let it go. "Campaign is running superbly, thanks to Miranda. Hopefully Ethan's article will clinch it for me."

"I saw your interview yesterday."

"And?"

Myrna sighed and pushed the button on the coffee maker. "You've done really well for yourself. Despite everythin'."

Not exactly what I was looking for. "I'm making a difference. That's what this election is for."

"As long as it's what you want, I'm happy for you."

"The day Dad feels the same way will be the day Texas outlaws guns."

"Oh, hush, girl. Of course your father wants you to be happy. He just has a hard time showin' it."

Audrey leaned against the counter and crossed her

arms. "It's been a decade, Mom. How long can someone hold a grudge?"

"You're in East Texas, darlin'. How long can the sun burn?"

The inside of her cheek was too soft to bite as hard as she wanted, but she tried anyway. Anything to keep from screaming. Rolling her eyes wouldn't cut it either. "Will Dad or Adam bite my head off if I try to deliver Sally's cider?"

"Probably not, but bring the tray just in case."

Carrying a tray of three ciders wouldn't protect her from their tempers, but Audrey complied. As she walked to the family room to drop off Ethan's, disappointment crept down her spinal cord. The miracle of having her father and brother welcome her with open arms didn't happen. Adelaide's youthful smile, the same she was currently giving Ethan while chatting and watching the end of the parade, was expected. Ignorance truly was bliss.

When Audrey entered the room, Ethan glanced over and practically started drooling. "Hot apple cider? I'm moving in!"

"As much as I'm sure Addy would appreciate another judge for her pageant costumes and Mom a guinea pig for her pies, you're not invited." Audrey handed him a mug, careful not to spill the next-to-boiling liquid on his Levi's.

"Since when do you have a say on who is and is not invited in this house?"

The entire room dropped thirty degrees instantly. The biting tone came from across the room, and Audrey didn't need to look up to see who spoke the bitter words. Adam's smooth and direct voice hadn't changed. As strange as it was to admit, Audrey missed hearing his voice. At least back when it wasn't filled with cynicism and disappointment.

Just as his face was covered with it. That, and much deeper wrinkles and a shadow in his sapphire eyes she didn't remember seeing before. Two tours in active war zones had a way of extinguishing the light in people's eyes. That and unending resentment toward a sister that wanted nothing but love between them.

"Hi, Adam." She smiled back. "I like your hair that way." Ten years and she'd never seen his crew cut in person. He must've been a vision in his Army uniform, with his bulky shoulders and slim waist. No wonder Sally fell for him. The Marlboro man had nothing on her brother. The Marlboro man couldn't scowl like Adam, either.

"Adam, don't." Adelaide whined from the couch, holding one of her pageant photo albums in her lap. No doubt bombarding Ethan with her glamour shots. "She never comes home. Leave her alone."

He leaned against the doorjamb, arms across his massive chest and biceps bulging through the long-sleeved navy shirt. The angel of death couldn't instill fear with one stare the way Adam could. Good thing Audrey and Adelaide were used to it by now.

"She doesn't come home for a reason. And don't go using your campaign talkin' just to butter me up. That crap won't work in this house."

Just the kind of homecoming Audrey hoped for with a bloodthirsty journalist at her side. A quick glance showed Ethan continued to drool, only this time it wasn't over the apple cider in his hands. What would his fingers do if that were a pen and paper in his lap?

Chapter Seven

Ethan had been skiing a few times before in the frigid hills of the Colorado Rockies. But that cold couldn't beat the one filling this room in the middle of East Texas, and they'd hardly seen a flake of snow. Audrey wasn't kidding. He definitely didn't want to piss off this bear. Never mind that he was as huge as a minotaur, but if he was also a deputy, he was certainly packing heat.

Damn, this article would make him a legend. The dirt materializing in front of him proved he had a gift for being in the right place at the wrong time. He could see the headline. "The Peacemaker sparks war in her childhood home." He'd save his introduction until after this developing scandal played out. Journalism 101: Never interrupt the story, just watch and record.

"Dad said you brought home a boyfriend," Adam's tirade continued. "Couldn't believe my ears."

"If he *was* a boyfriend, why would that be so hard to believe?"

Where the hell did that come from? Not that Ethan expected a fake relationship out of this. She was clearly using him as extra ammo for the argument with her brooding brother. But that didn't sound like The Peacemaker, retorting with false info. But a relationship with Audrey Allen, even only a few nights together, would be well worth it. Good Lord, he bet she'd be a legend in the sack. Ethan set his mug on the coffee table, just in case things exploded.

"*Your* history? I'd expect you to keep boys as far from this town as possible."

"Boys? I'm not a teenager anymore, Adam. Meet Ethan Tanner, journalist for the *Dallas Morning Journal*."

Adam's eyes almost popped from his sockets. "Journalist? You *have* lost your mind."

"Ethan is writing an article on Audrey as a candidate." Adelaide closed her photo album and plastered on her innocent smile. An attempt to lighten Adam's mood she and Audrey had probably used a million times.

This was his cue. Or maybe not. Either way, it was time to join the fun. Ethan stood and stuck out his hand, fully expecting Adam to ignore it.

"Nice to meet you. Audrey tells me you're an Army man. Must have been ugly in Afghanistan."

Adam shifted his glare to Ethan's face, then his hand. *Take the bait, man.* He could feel the women in the room hold their breaths. This was either going to be a lot of fun or really painful.

"Adam Houston Biddinger," Myrna entered the room carrying a tray full of cookies and wearing the perfect disciplinarian frown every mother mastered. "If you don't shake the hand of a guest in your mother's house, I will pull your father's belt right off his waist and tenderize your hiney to Christmas, deputy's badge be damned."

Ethan kept his eyes on Adam's combative stare. Only a southern woman could check a grown man into submission with one sentence. Finally, Adam gave in and shook his hand.

"*Was* an Army man. And Afghanistan was a pony ride in hell."

"I have a buddy who took photographs of the 34th Infantry over there. Did a nice spread for them in the *Times*."

"I'm sure they did. Those boys were puppets for the NATO Security Force. The *Times* would have lit them up like heroes."

An extremely pregnant woman waddled up behind Adam and wrapped her arms around his chest. She flipped her long, golden ponytail over her shoulder and kissed Adam's shoulder. This had to be Sally.

"You're all heroes in my book," her soft and airy voice cooed.

The only sign of affection from Adam was a light touch of his hand on hers.

"My wife, Sally. Hon, meet Ethan Tanner. He's a writer." The last part dripped from his tongue like acid.

Sally stepped out from behind her mammoth husband and shook Ethan's hand. "Nice to meet you."

Could this woman's accent be any thicker? Amazing how the long vowels made her seem sweeter than a glass of port. What he wouldn't give for a sip of the dessert drink he hadn't tasted in forever.

Finally Sally's gaze moved across the room to Audrey. Unlike her husband and father in-law, she gave Audrey a hug with a charming smile. "Your momma said you may be comin'. How was the drive?"

"Long." Audrey threw Ethan a glance. "But good." She handed Sally one of the apple ciders from the tray. "How's my future nephew feeling today?"

The instinctual grab of the belly. All women must

have that silly urge to place their hands on a pregnant tummy, even if that tummy belonged to a stranger. Ethan didn't get it. Everyone said pregnant women looked beautiful and glowing, but he thought they looked more uncomfortable than a nun in a titty-bar. Had to be, with a huge basketball stuck up your front only to be shoved out a tiny hole when the timer dinged. God had a barbaric sense of humor.

"He's got three weeks left." Sally held her belly with one hand and sipped her cider with the other. "Can't come soon enough, since he kicks like a bull in the Stockyards."

"Have you picked a name yet?"

"Bryson Paul." Adelaide answered for her, beaming. "Paul is for Daddy."

"I'm so sorry I missed the wedding," Audrey murmured. "I would've come had I known about it." Audrey threw a glance at Adam.

"Well, it was kinda…sudden," Sally replied, red-cheeked, as she glanced at her husband hesitantly.

"But it was beautiful," Adelaide interrupted. "I got to be maid of honor and wore my purple pageant dress from last year."

"So Ethan, what do you write?" Sally asked with a simple smile and waddled over to a free chair. Adam's assistance seemed unconscious and fluid.

"I'm a journalist for the *Dallas Morning Journal*. I'm writing a series on both Audrey and Wyatt Williams for the election." Ethan sat back on the couch. Adelaide seemed to be inching closer to his side with every movement. Not that he minded. Just as long as she knew she wasn't legal.

As soon as the first sentence escaped his mouth,

Sally's smile weakened. What was it with this family and journalists? Sally looked at Audrey, caution all over her face.

"Well, don't you give Audrey here any trouble. You're bound to regret it."

"Yeah, we all know what Audrey does to boyfriends," Adam muttered under his breath.

Perfectly timed, Audrey glared at Adam just as Sally smacked his wrist.

"What exactly do I need to be prepared for? That is, if I ever became her boyfriend." Ethan kept the joking tone in his voice. A sore spot for the family needed to be turned into something more lighthearted if he was going to get anything out of this guy.

But he didn't say anything. No one said anything. They all stared at Audrey, clearly biting their tongues. The sarcasm didn't work. Not the first time it hadn't worked for Ethan, but he'd figure out their weak points soon enough. This room wasn't pretty, despite the charming country décor.

Audrey continued to stare back at her brother, but the glare was now more of a sad frown. Quietly, Audrey set the tray on the table, took her mug out of the room, a stole a cookie from her mother's tray as she disappeared down the hall.

"You're such a prick sometimes, Adam." Adelaide threw a magazine at him. It ricocheted off his arm with the weight of a wadded napkin.

"You shut your mouth with what you know nothin' about," Adam shot back at her.

"Enough, you two," Myrna bit out and handed the tray to Ethan. "Addy, watch your language. That's no way to behave in front of a guest. Ethan, I'm so sorry.

Excuse me for a minute." She followed Audrey's trail.

"Well, I'm clearly missing something important." Ethan grabbed a cookie from the tray. These folks needed to talk, and he had a whole two days to accomplish it. One way or another. "But I assume she still has your votes for senator."

Adam scoffed. "Not from anyone in this town." And then trudged out of the room.

Bingo. Ethan's story was right here and he ate another cookie to hide the drooling.

Chapter Eight

Mom was right. They would never let go of their anger. But that's exactly why she needed to keep doing what she planned. As long as she kept breathing through the weekend and stayed out of the mud, she could get back home and focus on the Crisis Center. And this election.

The oatmeal cookie crumbled down her shirt as she took a bite on her trek to her father's den. *Sugar-free, yuck!* Must be Mom's way of reinforcing healthy foods despite Dad's rebellion and fight with high cholesterol. Oh well. Cookies weren't his problem as much as the daily case of beer. Mom had learned a long time ago to pick the fights she had a chance at winning. One of the few lessons Audrey valued.

The pregame announcers blared through the room as her dad nursed a third beer in his chocolate-colored La-Z-Boy. The lowered blinds darkened the bear's den with only a few rays of light bouncing off the wood-paneled walls. Just like Dad, this room hadn't changed at all. Which meant the answer to her first question would be the same as always.

"How's work treatin' you these days, Dad?"

Without taking his eyes off the television, he rubbed his chin and set down his can. "New rig this month, with a new crew. Ironing out the wrinkles."

"How far away is the rig?"

"Sixty miles north."

"Butch Clearwater still working for you?"

Dad took another swig. "D'you really come all this way to talk about my job and Sally's cousin?"

Audrey shrugged. "It's clear you don't want to talk about the other issue."

"And you do?"

"It's certainly on Adam's mind."

"Then tell him to get his butt in here and duke it out."

"You know he stopped listening to me a long time ago."

"Well, with a journalist in the house I figured it was the last thing you wanted to bring up."

Audrey forced herself to take a deep breath. "I can't change the past, Dad."

"I know that."

"That's why I'm doing what I'm doing. Trying to devote my life to making things better for others."

Finally, her father muted the television and looked her straight in the eye. "Is that what you're doin'? You sure you're not livin' someone else's life?"

Her feet looked so small in this room. Just as her voice always sounded so childish when she spoke to him. "Is that life so bad?"

"It ain't, as long as it's your own."

"Well, I'm *making* it my own."

Her father's grunt proved just how much he believed her words. A little less than she believed them herself. A second later, he un-muted the television and leaned back in his La-Z-Boy.

Audrey always knew when she was dismissed from a conversation. The moment only one voice was speaking and not heard.

"Sweetie." Her mother's softened voice caught her attention. Myrna stood in the doorway, arms crossed and massaging her wrist. "Don't mind Adam right now. You know how he gets when he's grouchy."

"It's all right, Mom. I expected it." Audrey stood and checked her watch. "If dinner is at four, I need to get Ethan checked in at the motel before then. We should head out."

"Why would you do that?" Myrna sputtered. "We have Adam's old room available. You don't stick guests in a motel." Audrey could tell the very thought of that went against all of her mother's southern sensibilities.

"Mom, I'd rather he stay in the motel—"

"Moot point, Audrey. Motel's full." Her father interrupted without looking away from the TV.

"What?" Panic flushed through Audrey's system. *Please tell me I heard him wrong.*

"Motel's full."

"How?" This is the tiniest town for a hundred miles in either direction. The motel should barely have any guests, let alone be full.

"Hunting season."

"But…it's Thanksgiving. That doesn't make sense."

"More busy this year since the wildfires down south destroyed their game."

"Well, isn't that fitting?" Ethan's gloating voice drifted from over Myrna's shoulder. "Guess we don't have a choice, Audrey."

The way he stared at her, like a delicious meal and his arm braced against the hallway, made Audrey want to slap that smug smile off his face. Despite how gorgeous he looked. There's no way she was going to sleep under the same roof as this sick opportunist.

"Well." Audrey took a deep breath. "We'll just go see if there's space anyway. I'm sure we can find him a room." She stared right back at the glimmer in his eye, ready to steal the light right out of it.

"Nonsense. Audrey, I know I raised you better than that." Her mother's face turned serious, resolute. "He'll stay here for the weekend."

"I promise to help with the dishes and take out the trash. I'll be just like family."

Audrey cringed inside. Both at the thought of him here, and his sultry pledge to be one of the family. "Mom, sorry. But there's no Internet access here and I know Ethan will need it. The motel can service his needs better." She threw a glare at Ethan.

"Moot point," her father muttered once again.

"The library has some," her mother claimed. "He can do his Internet stuff there. Problem solved." Without skipping a beat, Ethan smiled victoriously behind Myrna.

Where's an eraser when you need one? I can swipe that off his roguish face.

Her mother continued in one breath. "Now, can you please run to the store for me? I'm out of flour and sugar for the pumpkin cheesecake."

Highly unlikely. Her mother stockpiled baking items in her kitchen/bomb shelter. Before Audrey could open her mouth, Myrna turned around and started walking away.

"Oh, and take Addy with you. She's been watchin' TV too long this mornin'. You both can show Ethan around town a bit."

Yeah. Give Adam a chance to cool down. And Ethan a chance to warm up.

Audrey sighed and glared at the mistake she brought. Her mother and sister falling for Ethan's city boy charms was inevitable, but Audrey wasn't interested in only protecting herself. She had to protect her family. Dad would keep his mouth shut without altering from his normal routine. Mom loved to talk and flout her southern style, but she wasn't a gossiper. It was Adam and Adelaide who concerned her most.

Besides, if Ethan intended on interviewing her siblings as well as the whole town, Audrey wanted to be there right beside him and monitor his ridiculous questions. *Make* him keep his promise. The story was on Audrey, no one else.

****

Adelaide's constant chattering from the backseat was a relief for once as Audrey drove down Main Street. Spilling the beans to Ethan on her life in high school and pageant escapades meant Audrey could relax just a hair. But it was only a matter of time before Ethan asked the probing questions. Either way, Adelaide was a minor and he couldn't quote her without her parents' consent. Still, it would give him ammo for everyone else in town.

"What do you think of your sister running for senator?"

Yep, predictable as pumpkins in October.

Adelaide smiled at Audrey in the rearview mirror. "She'll do great! The only one with enough guts to tell the president how to do his job the right way."

Audrey bit back a laugh. "The governor, Addy.

Senator for Texas Senate. I won't be anywhere near D.C."

Audrey threw a glance at Ethan, who strangely studied her with a weird grin. What she wouldn't give to find out what thoughts ran through that sneaky mind of his.

"Oh. Well that's a little less glamorous." Adelaide's dejected tone was hard to miss. "But she'll kill the election anyway."

The grocery store came up on their left, a few cars scattered in the parking lot for last minute Thanksgiving feast items. But Audrey kept driving.

"You haven't been away that long to forget where the store is." Adelaide laughed from the back seat.

"We'll get there. First things first."

"The only things out this way are the library and motel."

Ethan started laughing. "I hope not in the same building. Disobeying your mother? Audrey, shame on you."

"There's no harm in asking." Audrey shrugged and flipped on her blinker to turn into the small motel's parking lot. Half of the modest two-story building was covered in tarp and flimsy construction platforms. The other half's faded paint and rusted windows needed renovations as well.

"Mom will tan your hide with a belt if she hears you even thinking about putting Ethan in the motel. Besides, this place is shabby and Adam's room is so much more comfortable."

"You won't be staying here, Addy. Just Ethan."

"You wouldn't want your precious hide tanned because of me," Ethan mocked, leaning against the passenger door.

Audrey parked in the only available spot, as the rest were occupied by beat up pickups and dooleys. Her hopes for an open room dwindled, but she wouldn't give up yet. Better a tanned hide from her mother than a shattered career from Ethan.

They all climbed out of the car. Ethan and Adelaide started to walk inside, but Audrey waited by the trunk. "You'll need your suitcase."

Ethan turned and shoved his hands in his coat pockets, wearing that conceited smile that became more irritating every second. "Not if they're full."

"They'll have a room."

"Let's just check first."

Everything started to itch. Her neck, arms, eyes, and throat as they battled each other with their stares. The undercurrent of heat from his laughing eyes hinted at other ideas probably probing around his brain, standing outside a motel. If she weren't so struck by the glimmer in those gray irises and nonverbal challenge, she'd be offended. Adelaide stood next to Ethan, a ridiculous smile growing on her cheeks, clearly amused by their childish display.

"Fine." Chin strong and high, Audrey tossed her hair over her shoulder and marched past them.

The motel lobby had seen better days, but knew nothing of contemporary furnishings. Floral wallpaper faded to a muted brown with paper-thin carpeting that made psychiatric hospitals more inviting. An occasional orange and yellow matted shag carpet broke up the dismal color scheme. The liveliest decorations in the room were the few stuffed quail and hawks mounted throughout the small dining area next to the check-in desk.

The town's only motel didn't require a concierge or bellman service. The clientele didn't need them for their early morning hunting and fishing excursions, or their late night returns from the bar. The only other amenity they may have appreciated was a taxidermy service. Other than that, a decent mattress and a place to lock their guns were enough to consider this a five-star hotel.

Perfect lodging for Ethan.

The hotel clerk was as seasoned as the *National Geographic* magazines lying on the counter. Circa 1960s variety and just as worn.

"Hi, there. Do you have any rooms available for tonight and tomorrow?" Audrey asked with her most pleasant political voice and Peacemaker face.

"All booked up," the clerk rasped out in a thick backwoods, East Texan accent, without glancing up from his newspaper. Cigar smoke trailed up from the ashtray resting behind the paper.

"Sorry, Audrey," Adelaide called from behind. "Can we go to the store now? I need more lip gloss."

Audrey ignored the sixteen-year-old beauty queen and lowered her voice. "Please, sir. It's really important and you'd be doing us a huge favor. Could you just please check? Anything you have. I'll pay double the going rate."

The man raised his eyes with a recognition that sent squirms down Audrey's spine. "We're all full, Mizz Biddinger. Run on home now and take your campaign and big city reporter with you."

Rough words from a rough man Audrey failed to recognize at first glance. Time hadn't been kind to Mr.

Packle's face and voice, and neither had the cigar smoking. But neither had he been kind to her, even as a scrawny tomboy chasing her brother around the school fields he was in charge of maintaining back then.

He glared back into Audrey's eyes with the condescending stare that every southerner seemed born with. Audrey merely smiled back, grabbing her keys from the counter. Before turning to leave, she looked in his stern eyes once more.

"Sorry for wasting your precious time, Mr. Packle."

When she turned around, Adelaide's frown matched her crossed arms and hip thrust to the side, whereas Ethan's eyes flew wide to study Mr. Packle. Audrey closed the distance between them, polite defeat on her face.

"You want me to try and ask him?" Ethan whispered, not bothering to hide his amusement.

"I don't think he'd be willing to give you an interview, big city reporter. Let's go."

Crawling back in the car felt like slipping underneath a rock to lick her wounds. If she were still seventeen, she'd have thrown back an insult at Mr. Packle and cared less of the repercussions. But things were different now. She was different. Some arguments weren't worth fighting. But it still felt shitty to give up.

"That grump has had an attitude his whole life," Adelaide defended from the back seat as she slammed the door. "He should have felt lucky to have a reporter stay at his motel. But that's okay. Now Ethan can stay in Adam's old room. I'm sure the bed is comfier."

"I'm still reeling there's another person in this town that the great Audrey Allen couldn't sway."

Ethan's dimples recessed into his face as his smile widened. Only a true cynic could gain that much entertainment from seeing her ego thrown into the Stone Age by a small-town curmudgeon. "He was all grins and giggles for you. Must be drinking the same whiskey as your brother."

"Adam doesn't drink whiskey," Adelaide interjected.

"All military men drink whiskey."

The tall pine and oak trees faded from Audrey's view as she steered the last mile toward the grocery store. Adelaide and Ethan bantered like siblings. Harmless, relentless, and annoying all at once. Just like she and Adam used to be.

She missed it.

It was a good thing she couldn't see Ethan's face as he razzed with Adelaide. She didn't want to watch the sparkle in his eyes or the charming smile of a not-so-straight-laced paparazzo. He had the perfect face for an artist's model. Clean lines, strong features, easily shaded, and enough layers in his eyes to keep a sketcher occupied for days. But they were also the worst combination for any woman to keep her guard up. An artist's greatest love was the politician's worst enemy.

There was no doubt in Audrey's mind which role she needed to play. Or at least which role took precedence over all others. Which is why her sketchbook sat on her windowsill back in Dallas.

The grocery store parking lot was even fuller than before and Audrey's gut squirmed as she pulled into an empty space. Another deep breath and a struggled swallow helped steady her mind. Flour, sugar, and lip gloss. Then back to the quasi-sanctuary of home. What could be simpler?

"It's just a Piggly Wiggly."

Audrey looked out her window only to see it wasn't there. Ethan leaned against the open door frame, smirking and waiting for her to step out. Was she really that distracted?

He held out his hand, casual and undemanding, much like the rest of his posture. But there was nothing casual about that gaze. Like he'd win the lottery if he could guess the exact number of freckles on her face.

Would it be so bad if a man paid that kind of attention to details?

Audrey swallowed again and shook her head.

"I'm trying to decide whether or not I want wine with dinner," she lied.

If the motel was any indication of the welcoming she'd receive in this town, she should shut the door and drive home now. The grocery store here was like the Galleria in Dallas. Women came here for their gossip and stopped off in the beauty salon for the rest. Audrey was about to give them enough gossip for the next year.

And in front of a newsman, no less. One determined to uncover the details.

Audrey stepped out of the car and gripped her purse. She followed Ethan and Adelaide to the automatic sliding doors and inhaled, plastering on her peacemaker face.

Let's get this display over with.

Chapter Nine

As Audrey Allen trailed them into the grocery store, Ethan thought he saw fear in her hesitant eyes. She wasn't supposed to be afraid of anything. Forget that she clutched her bag like a life raft, she didn't lead the pack into a room like her normal campaign routine. News conferences, public appearances, even when she assisted Congressman Nichols on the floor, she always entered through the door first. Except now.

The motel clerk's open-armed welcome must have rattled her more than Ethan suspected. Hardly the kind of welcome expected for a Senate candidate on the campaign trail. Ethan couldn't stop smiling as he walked into the grocery store.

Shit, this was going to be a fun weekend.

Adelaide skipped into the store ahead of him, waving to one of the two cashiers as she passed, and headed straight for the makeup aisle. *So this is what a Piggly Wiggly looks like.* Not an indoor pen for farm animals as the name suggested, but a six-aisled general store the size of a mainstream pharmacy. Well, five aisles. The sixth was strictly hunting gear and ammunition. Not the kind of store seen in Dallas. And definitely not in New York City.

Ethan stopped and shoved his hands in his pockets, waiting for Audrey to catch up. What were they here for again? Something for her mother. Audrey strolled past without a word or glance.

Her perfume trailed in her wake and its sweetness matched perfectly with her sultry stride. Not that she knew it. Women like her were rare: not completely ignorant to their physique's effect on a man's senses, but clueless to its magnitude. No doubt Audrey knew to keep the make-up natural and the hair simple, but perhaps didn't know how to accentuate her curves with the *right* clothing. But with Ethan's trained eye on the female figure, his imagination on what Audrey hid underneath those political suits and oversized sweaters dripped with anticipation.

It took a moment for him to realize the store went quiet; no beeping registers, no chatting customers. Dead quiet.

Everyone's eyes followed Audrey to the baking aisle, and no one smiled. It was as if the world had stopped to let Audrey shop.

Had they never seen a candidate before? Ethan followed her, smiling at everyone and amused by the stunned faces, waiting for a punch line from someone.

Audrey surveyed the limited selection of flour. The way she stood with her arm on one curvy hip accentuated her slender waist. She looked great in a business skirt, but those legs were made for skinny jeans. Or nothing at all. Her dark hair cascaded down her back in wavy curls. An inkling of warmth spread through his veins at the thought of her curling her hair just for him. Who else did she need to impress?

"I'm impressed. Your entrances keep getting more entertaining." Ethan grabbed a bag of marshmallows from the shelf. "They only sell one brand? How did you survive out here?"

"Simplicity has its advantages. Easier to keep the annoying press away."

Ooh, touched a nerve there. What else can I touch?

"What's wrong with the press? Am I too sweet for you?" He waited for her eyes to meet his and gave a devilish smile. He opened the bag of marshmallows and popped a few in his mouth.

Audrey rolled her eyes and grabbed a bag of flour. "You haven't paid for those yet." She turned around to swipe sugar from the shelf behind her. "And you're more sour than sweet."

"You think this whole bag would make me sweeter?"

Her mouth twitched as if she wanted to smile, but didn't. *Does she allow herself any fun?* A light glimmered in one eye, proving she was capable of it, if she really wanted it.

"This entire aisle of sugar isn't enough."

A marshmallow sailed into the air and he caught it between his teeth. He tilted the opened bag toward her. She didn't move. Just continued to watch him with those sapphire gems.

He grabbed another one and raised it to her mouth, a hair's width from those moist lips. Not that this woman needed any more sweetness, but there was something about hand-feeding a woman. The anticipation. The trust. Foreplay.

Would she take the bait?

When he cocked an eyebrow at her, she tilted her head, never once taking her eyes off of him.

Those delectable lips never parted. She took the marshmallow between two fingers and tossed it back in the bag. "Let's just get out of here," she murmured.

"Aud." Adelaide strolled down the aisle, holding two lip glosses in her hands, oblivious to everything else around her. "What shade do you like best, strawberry diamonds or plum paradise?" She held them out and pressed her lips together. Audrey barely gave them a glance.

"Either one, Addy. Let's go."

"But...you didn't even look."

"Plum paradise, definitely," Ethan broke in. Adelaide's eyes widened the exact way as her sister's. He picked the plum paradise shade out of Adelaide's hand and pretended to study it. "Strawberries are for little girls. Plums are more exotic."

Adelaide's blush matched her sister's, too. It went straight up her cheekbones into her hairline. But Audrey was quicker at hiding hers.

"Look what the coyote dragged home," a high-pitched voice drawled from the other side of the aisle.

Ethan and Adelaide turned simultaneously and focused on the short, skinny woman, clearly infatuated with dark make-up and cheap hair extensions. As if the longer the hair extensions the more it would make up for her short height, only accomplishing the opposite effect. With a small basket of groceries in one hand and a fake Louis Vuitton in the other, her sneer reminded him of a few nasty ex-girlfriends.

Sauntering down the aisle, her gaze moved from Audrey to Ethan and back again.

"Hi, Maria," Audrey said with a sigh and weary smile.

"You think it's a good idea to be back here?" Her voice was like fingernails down Ethan's spine, and not the good kind. At least for once the hatred wasn't directed toward him. Amazingly, it was all for Audrey. "Let alone with this handsome fella to take the brunt of your schemes."

"Maria, this is Ethan Tanner, reporter from Dallas." Audrey performed the obligatory introduction with little enthusiasm, but still wore her moderate peacemaker smile. "Ethan, Maria Gonzales. She and I went to high school together."

"Pleasure." Ethan held out his hand, despite the sugary powder on his fingers.

"It's Maria Fuente, now."

"Congratulations," Audrey replied without losing her smile, and without feeling.

"You brought home a reporter? *You?*"

"Why does everyone keep asking that?" Adelaide interrupted no one in particular.

Maria threw Adelaide a glance and shook her head at Audrey. "You really think this is the best example you want to set for your little sister?"

"Addy is doing very well, thanks for asking." Audrey replied. "Have a good Thanksgiving, Maria."

Ethan stood dumbfounded, but had at least dropped his unshaken hand. The Peacemaker wasn't glad-handing a potential voter or squashing this woman's direct attack on her family. *What is wrong with her?*

He normally loved watching Audrey Allen refute arguments in the middle of a debate or news conference in glorious fashion. To the point where opponents backed down within two questions and journalists lined out the door to make sure they recorded the legendary confrontations. But here she wasn't putting up a fight. In her hometown. With attacks on her sister, no less.

"Eric, be sure to keep a safe distance from

this…*woman*," Maria threw over her shoulder as Audrey walked away. "Lord knows what would happen to you given her history."

"Maria." Adelaide gave her the perfect teenage scowl. "Go shove one of your hideous hair extensions up your butt and mind your business."

Ethan couldn't help himself. The best way to "see the town" was get an inside look. "Maria, who will you vote for in the upcoming senate election?" He kept the best journalist tone in his voice, but could've guessed which way her answer leaned. *Let's see how the strong candidate handles this one.*

Maria studied Ethan, clearly confused. "Hadn't thought about it."

Liar. She doesn't have a clue there's an election at all.

"Well, Audrey is running for a Senate seat. Is it safe to say she has your vote? Or will you be too busy fixing your hair?" Ethan popped another mallow in his mouth.

"Ethan." The warning in Audrey's voice was soft, but obvious.

"I wouldn't help her if she were laying dead in the street!" Maria hissed with eyes flared. She spun around and stormed off, extensions shedding as she huffed away.

"That was uncalled for." Audrey's penitent eyes met his entertained gaze.

"Me? She was the one throwing insults at you." This wasn't a funny situation, but why did he have a hard time containing the laughter building in his chest?

"You baited her."

"Come on, she was asking for it. That ridiculous

make-up and hair? She looked like Prostitute Barbie."

Adelaide laughed, her eyes almost gleaming. Audrey gave her an admonishing look and sighed.

"Why didn't you defend yourself?" It was about time to ask Audrey the question she clearly didn't want to hear. The serious words hung in the air as Audrey stared at him, with eyebrows lowered and sad lips. Something shifted in her eyes and it went straight to his heart. Regret? Annoyance? Fear?

But it slowly faded into a polite upturn of her mouth.

"It's time to go." Audrey turned on her heel and marched to the checkout counter.

Adelaide followed slowly, casting unsure glances between them.

Peacemaker face was back in place. This weekend grew more odd with every minute. He needed to get to a computer with Internet access, and fast. Everyone alluded to something about Audrey's past, and Bose was right. Small towns were ripe for juicy dirt. The Internet had everything.

Audrey strolled to the register. Something ached in his gut as her cheeks swayed with every step. Bodies like hers were made for fantastic romps in the bedroom. Round, plump curves connected to legs longer than the Golden Gate Bridge. Legs that Ethan imagined wrapped around his waist and squeezing with wave after wave of pleasure.

Whoa. Get it together, man. Fantasies like that don't belong in the middle of the grocery store when the goal is to expose Audrey Allen. A different kind of exposure.

The seasoned cashier was friendly to every

customer, calling each by their first name as she scanned their goods. Amazing how small towns could remember everyone's name. Ethan envied that ability. It didn't take long for them to know not only names, but birthdays, favorite foods, and family quarrels. Of course they knew everyone's dirty secrets and favorite sex positions, but they liked to be a little more discreet. But they still knew it. Ethan could tell by the little smirks on their faces.

Towns like this could write bestsellers with real stories.

"Happy Thanksgiving, Gladice," Adelaide sang as she placed her lip gloss on the counter. Beauty queens were required to wear their winning smiles 24/7, and Adelaide had clearly mastered hers. Ethan noted it was the same smile as Audrey's when she wasn't negotiating political peace.

"Same to you, Miss Addy," Gladice replied with a grandmother smile and started scanning. The white-haired woman glanced up at Audrey and Ethan, losing an inch of her smile. "Full house today?"

Audrey opened her mouth to speak but Adelaide answered for her. "Audrey's finally home! You remember her, don't you? She's running for Senate. Not sure if you heard. Ethan here is a reporter and writing an article—"

"That's nice, dear," she muttered. Noticing the opened bag of marshmallows, she frowned and threw disapproving eyes at Audrey. "You're supposed to pay for these before you open them."

Oh, this could be fun. Would Audrey try to placate her, make excuses, or ignore it?

Ethan laughed when Audrey turned to him with a

smirk, hand on her hip. "Would you care to answer Mrs. Covington, Ethan?"

God, the fire in Audrey's eyes is begging for playtime. It was clear this woman could hold her own in a fight. Suddenly, all he wanted was to fight with her.

Ethan reached into the bag that Gladice still held and popped another one in his mouth. "You're the one who said I needed to be sweeter."

Audrey's smirk twitched into a smile for just a second. But she kept her gaze on Ethan's grinning face. "More considerate wouldn't hurt, either."

Gladice scanned the opened package and bagged the items together, critical scowl still intact.

"Gladice, which way do you plan on voting in the upcoming election?" *Is this grandma as distrustful of all politicians as she clearly seems to be with Audrey?*

The cashier fished out change from the register and set it on the counter, glowering. "My husband and I vote for the most deserving candidate...with the cleanest record." Gladice glared at Audrey from across the counter, using her bitter eyes to convey her obvious message. Audrey wasn't that candidate.

Audrey paused, absorbing Gladice's answer before she picked up her change. Something in her posture changed—sunken shoulders, slightly lowered chin. Almost like a nonverbal apology.

Come on, Audrey. Show her you're that deserving candidate, like I've seen you persuade others a hundred times. Answers like that warrant a come back, and you're the Queen of Zingers.

"Thank you, Mrs. Covington," Audrey replied softly. "Have a nice Thanksgiving." Without another word, Audrey grabbed the bag and strolled out of the store, not waiting for Adelaide or Ethan to follow.

The pair stood there for another second, glancing back and forth at each other and Gladice. This had to be about the marshmallows. Ethan pulled out a five-dollar bill from his wallet and placed it on the counter.

"For the inconvenience." He smiled softly and shoved his wallet back in his pocket.

"No, thank you." Gladice slid the bill back toward Ethan, the scowl still plastered on her face. Her eyes dared him to argue with her. With a tip of an invisible hat, Ethan smiled and led Adelaide out of the store, who fidgeted in her Ugg boots and lost the beauty queen grin. The bill still sat on the counter.

Ethan's feet quickened to catch Audrey, who'd already opened the door to her Acura.

"What the heck was that?" Ethan called as Adelaide followed. "Why didn't you say something?"

Audrey plopped herself inside and shut the door, turning on the engine. She gave Ethan a confused glance and waited for Adelaide to slip in the backseat.

"Where was the legendary debating skills of Audrey Allen in there?" The door slammed on his last few words. When Audrey placed her hand on the shifter, Ethan stopped her by covering it with his own hand. Her hands were burning and sweaty. "Answer me first."

"There was no point. She had her mind made up already," Audrey replied with a polite voice and blank face. But a muscle tightened in that soft jaw line of hers.

"That's never stopped you before," Ethan shot back. "And don't use that Peacemaker tone with me. You should have used it in there, where it would have done some good."

Silence filled the car. Only the humming of the engine broke through. *Why wouldn't she fight back? Where's the Audrey every politician knows?*

The warmth from Audrey's hand filtered into Ethan's fingers as he held it in place over the shifter. He felt her pulse racing, blood rushing through her veins like water through a hydrant. Something was alive inside her, but she refused to use it.

"I've seen you turn the most difficult room of bulldogs to eat out of your hands like puppies. It's what you're known best for. How is it you can't turn a single person in a small town who've known you their whole lives?"

The windshield somehow became the most interesting focal point and Audrey refused to look away from it. And it started to bug him. He wanted her to look at him. Show him what was really going on inside that beautiful mind of hers.

Audrey swallowed. "It's easy to turn a difficult room if they disagree with my ideas or opinions. It's impossible to turn a single person if their problem is with my very existence."

The confession hung between them like acidic smog. For the first time, Ethan was speechless. He should be drooling. But his mouth was dry. *Has to be the sugar.*

"What's going on?" Adelaide's innocent voice broke the silence. "Why did Gladice treat you like that?"

Audrey ignored her sister and looked at Ethan with expectant eyes. "You finished?"

Ethan couldn't take his eyes off of hers, but let go

of her hand. The fight lived in her eyes. "Not even close."

"Aud?" Adelaide asked again.

"Leave it alone, Addy," Audrey snapped and thrust the car into gear.

Chapter Ten

Small towns never changed. The same narrow-minded atmosphere mixed with the independent stubbornness ingrained in Southern blood. Along with the unique trait of unending memory. Not that she would admit that in a campaign speech or press conference. They were still voters.

Audrey tried to keep her smile intact when she dropped off the grocery bags in the kitchen, but her mother saw the break in her lips as she walked off. No doubt Adelaide filled her mother in on the gossip she just suffered. But she needed quiet, to be alone, if only for a few minutes.

The wood planks creaked as she rolled her suitcase through the upstairs hallway and pushed through her bedroom door. The same room in which she survived adolescence. Barely.

It felt smaller than she remembered. The white bedroom furniture with pink and green flowered bedspread clashed with the memory of her black and white sketches she had pinned on the pistachio colored walls. Now redone as a guest room, her illustrations didn't match her mother's palette for the décor.

She lifted her suitcase onto the bed and started unpacking, wondering if her mother had thrown out all of her sketches or stashed them somewhere secret. As if her daughter hadn't existed. Hadn't annoyed the town with her "unusual behavior," and hadn't disgraced the family's name ten years ago.

The small bag of toiletries was the last item unpacked, which she set on the dresser. Not *her* dresser. Not anymore. The only thing in this room that felt like *hers* was the window. More specifically, the rooftop outside that she'd made into her own personal balcony. Late at night when she couldn't sleep, she'd hide out there in the darkness, dreaming up her next sketches. The branches of the large oak tree spread under the roof, forming the perfect ladder to the grass below, where she'd escaped countless times.

Half of those countless times were hand in hand with *him*. The happiest times of her life, short lived and the memories now full of heartache. Audrey pulled the brush out of her purse and combed through her hair, as if each stroke pulled the tension from her mind. Then her cell phone rang.

Caller ID showed it was Miranda, and Audrey let out a relieved sigh. "Did you make it to Houston?"

"Nope." Miranda's annoyed voice bit through the phone. "Flight delayed due to mechanical problems. I could drive to Houston faster than these yahoos can fix a plane. How's it going with you? Ethan behaving himself?"

"Not exactly, but I was expecting it."

"Bombarding your family already?"

"Let's just say it's not as smooth sailing as I'd hoped, but I'm handling it."

The pause on Miranda's end would have sent nervous shocks through anyone else. But not Audrey.

"Anything I need to be aware of before he publishes his article?"

"No, Mandy. He has the ground rules and so far he's sticking to them. Begrudgingly."

"What ground rules?"

"I don't want to talk about that. Have you heard back from the investors?"

The sigh Audrey heard didn't make her feel better.

"Would I let you down, Aud? Two of the three came back and said yes. Checks will be in the mail tomorrow."

"Seriously?" Audrey's voice jumped an octave and she felt like bouncing on the mattress. The Crisis Center could actually make it. "You're not playing with me, are you?"

"Not only that," Miranda continued with just as much excitement. "They're donating two season tickets to both the Stars and Mavericks for the auction on Saturday."

Now Audrey started to jump up and down on the wood floor, not caring that her family below probably thought she was moving furniture around.

"Mandy, I love you! You're brilliant! This Crisis Center can finally get off the ground, all because of you."

"Nuh-uh, sweetie. Because of you! They said they weren't donating to the campaign or the cause, but to you. They believed in *you* and what you can accomplish. *You,* Audrey!"

"You've made my weekend, Mandy!"

"Let's just hope it makes our week! We're on our way, Aud. With a little luck, this is just the beginning. Keep that sexy journalist in line and we'll have the whole thing clinched."

"News like this can make me keep the devil in

line." Audrey kept the thought of the *sexy journalist* in the back of her mind. Miranda was right, Ethan was chocolate-covered sex in a cup, but he was also the devil she had to keep under control. While she was at it, she'd have to keep her heartbeat under control whenever he walked in the room.

"Tell me, have you snuck a peek yet?"

"What?" Audrey blanched. *Did I say those things out loud?*

"A peek at his package. His baggy cargo pants aren't so baggy in a certain spot and I wondered if you'd verified it yet."

"How exactly would you want me to verify that, Mandy? He's the journalist you claimed could make or break the election for us. I can't feel up his crotch to satisfy your curiosity and risk a sexual harassment claim."

The hearty chuckle on the other end took Audrey by surprise. "I bet that one would welcome any sexual harassment from you. His sexuality is just dripping."

Audrey's cheeks flushed with heat. "Well, when the election is over, *you* ask him out."

Another laugh. "I think you've already claimed him."

"What are you talking about?"

"Sweetie, I saw the way he looked at you at the studio and at the meeting. Like his favorite gift from Santa Claus. And it was also the first time I saw you blush in years."

"That was the look of a player trying to aim in on another target. You're screwing up your metaphors." A sliver of Miranda's words stuck in the back of her mind, and a flicker of warmth grew in its place.

"I've never seen you or heard of you going on a date with anyone since I've met you. Don't you think ten years of single life is enough?"

Yes. And not nearly enough either.

"I hardly think the middle of an election is the best time for a politician to start dating. Particularly not with a member of the media."

"You've always loved a challenge."

Audrey pinched the bridge of her nose and shook her head. "Stick to harassing airline executives. It's what you're good at."

"You didn't see the news at noon, did you?" Her tone switched to serious with a click of a button.

"No, why?"

"Never mind."

"Mandy?"

"They showed Wyatt Williams' interview with NBC5. And he was…typical Wyatt."

"Great," Audrey groaned. *Yet another fire I'll have to put out.*

"We knew ahead of time that Mr. Williams doesn't keep the gloves up."

"Well, Wyatt forgets that unlike most of his competition, my jewels are above the waist."

"Ooh, good one! I'll tell Canyon to include that in your acceptance speech."

"Leave him alone. He has enough speeches to write for the fundraiser this weekend."

"Audrey, that is what Canyon Wilde lives for! Oh, and he wants to talk to you about a few lines in Saturday's speech when you have a free minute. Also, let him pick out your dress for the event."

"He's my speech writer, Mandy. Not my stylist."

"But he should be. He's got a hell of a lot more sense than you. If you don't let him primp you up, I know you'll show up in one of those boring suits covered from head to toe like an Amish nun."

Audrey rolled her eyes. "I'll call him tomorrow."

"Well, cry out, Moses, they're finally boarding! I might just get to Houston before Hanukah."

"Be nice to the flight attendants."

With a quick laugh, Miranda hung up.

A cold spell swept down Audrey's spine as she stood in the middle of her former bedroom and realized Miranda was right. She had blushed in the news studio. Which was why Ethan took the signal to flirt and use his playboy ways to get answers out of her. Why else would he come on so strong with his sexy stares and charming smiles? She'd have to be dead not to react to the heat meandering through her veins when Ethan brushed up against her shoulder or touched her hand.

Or held that damn marshmallow up to her mouth. She was a heartbeat away from licking it from his fingers and finding out exactly what he tasted like. Ethan Tanner knew he could pulverize a woman's senses into submission. And it *had* been a long time since…

She wasn't dead. Sure, a lot of people in this town wished she was, but there were a lot of breaths left in her lungs, and plenty of beats in her heart. But she was determined to do something good with every one of them. And love wasn't part of it. Or sex. Sex had no place in her life while she was busy making up for her mistakes.

Especially not with Ethan. Even if it was clear he wanted it.

A soft knock on the door pulled her from her internal determination speech. Ethan leaned against the doorframe, a sly grin on his face and his hand shoved in his jeans pocket. The fabric pulled tightly across his hips revealing a bulge larger than—

Shit! Audrey forced her eyes to Ethan's chest, feeling the heat rise on her cheeks. *I really need to stop listening to Mandy's ideas.*

"See something you like?" Ethan asked smoothly, like warm silk tenderizing the air. And her thighs.

Yes, now stop rubbing it in. "Did you lock my car after you grabbed your suitcase?"

"Are there a lot of burglars out here where the paved roads end?"

Pressing her lips together wasn't a successful deterrent to Ethan's probing stares. Conversely, it seemed to reignite his attentions.

"We're right across the hall from each other. That should make my nights here very pleasant."

Audrey couldn't hold back her smile. "Every door has a lock on it, and East Texas practically requires a dozen guns in the house."

Ethan placed his hand over his feigned hurt chest. "You think so little of me. Besides, I'd have a hard time seducing you in this room. This is clearly your childhood furniture." He moved across the room like a teasing breeze and grabbed one of the white four posters of her bed, leaning a knee on the mattress. "Kinda dampens the mood."

The way his hip leaned onto her bed jerked the breath from her throat. The fabric pulled tighter across his crotch, accentuating the bulge.

"Oh, so you're more used to a raggedy mattress on

the floor surrounded by smelly heaps of dirty laundry and empty whiskey bottles?" Audrey needed any kind of grotesque image to snuff the flames ignited by her imagination.

His eyebrows almost met his hairline. "That's what you think of me?" Half a smirk grew on his lips. "I'm hardly a whiskey drinker."

"Why don't you freshen up before dinner? You can use the bathroom first," Audrey deflected with a deep breath. He was getting way too attached, and an arm's distance was the best place for a journalist, if a metal cage wasn't close by. "But please remember to leave the toilet seat down."

"We're *sharing* a bathroom? Now's there an image I can get in the mood with."

A buzzing caught Audrey's attention, pulling her electric connection to Ethan's smoldering eyes. A moment went by before she realized it was Ethan's phone vibrating through his back pocket. But he didn't bother to reach for it. His smolder continued to bore through Audrey's defenses.

"You gonna answer that?"

Ethan shook his head.

If he would just stop looking at me like that, I could think. "Might be important."

"Not as much as you...right now."

Roll your eyes, Audrey. Just roll them...stop looking at him.

But she couldn't. The steel cords emitting from his stare kept her glued to the spot, pulling her gaze back into his gray eyes, tinged with a hint of cyan toward his pupils. Like the calm center of a hurricane, damaging just to look at him, with the promise of even more destruction to break away. The only way to keep the storms from raging was to keep her focus connected to those eyes.

In the reflection of his irises, she could see his toned, naked body pressing against hers, hips thrusting her against the wall, while his lips devoured her nipples, both of them covered in sweat and heat. Suddenly, the room was twenty degrees warmer.

I'm not important to him. I'm only important for his article. He'll do or say anything to get what he wants for the article. Including seduce his target. You'll be left with nothing the morning after. Again.

Forcing her foot in front of the other, Audrey moved the few steps across the room, slowly, never breaking away from Ethan's gaze. Anticipation sparked in his eyes, clearly amused by her forwardness and waiting for the signal to reciprocate.

An inch from his chest, which started heaving at her closeness, his cologne filled her senses. The fresh woodsy aroma was uncharacteristic of what she expected from most media men. His expansive shoulders seemed wider since the last time she looked, each muscle intimately defined in her imagination. The urge to verify and open his shirt itched at her fingers. Millimeter by millimeter, she leaned closer into him and heard his knuckles tighten on the post. The vein in his neck pulsed, faster with every beat.

She lifted her eyes to the gray orbs devouring her face, now darkened to the shade of billowing rain clouds. Her hand brushed against his sleeve as she slipped it through his arm and reached behind him, grabbing her toiletry case from the suitcase.

"I'll take the bathroom first. You can answer your

phone."

Only when she reached the bathroom across the hall did she hear Ethan blow out a sigh.

One thing was certain—he wasn't boring. And this weekend would certainly have its moments.

****

"Why didn't you answer the phone?" Bose McGavin's raspy voice called out when Ethan finally dialed him back.

"I was busy. But boy is this one big. Bose, I've hit the jackpot," Ethan murmured into the phone. How he managed to keep his voice low with Audrey taking a shower on the other side of the wall was beyond him. He could think of so many other things he'd rather be doing with that scrumptious body lathering up only a few feet away from his groin. He definitely needed to change into looser pants. "Not only is her family completely disinterested in her campaign, but the whole town seems bent against her for some reason. And get this, Allen isn't her real last name."

"What?"

Ethan laughed. "Yeah. Well, it's real now, but she was born Biddinger. This is big. As soon as I get a chance to poke around on the Internet, I'll have details."

"Shit, Ethan. You really are a magnet for scandals. I should have given you a raise after the county commissioner story."

"You're right," Ethan laughed. "And then some. This is gonna be my dream article, I can feel it."

"Keep me updated." A rustling broke up his words.

"What are you doing?"

"Mind your business."

More rustling caused Ethan to pause. And then a muffled laugh.

"Why the hell do you call when you're with a girl?"

"Because up until a few minutes ago, you did the same thing. Now call me later."

Click.

"Horny little bastard. It's Thanksgiving, and he's hired another one." *My mother really would be pissed that I work for this guy.*

Through the sound of the shower on the other side of the wall, Audrey's airy voice joined in, singing Lady Gaga's *You and I.* Ethan couldn't help laughing at her decent attempt, despite the occasional flat note.

And then it hit him. Bose was right. Audrey's bedroom was the first time he hadn't answered his phone.

Chapter Eleven

Before heading downstairs, Ethan debated bringing his hand recorder to dinner. Consent from everyone would be required before he recorded, and they would censor their statements, either consciously or not.

He shoved the recorder back in his suitcase. Besides, as a deputy, Adam would never agree, and definitely not as a hard-ass brother. More than likely, Audrey's father was the same way.

The man in the mirror had considerably fewer wrinkles in his slacks and collared shirt than Ethan expected. Wrinkle-free suits would have to be added to his wardrobe, considering they made him look this good. Not that he loved to brag about himself. But it was amazing what a fresh shower and "proper attire" could accomplish. *Good thing I packed my only decent pair of slacks.*

The more formal clothing may not have been necessary for a country Thanksgiving dinner, but this felt more important to Ethan. For some reason, Audrey seemed more deserving than his traditional cargo pants and cotton shirt that was lucky to see a washing machine, let alone an iron. Perhaps she and her family would be more comfortable talking to someone who looked like he walked out of GQ magazine, not a back alley vagrant pushing a grocery cart.

The bathroom was so full of steam after his shower

he could barely see his face as he shaved, even after the second attempt. Or maybe it was because his blood was pumping from imagining Audrey in the shower that he couldn't keep his hands steady. He'd switched the water to cold and simmered for a few minutes to cool his aching hard-on. No other girl or coed in any bar had affected his imagination like that. The hairs on his neck stood just as high and hard as his penis when she prowled across her bedroom like that, staring at him with those cobalt irises, like she intended to lick a chocolate smudge from his lips. He never remembered buying pants that tight. Or feeling that desirable.

A knock came at his door. He could only imagine Audrey's face when she saw the polished Ethan Tanner simmering on the other side.

"Can't wait to give me a kiss, can you?" Ethan swung open the door and his mouth dropped. Adam's scowl filled the doorway, along with his red flannel shirt.

"I'd rather pummel you down the stairs, but I think my mother would object to the dents in the wood floor."

Ethan cleared the scratch in his throat. "Sorry. Thought you were—"

"Audrey?" Adam answered for him. "I'd think again before trying to pucker your lips at her, too."

Bingo. Get whatever you can out of this heap of muscle. He's clearly the one with the biggest grudge against Audrey.

"Why's that, Adam?" Keeping an innocent look on his face was hard with this minotaur burning holes into Ethan's forehead. His eyes were the same color as Audrey's, but much more vicious.

And they gave him all the answer Ethan would get out of him. At least directly.

"Dinner's ready," Adam growled between his teeth. "My mother wants you to sit beside her."

"Love to." Ethan followed Adam downstairs. This was not a guy to mess with. Despite the size of Audrey's brother, he trekked lightly across the floor with fast, nimble moves. *His training was well worth it.* Both in the army and law enforcement. If Ethan were to end up in a fight somewhere in his life, a friendship with Adam would definitely determine the winner. But he seemed like the kind of guy whose only friends were former military men. And Ethan didn't fit that description.

The further down the steps he went, the stronger the smell of roasted turkey and all the fixings filled the house. The amount of time that had passed since Ethan had a home-cooked meal like this, let alone with a family sitting around the table, could have been measured by the continental drift. Turning the corner, he saw the table was already set with fine white china, little blueberries and apples painted on every dish with matching salad plates and crystal goblets. The burnt orange tablecloth could barely be seen under the perfectly placed food-dishes and two white candlesticks.

Adelaide fluffed table napkins when Ethan walked in. She smiled at him, the light in her dark blue eyes reflecting off the already-lit candles and her whole face glowed. Every child of the Biddingers had the same dark blue eyes, but Ethan was only affected by the light shining from Audrey's as she strolled in from the kitchen carrying a bowl of buttered corn.

She stopped in the middle of the doorway and her gaze met Ethan's. Her lips parted an inch as she looked him up and down. A blush spread up her cheeks to her ears, and Ethan's heart thumped harder. The brick red silk blouse hugged and silhouetted her breasts, drawing his eyes into the slight V of her cleavage. The silk cinched at the side of her waist, drawing his sight lower to the curve of her hips accentuated by the black slacks that hugged her in a way that would have made spandex jealous.

"Happy Thanksgiving," Adelaide sang.

It took Ethan's strongest willpower to break his eyes away and look at the teenager smiling at him.

"Happy Thanksgiving," he replied, his voice softer with a slight break he didn't expect. Suddenly he felt inadequate. He should have brought flowers. Both for Audrey, Adelaide, and their mother. Or an expensive bottle of wine or champagne. Something.

His mother had taught him better, but it had been so long. Memories of her were now distant and faded. What was this ache in his chest?

He moved at the sound of shuffling behind him, and saw Sally waddling down the hallway, arm held closely by her husband. The scowl on his face wasn't as pronounced around his wife. And whose would, with the bright face of the southern belle on his arm?

"You clean up nicely, Ethan," Sally said breathlessly. They moved into the dining room as Adam guided his wife to the far side and helped her sit across from Adelaide. The closest chair to the bathroom door, Ethan noted.

"Thanks. You're practically glowing, Sally."

Adam's scowl deepened again. "You gonna flirt

with every woman in this house?"

Audrey glanced up at her brother as she set down the corn and moved to sit next to Adelaide.

"Oh hush, sweetie." Sally lightly swatted Adam's arm. "He's just being polite to a tired, pregnant woman."

Right on cue, Mrs. Biddinger came through the kitchen doorway carrying a steaming tray of a golden turkey, trimmed with cherries and parsley. The sweet aroma infiltrated the room and Ethan's nose, sending electric signals down his nerves straight into his grumbling stomach.

Adam squeezed into the chair next to his wife. Audrey's father was the last to stroll into the room from his man cave, and surveyed the table like a bear fresh out of hibernation. Myrna placed the turkey in front of her husband.

"You've outdone yourself again, Myrna." He adjusted his belt and kissed his wife on the forehead. The simple, yet intimate, gesture caught Ethan off guard. Every interaction he'd had with Audrey's father imprinted a gruff, almost-cold man into his mind, and this small glimpse into the tender pockets of this man's façade proved he may not be as unforgiving as he portrayed.

Then his somewhat-forgiving eyes rested on Ethan, and all the tenderness erased. Like a bucket of ice water on the first day of spring.

"Get what you came for yet?"

"Daddy," Adelaide muttered from the other side of the table.

"Do you mean Audrey or Shakespeare?" Adam tossed a glare at Audrey sitting in front of him.

"I think we're sitting down to the meat of the weekend right now...in more ways than one." Ethan maintained his cordial demeanor. *Let the games begin.*

"That we are," Myrna chimed in and grabbed Adelaide's and Adam's hands. "Let's say grace." Everyone held hands around the table. Mr. Biddinger's mouth twitched when he took Ethan's palm in a vice grip.

Audrey's fingers were soft and warm, spreading heat into his right hand. Her skin was like silk and a thought flickered that it was just as smooth in every corner of her body.

If there's a God, he'll strike me with lightning for thinking like this during grace.

"Heavenly Lord, bless this food which we are about to receive." Myrna, along with everyone at the table, closed her eyes as she spoke. "Bless all those who are less fortunate and bring peace upon them. We are thankful for Audrey's presence, and the gift of new friends."

Ethan had bowed his head like everyone else, but wasn't used to praying before a meal. He wasn't used to praying, period. Upon hearing "new friends," he looked up and saw Myrna wink at him from across the table. If her hair had been white, she would have been the embodiment of Mrs. Claus.

"We thank you for the new life you've blessed Sally and Adam with and pray for a healthy baby. We thank you for the constant presence and guidance you give Addy as she prepares for her next pageant. Above all, Lord, we thank you for your unending grace and love. In His name we pray."

Murmurs of "amen" around the table warranted

Ethan to follow suit, despite the strange feeling it brought. Or was it Audrey's faint squeeze of his hand before she let go that caused it?

"When's your next pageant?" Audrey pulled her napkin from the ring.

"Three weeks in Richardson. You gonna be able to make it?"

"I'll really try." Audrey smiled as everyone started passing the side items while Mr. Biddinger began to carve the turkey.

"If she wins the election, she might be committed to a billion events by that time." Plugging her politics into the conversation was the quickest way to start getting the goods he needed for his article. Whatever scandal resided in this family's dining room had to start there.

But the hurt on Adelaide's face after his comment made him wish he'd chosen something subtler. Audrey caught it, too.

"I'd rather not discuss politics at the dinner table." Mr. Biddinger held the serrated carving knife at an odd angle.

"Addy's pageants mean just as much to me as any campaign stop, if not more. Go ahead and reserve a seat for me. Where are you getting your formal wear?"

"Trudy's. She makes the best dresses."

"Yes, she does." Audrey sipped wine. "If Mom and Dad don't object, I'd love to pay for it when it's ready."

"Since when do you care about pageant dresses?" Adam chimed in. "You were always more interested in scribbling in that notepad and wreaking havoc across town."

Adam stared hard back at Audrey, who hadn't

paused in dishing up sweet potatoes on her plate. Sally placed her hand on Adam's arm.

"I care about Addy and what she loves to do. Just as I care about you and the things you love."

Peacemaker is back at it. So she's more willing to defend herself with her family than she is with people in her hometown. Something didn't add up, but the tension around the table thickened with every spoonful.

Adam snorted and plopped green beans onto his plate before passing them and serving up corn. "Don't use that politician schmooze with me. You already know I won't be voting for you. You don't give a sh—" A quick glance to his mother stopped him with a stern look. "…crap about what I love. Nor anyone else's."

"Adam…" Myrna's warning, though soft, was just as forceful.

"White meat or dark?" Paul announced. "Pregnant ladies first. Pass me your plate, Sally."

"White, please. Thank you." Sally smiled as Adam picked up his wife's plate and handed it over.

"I was thinking royal or cobalt," Adelaide continued the passing plates. "I think one-shoulder would look best with crystals across the bodice and then 'flowy' silk cascading in the back, like a waterfall."

"That sounds gorgeous," Ethan broke in. "That color blue would really bring out your eyes."

Everything paused at the table as everyone stared at Ethan. Adelaide's smile beamed across at him. His attention was pulled away with another squeeze on his wrist and Audrey gave him a wink.

A corner of his gut tightened at the sight. Her legs and curvy figure had nothing on that wink. It could melt a man's skin in the middle of the Arctic. Ethan bet only a spare few people in her world received it.

"Ethan!" Paul barked.

He jerked his head up. "I'm sorry. What?"

"White or dark?" the man asked roughly.

"Both please." He passed his plate.

"That explains a lot," Adam muttered as he shoved half a roll into his mouth. He barely moved when Adelaide elbowed him in the ribs.

"Ethan, dear," Myrna chimed in with an upbeat voice. "Tell us about yourself. Were you born in Texas?"

Not that Ethan wanted the conversation directed at him. He avoided talking about his past and the questions everyone inevitably threw at him. But he had to play this part if he was going to get something out of this family. And there was no missing Audrey's intent gaze at the question, which made his mouth a little dry.

"In Houston. Got my undergrad at UT Austin. Then my Masters at Brown before I started at the *Dallas Morning Journal*." Simple as possible. What kind of questions can they come up with from that generic response?

"Are your mother and father still in Houston?"

Damn. He squirmed in his chair and cleared his throat. "No, my mom passed away a few years back and my father left for Chicago a long time before that." Forcing his voice to stay flat and unemotional had become second nature over the years when this topic came up. Particularly as he bit the inside of his mouth to push the resentment back down his throat.

"Oh, I'm sorry," Myrna replied with sincere sympathy. Ethan relaxed when she quickly changed the subject. "Did you always know you wanted to be a writer?"

"I was on the Yearbook Committee in high school and realized journalism was my forte." A bite of turkey almost dissolved on contact in his mouth with a sweet flavor only a premier chef could identify. "This is delicious. What did you marinate this with?"

"Cream sherry," Audrey answered for her mother with a smile, followed by a bite herself.

"And a few other things," Myrna added.

"Audrey was on the Yearbook Committee at her high school, too," Adelaide interjected. "For a while."

"Yeah, during the brief times she wasn't terrorizing the village and breaking hearts." Adam sat back in his chair.

"Audrey was a heartbreaker?"

"Yeah, but she looks way different now," Adelaide clarified. "I'll show you." The kid darted out of her chair.

"Not right now, Addy, please." Audrey put down her fork and shook her head.

In less than five seconds, Adelaide bounded back into the room carrying a thin brown leather book and flipped the pages. "This is her senior yearbook. Daddy says she was a 'rebel' rouser."

Ethan chuckled at the term while Adelaide found the page she wanted. When she passed the book to him, he reached out with wide eyes and a lopsided grin.

"Addy, does this really have to be done at the table?" Audrey went to swipe the book from her sister's hands, but Ethan jerked it away. The woman flushed and pursed her lips, in that adorable way only little sisters could create.

Across the page were color photos of the senior class, and toward the bottom, mixed among bright smiles, black robes and perfectly coiffed hairdos— Audrey's dark blue eyes beamed out, crossed, with red and blue strands streaked through her short hair, slightly longer than pixie cut. All it needed was a tongue sticking out, and she would have been the perfect fourth stooge. Larry, Curly, Mo and Bozette.

Ethan laughed and looked back at Audrey, trying to find the resemblance in her now-dark hair plummeting past her shoulder blades. "This is hardly the usual senior portrait."

"Exactly." Audrey tried to yank the book out of his hands. "That was the point."

He pulled the book out of her reach and read the text beside her photo. "Audrey Biddinger, Personal motto: 'Think outside the cage.' Aspiration: Art school."

"Art school. Politics wasn't your plan from the beginning?"

As the table fell silent, Ethan's eyes caught the photo to the left of Audrey's. Adam. The young, unwrinkled and easy smile on the adolescent Adam's face didn't match anything he saw in her brother today. It took a second for Ethan to remember the two were in the same grade. He read the text to himself. *Adam Biddinger, Personal motto: 'Never back down.' Aspiration: Army officer.*

That part fit perfectly with the image Adam embodied today. Another second went by before Ethan realized the table was still silent. Not even the sound of utensils clinking on the plates.

"Nope," Adam answered for his sister. "She stole

that dream from someone else, among other things."

"Adam," his mother whispered.

"More like living the dream *for* someone," Audrey replied softly, spooning corn between her teeth.

A fork clanked as Paul put down his silverware and crossed his arms, staring at his only son. "You really want to talk about this right now?"

"It's clear Adam doesn't approve of my profession." Audrey kept her voice even and tender. As if defending herself in her childhood home required careful plotting, just like any politician delicately considered each word before they spoke. "And I can't change his mind." Audrey wiped her mouth with a napkin. "But either way, I'm proud of him and what he's accomplished. You're living your dream. But I take it you don't care that I'm happy for you. It's clear you're holding onto an anger so deep that nothing I say or do will ever be good enough for you to be proud of me. Or at least accept me. And I've accepted that. I'm not here to have you approve my decisions."

"Then why are you here?" Adam crossed his own arms and stared harshly into Audrey's empathetic eyes.

"Because I love you. You're my family, no matter what happened."

"You're a liar."

Audrey's jaw clenched, the muscle twitching up behind her ear, and the empathy in her eyes now faded into bitterness. "I never lie."

"You sure as hell chose a profession that required it. It made sense to me when I heard you were running for office."

Ethan swallowed the food in his mouth and leaned back slightly. This was no simple sibling quarrel.

Audrey Allen, the candidate, never grew defensive. But with family, Ethan knew better than anyone these could be the most painful and vicious.

"You're one to talk," Adelaide bit out.

"That was different," Adam replied without taking his eyes off the target of his anger.

"What are you talking about?" Audrey glanced at Adelaide, who looked warily at her father.

Sally pushed a green bean across the plate with her fork, holding Adam's clenched fist on the table. When no one answered, Audrey turned to her father. "Adam ran for an office?"

Paul leaned back in his chair and sighed. "He ran for sheriff last year."

Audrey blanched. Seeing her surprised was a different angle than Ethan expected from her. Audrey Allen knew everything that went on her district, had responses for every difficult question before they were even asked. But apparently not within her own family.

This was getting better with every second. *Then why am I not as excited as I thought I would be?*

"And?" Audrey waited for Adam, but he clearly bit his tongue hard inside his piercing scowl.

"He lost, sweetie," Myrna replied sadly.

"I'm sorry. Sheriff Mallory has held that position forever. He's a hard man to beat."

"No, Mallory retired. Adam ran against Billy Buck." Paul picked up his fork and shoved in another bite of turkey.

"Billy? The guy who toilet-papered every cheerleader's house in high school?"

Her father grunted and took a sip of wine.

"Well…was it close?"

"No," Adam bit out.

"But...you're army. Billy never served, did he? What was his campaign strategy?"

Her family all looked down at their plates, except Adam. His glower darkened over the steaming plate of food. This guy screamed for anger management courses.

Ethan took a small sip of water, something to fill the uneasy silence.

"No one voted for the brother of a murderer."

Ethan snorted what little liquid was in his mouth. Before he dropped the glass, he managed to set it on the table and stared, dumbfounded.

Murderer? Talk about a fucking bombshell.

The room roared with silence. Instead of defending herself as Ethan expected from the prodigal politician, she gaped at him, with a touch of moisture at the corner of her eyes. There was no movement in her chair, except for the slightly faster lift and drop of her chest. Eventually, her eyes dropped to the table.

"You have nothing to say now, do you?" Adam glared at her. "Miss Always-Have-Something-To-Fight-About is finally speechless."

"I'm sorry he used that against you." Audrey's voice lowered an octave. "Guess he figured throwing lies like that was his only chance at beating you."

"I never had a chance!" He pounded his fist on the table, clattering every dish and spilling droplets of wine on the tablecloth. "It doesn't matter who I am, what I do, or my experience. My potential has already been determined because of you!"

"I'm sorry you feel that way, Adam." Keeping her voice calm and steady in the face of a screaming madman was the mark of any true negotiator or mediator—or a sister who truly loved her brother. If anyone screamed in Ethan's face like that, he normally matched their volume with insults or threw a punch. Especially in his drinking days. That's why Audrey was the one running for office, not him.

"Don't placate me," Adam spat back.

"I'm not. I hope you don't think that of yourself. I know how great your potential is, even if some people here don't."

"So now the people in this town aren't good enough for you? You sayin' you're better than everyone in this place?"

"Not at all. But clearly they don't have a clue what really happened that night and chose to make up their own conclusions." The pause in her voice showed the ache in her heart. "I thought as my only brother you knew me better."

Adam threw his napkin down onto his plate and pushed his chair back. Lifting his husky frame out of the chair, he leaned his fists on the table and glued fiery eyes on Audrey. "As far as I'm concerned, you're just an unwelcome guest in my parents' house." His fury switched to Ethan for a second. "With another sorry fool at your side bound to suffer the same fate."

Raising her chin to meet his gaze, Audrey refused to react to Adam's dig.

"Why don't you do us all a favor and leave? It seems that's what you do best."

Adam's feet clomped on the wood floor as he stormed out of the room and down the hallway toward the back porch. The screen door squealed and banged against the white siding, and then slammed shut.

"You told me Adam lost because Billy Buck had more advertising money," Adelaide said to her mother softly. "Audrey didn't murder anybody. Did you, Aud?"

Only Ethan and Adelaide waited for Audrey to respond, but she clearly wouldn't open her mouth now. The faraway look in her face as she looked at the empty chair across from her was all she would give. A last wipe of her mouth with her napkin, Audrey stood slowly, taking her wine glass with her.

"Mom, everything is delicious, as always. But I've lost my appetite. Excuse me." Leaving her plate full of food, her footsteps were mere taps on the planks as she climbed the stairs, and the distant sound of her bedroom door closed.

Good God, the story here was epic. As was the pain, resentment, and a need for family therapy. But as the journalist inside Ethan drooled over the potential story, a stronger urge to follow Audrey upstairs and hold her gripped his conscience.

"Ethan." Myrna cleared her throat as she quietly said his name. "As you can tell, this family has been through a lot. Small towns are notorious for talkin' and pretty soon a small creek is as wide as the Mississippi. But no matter how false rumors are, squashin' 'em is like unringin' a bell."

Chapter Twelve

There weren't enough wine bottles or warm blankets in the world to comfort Audrey as she curled up on her old mattress and tried to shove her shoulders as far into the corner as they would fit. Her mother had painted over the smudges on the wall where she'd used to doodle with a pencil—her usual juvenile coping mechanism.

Only this time instead of using a pencil, she coped with a full of glass of red wine. It was a much more effective therapeutic tool. Even if only temporary.

"An unwelcome guest," he called me. Of the few who were supposed to support me, he was the first to cast me out.

No matter how hard she fought it, a tear slipped out of her eye and rolled to her cheek. She wiped it away, only to have another one follow behind it. *Snap out of it, Audrey.*

She'd spent years of her life in depression, crying in solitude and desperate to keep her mind occupied and out of the depths of darkness to relapse again.

The phone vibrated in her pocket. Wiping her face again, she yanked it out and squinted through the mist in her eyes to see the screen. Miranda.

After clearing her throat twice, she answered. "Did you reach Houston intact?"

"Barely. Flight attendants are mean."

"It's Thanksgiving. They have to put up with a lot more crap than you." Audrey rolled off the bed and groaned at her pitiful reflection in the mirror: splotchy skin, puffy eyes, and slightly running mascara. Black lips would have made the zombie-look complete. "You didn't kill any of them, did you?"

"No, although one wench was asking for it."

"We won't be getting any complaints to our campaign office, will we?" Audrey wiped the mascara away and cleared her scratchy throat, again.

"If we do, we'll move Airline Passenger Bill of Rights to the top of your platforms list."

"Behind the Crisis Center, of course." Audrey laughed.

"Anyhoo, we're about to sit down to turkey, but I just wanted to check in with you and make sure Ethan is behaving."

"He's not the one you should worry about."

"What do you mean?"

"My brother isn't...cooperating." The pressure between her eyes grew, and she pinched the bridge of her nose to suppress it.

"He's the Marine turned cop, right?"

"Army, but yeah."

"Not surprising. Cops don't like the media."

"Not just that..." The silver frame on her dresser caught her attention, and she picked it up, staring at the happy faces of her parents holding her baby sister, while Adam and her younger self wrestled in the foreground, laughing. "He's had this longstanding grudge against me and is unwilling to help."

"He's not making things worse, is he?"

"For the campaign or for my family?"

"Either."

It became hard to breathe, suddenly. The thought of her family torn apart further by the tragedy a decade ago ripped at her heart, and even more by Adam's contempt. It was one thing to have the whole town believe the worst in her, but quite another to have her brother believe she was capable of anything malicious. And to top everything off, her insecurities were stripped bare in front of the first man she was insanely attracted to in ten years. As hard as it was to admit she was attracted to someone, let alone a newsman, being embarrassed in front of him proved there was not only no way he'd be interested in seeing her in the future, but also wouldn't paint a positive light for her campaign.

Salvage what you can. You can't pursue both, so pick one and save it.

"It's nothing I can't handle. Say hi to your family for me, and enjoy the turkey."

"Hang in there, girl. It's almost over."

Audrey sighed, amazed she was able to draw in a breath. "It's only just begun."

****

"Throw another log on that pit, Ethan," Paul ordered from his patio chair on the back porch. It was just the two of them, Adam and Sally having departed shortly after he simmered down and her heartburn kicked in. As cute as babies were, they sure caused a hell of a lot of problems and inconveniences. Not that Ethan would admit that to the heavily showing woman. Pregnant girls were overly emotional, to boot. And Adam wasn't much better right now.

Ethan grabbed a piece of wood from the cut stack

and tossed it into the metal pit just off the porch, then resumed his seat on the thin cushion behind him. If there was a full moon out, no one could admire it with the sky now covered by clouds in the dark night. The fire cracked and sparked, casting a whitish-orange glow on Paul's face and across the lawn. The sound of trickling water filled the air from the creek just beyond the glow of the firelight.

Men abided by unwritten rules, including never looking at each other when surrounding a fire. They were required to look at the pit, or the sky, or anywhere else when talking of profound things. They were lessons Ethan never learned from his father, but from his friends and colleagues as he meandered through life. Even though his career goal required ripping Audrey Allen's campaign to shreds with any unpleasant details he uncovered this weekend, he still respected her father as the man sipped on his beer nestled in his own patio chair. He'd continue to respect him simply because her father never left his family. He may have been a quiet man at the table, hard on his children at times, but he didn't leave.

A trait Ethan hadn't seen in his own pitiful excuse for a father, despite the asshole's success in business.

But Ethan was never one for small talk, and getting to the center of tootsie pop was best achieved in one bite.

"Your son has a lot of anger, but calling his sister a murderer is something you don't hear every day."

A long pause filled the space between them, but Ethan knew Paul was a man of few words. Careful not to fidget or move his gaze from the fire pit, Ethan waited. Some people needed coaxing to speak up, but

Ethan knew this man needed time. And silence.

"For most people, you'd be right," he finally answered after a long sip of beer.

"You don't see many murderers running for office."

One grunt was laugh enough for the old eyes gazing across the lawn. "I'm sure I don't want to know the real answer to that question."

"Even something as dramatic as Adam's accusation, in front of a journalist no less, I'm smart enough to know there's more history than what was said."

"Then as a journalist, you know people love dirty laundry, as long as it's not their own hangin' on the wire for everyone to see." He crushed his empty beer can on his leg and threw it in a bucket behind him.

"That's the truth."

"No, I'll tell you the truth." Audrey's father leaned forward in the chair and broke the man rule of the night by looking him straight in the eye. The direct connection from his hard stare made the fire stop crackling in his ears. "I'm not ignorant to the kind of things you write. I know what you're here for and I don't like it. My daughter has been through enough in life. This town has been through enough. I'm askin' you to leave this one alone and find whatever dirt your lookin' for somewhere else."

Saliva filled Ethan's mouth, but he wouldn't dare swallow. Paul hadn't broken the man rule, but instead used the one exception men were allowed: to look a man in the eye when he was threatened. Where the magnitude of the message was of the utmost importance. But all media junkies lived for stories like this, and Paul's insistence to stay away only made Ethan want to push more.

"She's running for a public office. Opening this can of worms was her doing." Despite the meaning of his words, Ethan made sure to keep his tone sympathetic, even softened.

"No, you opened it."

"Then why'd she come home and let me see this if she didn't want the worms set free?"

"You should ask her that."

"I did. She said she wanted me to see her family. Said you had big hearts, bigger hospitality, and you were the best people she knew."

For a man who showed no other emotion than condemnation, Paul displayed shock well enough. The wrinkles on his forehead pointed upward for once and Ethan could see the full white of his eyes instead of a half-squint.

Eventually, he looked away and cleared his throat. He reached down beside his chair and cracked open another can. "Hard to hear that." Long sips filled the break between his words. "Words I don't really deserve. It's been a long time since my daughter has done something with her life I could get behind. Her teenage years were my toughest as a father. She did a lot of things I didn't approve of."

The normal response for someone without an agenda would have been "don't most teenagers?" It's what Ethan wanted to say to console a doting father. But his dirt-digging job had trained him otherwise.

"Like what? She didn't want to join Junior League?"

Paul shook his head and focused on his boots.

"That was her mother's dream, not mine. She was rebellious, headstrong, stubborn...desperate to show her independence. I lost track of how many times we were called by parents upset with something Audrey said to their daughters, or just generally complaining. But underneath it all, Audrey had a good heart and meant well. She was the first to help a hurt stray or give her lunch money to a kid whose parents were laid off."

Sounds familiar. With how hard and heavy Audrey pushed for this Women's Crisis Center, it was bound to be the grand slam of philanthropy. Perhaps a trait she inherited from her family, or maybe just born with a golden heart among a town of bronze pellets.

"But any ruckus that went on in this town was put on Audrey's shoulders, whether she was responsible or not." Paul grabbed another beer and tossed it in Ethan's lap as he continued. "It didn't help that senior pranks were her specialty, all four years of high school. But at the end of the day, people just disapprove of anyone different. And Audrey was different."

Yes, she is. Which is probably why I can't stop thinking about her.

Ethan stared at the beer can in his hand. Four years without a drop of alcohol, but he didn't want to insult the man who had just started to squeeze out the juice he needed for his article. So he just held the frigid metal in his fingers.

"But as hard as I've been on Audrey, Adam is tenfold. He *does* have a lot of anger and he has his reasons. Just like many people in this town. The way I see it, there are three things that run deep in this place: that creek over there, memories, and grudges."

The clouds moved with the wind, allowing a sliver

of a half moon to shine across the grass into the heavy woods on the other side of a large crevice. The branches in the large oaks creaked and swayed to the rhythm of the flowing water that Ethan could hear, but not see within the fracture's dark space.

"My daughter is many things, but not a murderer. She was just in the right place at the wrong time. People made assumptions, chewed on it like tobacco to an outlandish story, and stuck it to the bottom of their boots."

"What kind of assumptions?"

"You'll have to ask her."

They sat staring at the dying fire. Maybe it was another *man rule*, or maybe it wasn't, but leaving a fire before it dwindled felt disrespectful. At least out here where the stars were brighter, even if hidden above a layer of clouds.

Chapter Thirteen

Nothing I can't handle.

Audrey had been saying those words for the last ten years, so often it felt like her personal motto. At what point would she run into a situation she couldn't handle? And how would she respond? Explode into a raging tirade of expletives, throw punches and karate kicks, or withdraw completely like a scared rabbit?

It was a wonder she *handled* the events that had led to this point without losing her sanity. At least, when in public. Distraction was a useful tool in times like that.

So Audrey buried herself in the paperwork she had brought along for the weekend, while snug in her green flannel pajama pants and loose T-shirt. Speech notes, campaign funding reports, and upcoming interview agendas. She would have much rather reviewed legislative bills or construction plans for the Crisis Center. God willing, this election would help her achieve both.

Wyatt Williams was a fierce competitor with years of experience in the House of Representatives. But all of those years proved he was nothing more than a bull in a china closet, or a snake in a rat's nest. Audrey just needed to show the people she was more capable of getting things done in Austin without blowing up the bank. Which would be a lot harder now that her own brother had accused her of murder in front of a reporter.

Canyon's notes on her latest speech blurred red across the black and white text. The guy was a genius in pinpointing statistics to prove a platform, and putting them in words that swayed even the most confirmed disbelievers. Her campaign team was the killer combination. Miranda found the right venues and audience, Canyon wrote the words with which to influence people, and Audrey closed it. But the fourth companion on her team started to fail her: the empty glass of wine on her desk.

The clip in her hair itched her scalp, and when she pulled it out, the ache permeated down each strand of hair. She massaged her head and grimaced at the split ends. She'd need to cut them before the awards ceremony on Saturday.

"You hardly look the murdering type."

The soft words made her breath stop. She stared at her bedroom door, now open with Ethan's eyes boring into hers. The dim light reflected in his pupils, dilated and playful. She didn't remember hearing a knock or the door squeak open, and his stare felt like an intrusion. One arm braced on the frame, he held a glass of clear liquid on the rocks in the other. But what unnerved her most were his eyes waiting for a response to the uncomfortable question.

"You must be used to not knocking, as a scandal seeker. But please remember you're in someone else's house and etiquette rules apply." Audrey pushed up from the chair and steadied herself, trying to wince out the needles in her leg, which had fallen asleep. And it was the wrong moment for her nipples to react to his manly presence.

"Etiquette?" His eyes laughed back at her. "How

about answering a question?"

"You didn't ask one." She crossed her arms, hoping it hid most of her body's unwanted response.

"Touché. I never thought I'd see The Peacemaker crying."

"I'm not crying. And don't call me that here."

"Oh, okay. Then I'll just take the wetness in your eyes as allergies and the empty wine glass as medicinal."

"There's no story from what you heard downstairs. Nothing politically related, anyway."

"Everyone has family crap. It's required if you're a human being." Ethan stepped forward and swung the chair around, straddling it like a horse—slowly—and crossed his arms over the back. The junction between her legs reacted with a traitorous clench and warmth. She refused to acknowledge it.

"Including you?"

"I don't have a family. I'm exempt."

"Didn't you say your father was in Chicago?"

"He's not my family."

Audrey nodded. "Yep, including you."

"I take it there's a lot of history from what happened downstairs."

Audrey shrugged and held the glass in one hand, cradling it between her fingers. "Everyone has a black swan in the family."

The man's eyes studied her for several moments, and the feeling of intrusion took over again. Like an unwilling patient being examined by a curious doctor who just started worrying about how his pokes and prods could hurt. Another heartbeat later, as they continued to stare at each other, his gaze took on an entirely different characteristic. Whether it was his deeper breathing or the moisture on his lips thickening, with the corners of his mouth turned up a hair, suddenly all she wanted was for him to stay right where he sat. Legs spread and hot pheromones dripping from his gaze. Her T-shirt tugged against her nipples, now starting to ache. Heat built inside of her body, though from the wine or his presence, she couldn't tell. It didn't matter. Just as long as he kept looking at her. Testing the limits without questions.

He took a long sip from the glass. It could have been vodka, or possibly gin, but there was no smell to it, only a few feet from his penetrating stare. Water was the best guess. Why just water? Guys like him probably lived on beer or Coke and rum.

The great watcher licked his lips, deliberately, taking his time in conjuring up his next move. But unlike her body's responses, she wasn't going to make it easy on him.

"I take it the right place at the wrong time ended in someone's death. And perhaps that was also the last time you were here."

Audrey kept her eyes on his face, trying to capture a glimpse of gloating that he was sure to reveal. But her only answer to his affirming face was more silence.

"Two for two. Which would explain the name change. To hide whatever happened here."

"I never said I was hiding."

There he goes again. Making assumptions of the most unimportant details. Journalists were all the same. *Don't trust him, Audrey. He's out for the story, and not you.*

"There's obviously a lot of pain there. Your brother

called you a murderer. How does that make you feel?"

Disappointed, hurt, unloved. All of the above she wanted to admit, and had to her therapist over the years. But not to the journalist. If the human with a heart ever showed up in Ethan's place, she'd probably spill everything.

"To be honest, nothing I wasn't expecting. I *hoped* for something more sibling-like, but I'm not surprised." Audrey sat on the comfort of her bed, hoping a brace could offer some kind of support, anything to get her mind off how damn hot this wolf looked.

"You said Adam was the protective type. I don't think calling your sister a murderer is very protective."

"He *is* protective, just not of me. Not anymore, anyway."

"What causes a brother to lose that instinct for his sister? For you?"

"I know what you're targeting." Audrey's eyes narrowed in on him. "And you're not going to find the answers you're looking for. You said you'd leave my family out of this."

Adam let out an annoyed sigh and uncrossed his arms, now gripping the sides of the back of the chair. "We're not talking about your family. We're talking about you. So let's cut to the chase. What exactly is everyone talking about? What happened?"

"You're the journalist. Why don't you dig it up for yourself?"

"You know I'm going to. This is me asking for your side of the story."

"What's the point? You'll write the worst image of history, whether it's true or not. So why should I help you?" Fire raged in her stomach, as well as her mind, knowing the calm and collected Audrey Allen was losing it with this too-handsome-for-his-own-good reporter sitting in her favorite chair sprinkling gasoline on kindling embers.

"Because you need my help for your campaign. Because you're the one with the most to lose."

"Like you have nothing to lose."

"Nope. I didn't kill anyone."

"Neither did I."

The gleam in his eyes could burn cities to the ground. And enflame a passion more raw than anything Audrey had ever felt.

"I don't have a grudge against anyone," Audrey continued. "Well, except the media, because of this very reason. And I'm not going to let you hurt anyone in this town by scrounging for more scandals."

Ethan's eyes flared and his mouth dropped open, stealing the breath from her lips.

"You're not going to let *me* hurt…after what they did to you today?" His voice turned angry and biting. "After what they said? How can you protect them?"

Though he hadn't moved from the chair, his presence doubled and his face turned darker, more primal. The change was awing and intimidating. Why was he so passionate? Almost defensive.

"Adam isn't the only protective one in my family." Audrey stood from the bed and placed her wine glass on the dresser. The hair clip was her next distraction. Her next way of *handling* things, as she twirled her hair above her neck and secured it to her scalp.

Like a jaguar, Ethan silently slipped from her favorite chair and stopped only an inch from her face. His warm breath singed her lips as he pinned her to the spot with his gaze, and the hairs on the back of her neck stood up. Her palms grew sweaty and her knees weakened. Somehow she forgot to breathe with those sea-gray irises holding her in place.

"I'm going to find out the truth, Audrey." His silky voice conflicted with the dagger-like words. Just as the desire in his eyes conflicted with the very purpose of his presence. "When I do, you'll *want* to spill everything to me then."

His lips parted and his gaze moved to her mouth. The inch between them became a millimeter. If only her mind wouldn't let her care anymore, she'd let her body loose. Explore every wild thought in her mind.

"*If* you find out the *whole* truth, I won't have to spill anything. To anyone."

His gaze moved back to her eyes and suddenly she found her own lips parted. A tender touch slid through her fingers, shooting tingles up her arm and into her chest. Ethan's hand inched up to her wrist, where the full heat of his palm lightly closed around her arm. Instinctively, he pulled her against him and her waist moved against his hips, their mouths still barely a hair a part.

His grip moved from her wrist to her waist, both hands, and pressed further. The thickening against his pants grew harder, longer, and unmistakably hotter. Her core sparked and a red flame pooled in her groin. Just once, she wanted to let that side of her take over and quench it. Their hips ground against each other and their lips, hot and anticipating...

Thump.

A muffled laugh filtered through the door.

Ethan frowned and glanced down to the nonexistent space between their bodies. And his raging erection. Audrey couldn't catch her breath and realized the thump wasn't from either of them.

She glanced to the door and recognized the repeated muffled laugh as Adelaide's. And then a much deeper "Shhh" followed.

Audrey flattened her hands against Ethan's chest, his chest strong and hot, and then clenched his shirt in her fists. His breathing quickened under her fingers and he squeezed her hips harder. As if he refused to let her go.

So damn close.

She pushed away from him, as if space were her only salvation, and then moved to the door. A few steps later, she was down the hallway and ready to knock on Adelaide's door, when muffled whispers came through again.

Two voices. One she recognized, and the other not at all. "Keep quiet, Brace. Gimme your shirt."

Adelaide's playful whisper to the enigmatic "Brace" stopped her breathing. The hot arousal lingering in her body chilled instantly. Painful memories filled her mind. *Not again.*

Audrey knocked lightly and didn't wait for a response. She opened the door and caught Adelaide kneeling on her bed wearing boy shorts and a pink lace bra. An adolescent wannabe body builder Brace stood at the end, wearing even less. Shock filled the boy's face, too stunned to cover his naked self, while fear filled Adelaide's eyes as she held Brace's T-shirt.

Before anyone could make a sound, Ethan moved behind her and witnessed the teenaged hormone exploratory session.

"Oh shit," he murmured.

"Oh shit," Brace repeated.

Not again. Audrey sighed as the only means to keep from groaning aloud and having her parents hear the commotion.

"Brace," Audrey snarled. "You have thirty seconds to get your clothes on and get out of this house before my father sees you. Addy," her fierce gaze flickered. "We need to talk. Now."

On the verge of tears, Adelaide nodded, covering herself with her arms.

Audrey closed the door and waited, as she heard movement around the room on the other side.

"Relax. They're just kids," Ethan whispered behind her.

"Exactly. She has no idea what fire she's playing with."

Ethan giggled. "That was hardly fire between his legs. More like the Oscar Meyer Weiner whistle."

"This is serious," she hissed.

"All right, I'll admit it wasn't smart to try that in her parent's house full of guests, but it's not like they're the first teenagers to bump uglies upstairs. I did worse at his age."

Audrey's eyes narrowed on him. "Oh, I have no doubt. Which is exactly why you should keep your butt out of this."

"Give them a few minutes." His voice darkened a shade. "Let's finish what we had starting in there." He lifted his hand to cup her cheek and her face burned.

"Go back to your room."

"Fine," he groaned. "But talk loud so I can hear you through the wall."

Chapter Fourteen

It didn't take long for Audrey to sober up after catching her sister on the verge of sex. A perfect glass of wine wasted. But the next conversation would surely instigate the hangover headache several hours ahead of schedule.

Adelaide curled herself up on the window seat peering out the same window that Brace had crawled through only fifteen minutes earlier, anxious for their tryst. The pink cotton robe wrapped around her torso down to her knees, and through the tears she couldn't control, her eyes raged.

Sitting on Adelaide's bed didn't appeal to Audrey at the moment. Particularly not after what she just witnessed. So she sat on the other side of the window seat, careful not to invade her sister's personal space. Well, not as much as she already had.

The box of tissues was her first peace offering. Hopefully it would ease a little of the tension before Audrey asked questions to which she probably didn't want to know the answers. Adelaide plucked a few tissues and wiped her face, clearly fighting hard to hold back more tears.

"I take it this wasn't the first time." Audrey kept her voice soft, but wouldn't let her sister make the mistake of thinking she wasn't serious by using the same look of competition she used in debates.

Sniffles filled the room as Adelaide refused to look at her sister. A moment later, she shook her head. "Are you gonna tell Mom?" Adelaide's voice cracked through the sobs buried in her chest.

Audrey pursed her lips. "I *should*." She really should. No one had warned her that moving too fast at this age could cause immeasurable heartbreak. Not that she would have listened. Which worried her the most, knowing Adelaide possessed the same stubbornness.

And then her sister rested her eyes on Audrey's face, burning rage through her pupils. "I don't think you should be allowed to, since you just burst in here without permission." Each word grew louder, as much as she was willing to prevent being heard by their parents.

"I understand you're upset. You should be," Audrey replied calmly. Never raise your voice in an argument, or match the venomous tone. Audrey had learned the hard way it made things worse. Even if the argument Adelaide used was flawed and juvenile, she couldn't dismiss them. She chose her next words carefully, and spoke slowly. "But you have no idea what fire you're playing with."

Adelaide glared out the window and wiped her face with the tissue.

"Were you using some kind of protection, at least?"

"Uck! You really want to have this conversation?"

"Would you rather have it with Mom?"

"No!"

"Well, then you get me."

"You were my age not that long ago. You understand what this is like. Why aren't you on my side?"

"Because I know *exactly* what you're going through, and I'm trying to help you not make the same mistakes."

Adelaide closed her jaw and stared wide-eyed at her sister. The sympathy built in Audrey's chest as Adelaide wiped away more tears with the wadded tissue. Audrey had hoped she wouldn't have to reveal the details of her past to Adelaide, who was only a toddler when everything happened. But her sister was in the dangerous realm of repeating history. How could she let Addy suffer the same anguish if she had the power to prevent it?

"You were too young to understand what happened to me, but I know you loved me. Just as I love you. Because I love you, I'm telling you that you should be more protective of your childhood."

"I'm sixteen, I'm hardly—"

"But you are still a child, Addy." Audrey touched her hand, which Adelaide pulled away. "You wear adult dresses in those pageants, wear stage makeup, and give adult answers, but inside you are still a *child.* You have so much life ahead of you to make those decisions. Don't sacrifice what little childhood you have left."

"I'm not sacrificing anything. I'm on the pill, so I can't get pregnant. And I love Brace. I'll lose him if we stop."

Audrey blanched, but covered it by reaching for another tissue and handing it to Adelaide. "First, if you loved Brace, and he loved you, then sex would never be a condition of your relationship. If you think Brace will leave you just because you stop having sex, then it's not love. And you're better off without him. And your whole bit 'on the pill prevents pregnancy' is only the tip of the iceberg."

Adelaide rolled her eyes and wiped her face again. "Nothing's going to happen. I'll be fine."

"Yeah, those were the exact words I used, too."

Finally, that got her attention.

"Look, I know I can't stop you from doing what you want. But at least listen to my warning. From someone who understands the agony of what could happen from what you think is harmless. The consequences are far worse than you can imagine. And I don't want you to suffer the same way I did."

"You just left," Adelaide sniffled. "I thought when you got better, things would go back to the way it was before. But you just left."

The childlike tone in which Adelaide used nearly ripped Audrey's heart to shreds. The tears built again and Audrey bit her cheek to hold them back.

"I'm sorry I let you down, Addy. But I didn't leave." She paused, debating whether she should tell the full truth. The last thing she wanted to do was place blame, but Adelaide needed to hear it. "I was sent away. That way you could live your own life and not follow in my wake."

"What do you mean?"

"If I stayed here, people would have judged you and held you back from your dreams simply because I was your sister. I'm the reminder of what was lost. And we didn't want people to hurt you because of my mistakes."

"Mom and Dad sent you away? What is this, the Dark Ages?"

"No, it's East Texas. And right now you have one

foot on the same high-speed railroad tracks I went down. Please step off of it."

Adelaide stared hard out the now-foggy window for long moments. The tears had stopped, but her face was still red and puffy. "Are you gonna tell Mom?"

She should. Everything she'd read about adolescent deviant behavior instructed her to tell their parents, but something in her gut stopped her. Maybe this talk was enough. Enough to get her thinking, anyway. "No," she finally answered. "I love you. I won't say anything. I'm going to trust you, and hope you'll do the right thing."

Adelaide shifted slowly across the window seat and wrapped her arms around Audrey's shoulders. The hug tightened as Audrey smoothed her hand over Adelaide's soft hair. A moment later she pulled away and wiped her face again.

Audrey stood and noticed a pair of white underwear peeking out from underneath the bed. "Addy—" Audrey pointed at them and smirked. "Make sure Mom doesn't see Brace's tightie-whities."

****

The clock on the nightstand struck 11:30 as Ethan stared at his laptop, the blank document cursor blinking at him. Every beat blinked in rhythm with the coaxing in his mind. *Just…write…it. I dare you.*

This was major. Colossal. A senate candidate was just accused of murder by her own brother. All it took was a definitive source and the article of Ethan's career would practically be written for him. And he'd be on his way to New York. Just as he dreamed. Premier journalist for a major publication was one exposé away.

But for the first time in his life, Ethan struggled with some splinter buried at the back of his psyche. He couldn't even identify what it was, or what it signaled, but he didn't like it. Maybe it was his body's retaliation for smelling beer tonight, or Audrey's empty wine glass, and Ethan's refusal to join in. They had once been his best friends, but now coffee was his surrogate confidant. Or the painful joystick between his legs left unattended in Audrey's bedroom.

All he could see was Audrey's smile and the tiny sparkle in the middle of those sapphire eyes as they stared back into his. His fingers craved to pull the clip out of her hair again, and watch the dark waves drape down her shoulders. And his loins ached when he watched her nipples push against her T-shirt. Did she notice his dick stand to attention?

When she ground her hips against him, he almost lost it. The first time he would have ever lost control, when sober. The woman knew exactly how desirable she was, and those pink cheeks and wet lips were enough to make a man beg. Which he was almost forced to do in the hallway. He wanted to ease the pain in a hot shower, but decided against it after the display in Adelaide's bedroom. Whacking off at that point would have made him feel like a pedophile, even if Audrey was the Biddinger that filled his imagination.

The laptop beckoned his fingers to open his internet browser, but every window came up blank. The annoying error message splayed across the screen. "No Internet Connection Detected."

Stupid rural towns. How did people survive without internet? And what kind of childhood was Adelaide suffering through without it? No email? No social media?

The library was definitely his first stop in the

morning.

How long can a sister's lecture on safe sex take? Surely an hour was enough. Oh, wait. Audrey's pet project was a Women's Crisis Center. This could take *days,* let alone hours.

Ethan couldn't see what the big deal was. As long as the two horny kids were being safe, who cared? Sex was about pleasure. Instant gratification in its most primal form. Women were the ones who dragged *feelings* into it and grew attached. Besides, how else were these kids going to learn to navigate their twenties? There were sick people out there who exploited the ignorant ones. Audrey should be glad Adelaide wasn't jostling with an older guy, or worse, a pageant judge or consultant. That really messed things up.

By the time his thoughts returned to Audrey's T-shirt, or rather the curves he imagined beneath them, a ruckus sounded through his window. First were creaking brakes from the street, and then pounding footsteps across wooden planks, followed by muddled voices. The view from his window spanned across the side yard where darkness enfolded the large oak tree, but the beams of truck lights were unmistakable.

Then glass shattered. A lot of it.

In Audrey's bedroom.

Squealing tires filled the air outside his window and the lights faded.

Ethan jumped off the bed, dashed out of the bedroom, and raced into Audrey's room.

Glass and chunks of brick littered the wood floor and across the bed. A cold air blew through the window, fluttering the ripped curtains, and Ethan saw the jagged lines of a broken pane.

Audrey wasn't there.

Where is she?

Panic gripped him and he stepped forward to look out the window, bare feet be damned. He couldn't think of anything except a prayer that Audrey hadn't fallen, or worse...

Before he could take another step onto the broken glass, Audrey's perfume filled the air. She appeared beside him and gasped.

Without a thought, he wrapped her in his arms and fought to stop shaking.

"What happened?" she whispered.

"Something shattered the window. I thought you..."

She pulled back and stared into his face, eyes wide and lips parted. Only when he took a deep breath, did she peer around him and saw the damage.

"Everything okay?" Paul's clipped voice called from the stairs.

"We're okay," Audrey called back. "Are you?" she directed to Ethan.

"Sure," he replied with a steady voice he didn't feel.

When his hands stopped shaking, he turned back to the room and spotted an old brick, red and faded with a paper rubber banded around the largest piece. Careful not to step on the shards of glass, Ethan moved the few feet to grab it. "I assume this is Brace pissed off for being caught?"

Audrey took the paper off the rubber band before Ethan could read what was scribbled in black marker. Her jaw tensed and she shook her head. "No. Much more pathetic." She crumpled the note and turned out of the bedroom, trekking to the stairs. Ethan could only follow.

From the top of the stairs, he saw the front door sitting open and Paul messed with something on the porch, a faint glow in front of him. Myrna gripped her robe and watched him with a disgusted grimace on her face.

By the time Audrey and Ethan reached the bottom of the stairs, a rancid smell overtook his senses and he covered his nose. *Burning shit.* Paul stepped to the side of the house to grab something. A brown paper sack on fire no more than two feet from their threshold. Ethan didn't have to guess what was inside.

Paul returned from the side of the house, hose in hand. He doused the flames and used the high spray to push the remnants into the grass. Eventually, he came back into the house, muttering something about "stupid kids" and "minding their own business." The stench still hung in the air, but mitigated when he closed the door.

"You two all right?" he asked. "Which window?"

"Mine," she answered quietly and squeezed the paper in her fingers.

Her father's eyes dropped to her hand and his jaw tightened. "Give it here."

Audrey hesitated, swallowing back whatever she was about to say. Instead, she descended a few steps and handed over the note. As it exchanged hands, Ethan read the big letters scratched across the paper.

RUN AWAY, MURDERER

His jaw dropped.

Paul's brow furrowed. The pain couldn't be

masked by the growl he swallowed.

Myrna appeared beside him with a broom and dustpan, and then stopped when she saw the note. There wasn't enough make-up to cover the embarrassment and torture on her face.

She pulled her daughter into a sideways hug and patted her shoulder. "We'll get this cleaned up and go back to bed."

Paul muttered something else that Ethan didn't catch, but Audrey had. She stepped forward and stood before her father. He stood a good foot and a half over her, making Audrey look younger than she was. He touched her chin and checked for cuts or scrapes, like every father would.

Every father but mine.

In one motion, Paul wrapped one arm around her and pulled her close. He glanced up at Ethan and then grimaced. With a final kiss on the cheek and a strangled sigh, his impassive self returned.

"Does this happen often?" Ethan's question suspended in the entry hall, waiting for someone to say "Of course not. Who gets bricks through windows and fiery bags of shit on their front porches like this?" But no one said it.

Audrey didn't look scared anymore. Only disappointed. She gave her mother one last sideways hug, took the broom and dustpan from her hands, and climbed the stairs. She brushed past Ethan's shoulder and her own sweet perfume briefly allowed a reprieve of the horrible smell from the porch. But she never looked at him and just kept climbing. Myrna retreated to her bedroom in the back of the house while Paul lingered behind with Ethan.

"Adam isn't alone in his interpretation." Ethan finally broached the subject.

Paul sighed heavily, as if the world's judgment rested on his house.

"Mackineer is probably the only town where Audrey Allen won't receive a single vote."

"Not even yours?"

"I don't vote."

Unbelievable. It was the kind of answer Ethan expected from his own father, who'd never given him a day's worth of validation or compassion in his life. But he had hard time accepting Paul Biddinger as the same type of cowardly man. The brief moment of concern he showed his daughter was proof of that. But it still wasn't enough. Not to Ethan.

"Well then, how do you expect her to do it?" he asked. *Prove me wrong.*

"Do what?"

"Go through life without her father's support?"

Ethan's accusation appeared to hit Paul like a bale of feathers. A pathetic pillow fight, imploded on impact. And he just stood there.

"I may be a vicious, scandal-seeking writer, but even I expect all parents to support their kids in whatever they do."

This pillow was filled with a lot more than feathers. More like lead marbles. *What would it take to get a reaction out of him?* A red face, clenched knuckles, a series of profanities shouted at the guest who dared insult the man in his own home about his parenting skills. Something.

But Paul just stood there, emotionless. "This isn't the first window I've had to replace. Or the first wash-off of my porch. She didn't ask for this kind of treatment, but there's nothing I can do about it, either."

"That could have been a shot gun shell instead of a brick," he barked. "Stand up to it. If you know who did it, why not press charges?"

He sighed and scowled. "She hasn't told you yet. Or, did you even dare to ask?"

Ethan blanched. As much as this man liked to shut out the world, he had a sturdy grasp on the meaning of things.

"If you did," Paul continued. "You've got more guts than I expected. But if she hasn't told you now, she never will. Especially after this."

"You seem to know her really well for a father who hasn't seen her in, what…ten years?"

"I know Audrey Biddinger. She has too much pride to admit faults after something like this. It only persuades her to fight more."

"And what about Audrey Allen?"

Paul stared back him, his piercing gaze unwilling to admit defeat.

If her own father wouldn't stand up for her, Ethan felt the necessity to do it for him. Why? He doubted he could ever explain it to himself, but something compelled him to open his mouth and say the words her father couldn't.

"Audrey Allen has accomplished a lot. Probably more than Audrey Biddinger could have hoped for. One of the youngest state senate candidates ever, and a woman, doubly hard. Even more incredible, a lot of people expect her to win. You might be surprised at what else she can accomplish if she didn't have to worry about bricks being thrown at her. If she had a little more support from you."

Paul's deep sigh finally triggered the animosity Ethan expected.

"Good night, Ethan," he bit out, tying his housecoat with one final glare before he trudged off.

Chapter Fifteen

The breeze through Audrey's window was frigid, but there was nothing worse than her stiff backside while they cleaned up the debris in her room. He desperately wanted to talk to her, to wrap his arms around her and forget the horrible sound of shattering glass. It was the one time he cursed the vivid imagination of a journalist.

Audrey swept the broken pieces into a pile in the center of the floor. She'd already slipped on a pair of shoes and stripped the comforter and pillow from the bed, just as she'd stripped the emotion from her face. A skill she'd mastered.

"Where's the linen closet?" Ethan hadn't expected his voice to sound so harsh.

Audrey just pointed to a door across the room.

Ethan fished out a spare set of sheets and the biggest blanket he could find. Someone knocked on her door and Adelaide stepped in, clutching a piece of cardboard, duct tape, and a weary frown.

The sisters gave each other a silent hug. Audrey took the items and laid them on the bed. With a worried glance, Adelaide closed the door and left Ethan alone with the continued silence.

This isn't my first broken window. Paul's words rang in his ears while Audrey scraped the first pile into the dustbin. The glass clanged against the metal trashcan in the corner.

What kind of fear did a teenage girl have to suffer through with a window shattered while she slept? No child deserved that kind of treatment, that kind of terror. Ethan's hands trembled at the image and the rage flowed through him.

He'd covered these kinds of stories on violent intimidation with rape cases and victim retaliation. The photos were never pretty, and neither were the outcomes. They were the kind of stories he hated to cover. Mainly because he finished the articles more angry than when he started. It didn't matter that journalists weren't supposed to show emotion—only report the facts and their interpretations. Despite his reputation, he had a heart. Maybe not a conscience, but at least a heart.

To stop the trembling, he had to keep his hands busy. So he grabbed the cardboard from the bed and taped it to the window frame, careful not to catch his fingers on the remaining shards of glass. When he was finished, he lowered the blinds and drew the curtains.

The air was still cold, but at least the wind wasn't blowing as hard.

"I'll sleep in here tonight," Ethan said to the window. "You can have my room." It was the first logical thing that popped in his mind. His mother would have demanded it, and he hadn't lost all of her lessons.

"No." The refusal was quiet, but adamant. He turned, but Audrey continued to sweep the debris into the trash bin.

"You can't be serious."

Audrey moved to the bed and grabbed the pillowcase, shoving the pillow inside. It was obvious she ignored him. It pissed him off.

In one move, he reached her side and grabbed her arm, though harder than he intended. Her eyes flared, but at least now she was looking at him. So many emotions battled each other in those blue orbs: it was hard to tell which one she directed at him.

"That could have been a bullet, Audrey."

Moisture billowed on her lower lids, but she blinked it away. "This is *my* room. *No one* is going to keep me out of it tonight. Not you, not that damn brick, and certainly not some ridiculous ten-year-old grudge."

The first thing to grip his gut was the passion in her face. Not fear or sorrow or a guarded scowl. Only a raw determination that awed him to the bone. The second was a primal instinct that had no rational explanation.

He crushed his mouth to hers. As if connecting was the only way to verify he was still sane. A sliver of panic rang his brain at Audrey's stiffened posture. This was serious out of bounds. She could launch more than a reasonable complaint against him for this. For a second, he expected her to pull back and slap him across the face.

Until her tongue slipped between his lips. Then her hand wrapped around the back of his head and pulled him deeper into her mouth. Their tongues collided, dancing against each other in a fervent craze more urgent than breathing. She was sweeter than the marshmallows and infinitely more addictive.

She'd dropped the pillow and now gripped his waistline, pulling his rock-hard groin against her abdomen. He didn't need any other cues than that. He slid his hands up her back; her breasts pushed against his chest, her nipples hardened, peaking through her shirt. He growled low in his throat when her fingernails scraped against the back of his head. He was certain this wasn't the kind of in-depth look Audrey had expected from him, and knowing her, she'd regret this in the morning. But Ethan couldn't help himself. This was a better view of her than he could've hoped for. All flushed and hot, breathless and hungry. Because of *him*.

The curls of her hair were soft as he swept his fingers up her neck to cradle her head, molding her face to his. Audrey was better than any aphrodisiac or sweet glass of liquor.

Either from his momentum or her urgings, they danced backwards. Her back brushed the curtains and leaned against the windowsill. His hand glided down her frame and cupped her thigh, pulling it up to his waist as he ground into her.

Audrey gasped and winced away from him. "Damn!" She hissed, clutching her hand.

"What?" It took a second for the fog of lust to fade. But it evaporated the second he saw the blood trickling from Audrey's palm. A glass shard dropped from her hand and landed on the windowsill, a few remnants still littered across the wood.

"Shit. Is it deep?" He clasped her hand, now covered in sweat and clammy. He felt her breathing change, rather than heard it. Now shallow and quick. Glancing up to her face, her skin had gone white and her eyes glazed over.

"Audrey? It's just a cut. We'll clean it up." He pulled a chair over to the window and urged her to sit. The distant look in her eyes kept her from seeing him, despite being only three inches in front of her. He pulled several tissues from the box on the dresser and pressed them against her wound. She never flinched.

"Audrey?"

Finally she blinked and pulled her hand away, covering the wound herself. "I'm fine." A little color returned to her face, but she still refused to look at him.

"You don't like the sight of blood, do you?" Ethan knelt in front of her, resting his hands on her thighs. The gesture was casual and intimate simultaneously, and a position he was thoroughly unused to. "I'm that way with needles."

"I need you to leave." Her voice was clipped and quiet. Too quiet.

"Audrey, it's okay. Let me help."

"I can take care of myself," she rasped, turning away. Her entire body closed off right in front of his eyes, the defenses re-erecting themselves ceiling-high. It ripped at his heart. "Good night, Ethan."

As he stood and walked to the door, the room felt colder and more unforgiving. Audrey kept her face turned, the radiant hair tumbling over her shoulders. When he closed the door, he swore he heard her sniffle on the other side.

He scowled.

This is what I get for caring.

Chapter Sixteen

Pain seared through every muscle as Audrey's freezing body shivered against the icy wind. Except for her toes and lips. She couldn't feel them anymore. A burning flood covered her right side, emitting the only warmth in her existence.

"Hang on, Audrey," a dark voice murmured above her. The raspy words were meant in comfort, but she felt no relief. The sky moved above her bleary vision, blackened clouds swirling in the shadows of night. When her neck fell over the arm of the voice, her vision cleared to the sight of an empty road, careening into oblivion, littered with scraps of debris.

Heap after twisted heap, milliseconds of clarity revealed remnants of a car. A metal bumper, a tire, some kind of axle, and a chair. Shivers rocketed through her limbs as the winds kicked up against what felt like her naked flesh. A larger scrap looked like the dashboard, with the steering wheel still intact.

"Audrey, can you hear me?" The dark voice spoke over her again, and the world swirled before her bleary eyes. A long moment later, her eyes focused on a lump in the distance. Something pulled at her soul, but her body wouldn't move.

The voice carried her closer to the mound, a breath huffing over her at an even pace. The world focused and the lump was now distinctive. A boy. A boy lay on the ground with another man leaning over him.

The man pushed on the boy's shoulder, turning him onto his back. Another freezing gust of wind raked her cheeks as the boy fell to the side, and the bloodied, lifeless face staring back at her with blank eyes was Ethan, the light in his gray irises extinguished.

Audrey screamed.

She woke to the sound of her phone buzzing at 7:15 a.m. A small twinge of light barely poked through the ripped curtains, casting a whitish purple glow on the wall across the room. The cold air infiltrated across her bed. The taped cardboard to the frame did nothing for insulation.

Cleaning the debris last night hadn't taken long, and neither did falling for Ethan Tanner. She'd melted right into him at the first kiss, her defenses battered from the genuine tenderness and concern he showed. He was right; it could have been a bullet through that window. And instead of pity or a barrage of questions, he moved right into her vulnerability and declared residence.

She'd never been more turned on in her life. On the wake of rage and determination, her arousal by Ethan could only be described as animalistic. He tasted better than she thought he would. Then the glass cut into her hand. And brought everything tumbling back into perspective. Seeing the blood trickle down her palm, dark against her white skin, triggered that damn nightmare.

Her chest ached and her mind still whirled from it. Something stuck in her throat like a chicken bone that she couldn't swallow. Audrey felt like she'd been sobbing, but there were no tears on her face. The pillow was dry.

Audrey reached over and shut off her phone alarm. Nightmares were constant, now. One in particular. But she had to keep living her life, no matter what therapists claimed. Recurring memories were normal in tragedies, even if victims didn't consciously remember them. That was one thing the therapist drilled into her immediately after...

The cold wood floor seeped into her socks as she tiptoed to the dresser and grabbed her hairclip. Toiletry kit in hand, she opened the door to the much warmer hallway and into the bathroom. One glance in the mirror and she winced. The dark circles under her eyes would need extra concealer, and her pale lips needed a bolder color today. Her hand still throbbed, but the cut wasn't as deep as she thought. At least not physically. Another quick cleaning and a fresh bandage, she was as good as new.

A few minutes later, she was at least presentable to venture downstairs for coffee. Ethan was an early riser, or at least a morning person, and in case he beat her to the coffee pot, she didn't want to resemble a zombie.

Just as expected, Ethan was already in the kitchen, fully dressed in a long-sleeve burgundy rugby shirt and those hideous cargo pants, chatting with her mother, each holding their own steaming mug.

"Mornin', Starshine," Ethan smiled. The rest of his face was unreadable, except his eyes. The dark glittery stare proved he still craved something from her. But her body or the story, she couldn't tell which.

"Mornin'. How'd you sleep?"

"Better than you, by the looks of it."

Ouch. This guy doesn't do subtle.

"There's a full pot of chicory ready. Would you like a blueberry muffin?" Her mother's voice hadn't lost an ounce of soothing gentility. Audrey missed waking up to that every morning.

"I'll get it, thanks."

"Your father left for the rig early this morning. Wanted to stop by the store to pick up materials to repair the window. He'll be back around dinner. Can you and Ethan stay that long?"

"Sure," Ethan answered before she opened her mouth. "I'd like to peruse around a bit today, after a stop at the library, of course. Need to check my email."

"Well, if you don't mind a small drive, can you bring your father his lunch on the way out there? He left it in the fridge."

"Sure," Audrey replied noncommittally as she poured herself some coffee. Chicory wasn't her favorite, but it would help to dissipate the images of the nightmare. And her peace of mind from a lousy brick and the world-spinning kiss.

Sugar and creamer later, she turned and leaned against the counter, waiting for her mother to spill something. The anxious look on her fresh face only meant one thing.

Doubt.

However long her mother had been conversing with Ethan alone this morning, Audrey had no doubts that Myrna had tried to convince him of Audrey's proud nature and honest intentions. How the misinterpretations of a few people regarding an unspoken tragic event in her past shouldn't deter anyone from believing in her. It was the same attempt she'd given to several reporters after that day.

But she was the mother of a suspect, no matter how innocent in reality. So taking Myrna Biddinger on her word—which used to be sufficient in a small town—no longer sustained.

Uneasiness grew more awkward when Adelaide strolled into the room, sleepy-eyed and still wearing flannel pajama pants and spaghetti strap shirt, and refused to look Ethan or her mother in the eye.

As she walked to the fridge, her cheeks pinked, probably all the way to her toes, and pulled out the milk.

"Sleep well?" Ethan asked politely, a knowing smile spreading his lips.

Don't rub it in, jerk!

Adelaide stopped and looked at him, eyes widening for the deer-in-headlights fear.

"Fine, thanks."

"What do you have going on today?" Her mother asked, oblivious to the visual war as she sipped more coffee.

"Oh, not much. There's a bunch of friends going to a skating party at the roller rink this afternoon."

Ethan gave Audrey a doubtful stare over the rim of his mug. *A skating party? Brace hardly seemed the skating type. Did Mom really have no idea?*

"I'll drop you off, if you'd like," Audrey chimed in. "Just let me know what time, and I'll be back to pick you up."

"That's okay," she pleaded Audrey with her eyes. "I'll drive myself."

"No, really. I'll drive you." Audrey enunciated every word, making her refusal perfectly clear.

"Maybe we could crash the party," Ethan smiled

playfully at the sisters. "I haven't been skating in decades."

"Shocking," Audrey mocked. "I'd expect someone as dedicated as you to have mastered the sport."

"Well, you three have fun. I'm off Christmas shopping in Tyler." Myrna stood and set her mug in the sink, clearly oblivious to Audrey and Ethan's insinuation. "There's leftovers in the fridge for lunch if I'm not back in time."

When their mother walked out, Adelaide poured herself a glass of milk and then glared at her sister. "I'd rather go alone today."

"And I'm saying it's not gonna happen." Audrey's glare was much more convincing, having more years of practice, let alone time in politics.

"Then I'd rather not go."

"Fine. In case you change your mind while Ethan and I are running errands, I'll bring along your car keys."

Unadulterated rage was the mastered emotion of every teenage drama queen. "You can't do that! You're not Mom! You have no right to exert authority over me!"

"True," Audrey replied calmly, with firmness implanted in her eyes. "So why don't we go talk to Mom."

Adelaide practically growled as she stomped her socks on the tile.

"Didn't you listen to anything I said last night?" Audrey pleaded.

"Of course I did! It's just a skate party."

Audrey threw daggers with her eyes. "Don't lie to me."

Adelaide flounced out of the kitchen, milk glass in hand. "Adam's right. You *have* become a boring, tight-ass cheat!"

When Ethan's arrogant smile was the only other face in the room, Audrey felt like smacking it off his face. Or pressing her lips against it. This man looked too good for the crack of dawn. She'd seen a brief glimpse of his protective nature, and tasted the raw passion simmering under the surface of his skin.

She'd fallen asleep to the mental image of him a breath away from her mouth, and then the illusion of finally joining together, tasting his sweet sultry tongue and her flesh tingling against his silky hands on every inch of her body. All before the nightmares took over.

"I think that's the exact definition in the dictionary for a politician. How do you feel to be pigeonholed? Oh wait, that was your sister."

"Watch it," Audrey smirked and sipped her coffee. *He's such an ass sometimes. I should kick him to the bus stop, but I'm trapped by those gray eyes of his, again.*

"You think Brace will be wearing clothes this time?" Ethan muttered quietly. "Skating naked is hardly comfortable on developing genitals."

Audrey rolled her eyes. "I'll finish getting dressed, and then I'll drop you at the library." *For good, if I know what's best for me.* "How long do you think you'll need?"

Ethan shrugged and stood. "I'll call you when I'm done. What are you gonna do?"

"Oh, I've got a hot date."

"At 9 a.m.? That's the time hot dates should be *ending.*"

"All right, Romeo. I'll meet you back down here in twenty minutes."

Before she could turn out of the room, Ethan touched her elbow and pulled her back. His smirk had vanished and Audrey couldn't tell which was warmer, the coffee mug in his one hand or the look he gave her. Sincere and gentle.

He turned her palm over in his hand and tenderly grazed it with his thumb.

"Are you all right?" His voice was even gentler.

"I'm fine." Instinctual answer, practiced over years of grunt work in politics. From the continued focus of Ethan's stare, he didn't buy it.

"Are we going to talk about what happened last night?"

"Which part? The brick or the kiss?"

His gaze darkened and pulled her in closer. It nearly stopped her heart. Brushing this off wasn't going to work.

"Is this Ethan Tanner the journalist asking?"

He rolled his eyes. "Enough with that."

The cologne he wore was different this morning— stronger, more crisp. Yet equally distracting.

"Tell me what that was last night." The hard edge to his voice surprised her.

"I'd rather not." His hard gray eyes bored into hers, but she'd fortified her resolve the previous night. "Thanks for your help, though."

Less than a half hour later, Audrey drove down the frost-covered roads with Ethan thumbing through his phone, hoping an internet connection would materialize the closer they got to the library. Her cowl-neck sweater matched the evergreen trees lining the road as she curved and cut through the fallow brown fields. Staring at a phone or reading anything if in Ethan's seat would have made her carsick. Which is probably why she wasn't a writer.

A small, historic graveyard passed the driver's side window, a short, iron-rod fence surrounding the slight hill up to an expansive oak tree, spreading its amber limbs across a pond's edge. Audrey could hardly wait to see the spot that fulfilled her soul, and yet almost dreaded the familiar sorrow that was sure to follow. But she didn't gaze too long, not wanting Ethan to ask questions. Or see her weakness.

The small, one-story library appeared another half mile down the road, nestled among tall pines and cedars and desperately needed an update. The corners of the foundation crumbled into the gravel parking lot and deep cracks in the brick façade cut like tributaries stemming from a main stream.

"How charming," Ethan said as he finally looked up. Still no Internet connection.

"Are you saying you're too good to use a facility older than your ratty tennis shoes?"

"Not at all," he replied, replacing his small frown with a grin. "The older they are, the more secrets they have."

So the genuine concern was gone. He was back to the journalist.

"Ha, ha. Call me when you're done with emails. Try not to piss of the librarian."

"Oh, I'm sure I'll be her best friend by the time I'm done. See you later, honey." He blew her a mock kiss and climbed out, laptop bag in hand.

The uneasy, I'm-gonna-regret-this feeling in her

gut didn't hit her until she saw Ethan grinning after her as she glanced in the rearview mirror pulling onto the paved road. That grin was both unbelievably attractive and annoying simultaneously.

The rumbling in her mind didn't stop when she pulled onto the side of the road, climbed out of her car and approached the wrought-iron fence in front of the graveyard. Her black coat provided less warmth than she expected, but she had to do it.

The chill seeped further into her clothes as she climbed the small hill between gravestones, her feet leading the way as if they knew her mind didn't want to think. Didn't want to remember.

Leaves blew across the moist earth and thickened as she approached the top of the hill, where the trees grew higher surrounding the pond. Her place of refuge and inspiration, just beyond her ultimate spot of sorrow.

Finally she reached the one gravestone she both craved and regretted, sitting at the crest of the hill. The black marble among a field of stone and concrete markers stood out, much like its occupant used to do in life. The small, metal vase imbedded in the ground next to it held wilted yellow roses, less than a week old.

Etched across the marble in bold letters read the one Audrey missed most:

JACKSON ALLEN DAVIS
June 12th, 1985 - November 28th, 2003
Perhaps they are not the stars, but rather openings in Heaven
where the love of our lost ones pours through and shines down upon us
to let us know they are happy.

Audrey brushed the leaves off the marble, and let

her hand rest on the cold stone. "Hi, Jack," she whispered.

This time she let the tears flow. Fighting them wasn't allowed here.

Chapter Seventeen

The smell of old libraries should be made into a home fragrance scent. Maybe there wasn't a large enough market for it, but Ethan would be the first to buy ten cases.

As he approached the stacks, he couldn't help wondering if it was the volumes of old books on the shelves that emitted the lovely smell, or the building itself. Places like this were jackpots for media gold, but people had to be willing to sift through dirt to get it. And Ethan was more than willing.

An older woman, short white hair holding her spectacle lanyard in place, peered up from the cart of books she perused behind the reference desk and stopped. Her thin and fragile frame looked as if she'd blow over at the first sneeze. The deep wrinkles proved she may have been as old as the building itself, and might know the stories he itched to uncover.

"Good morning," Ethan drawled, his buttering smile in place.

"Good morning," she replied, still considering him. "Can I help you find something?"

"I hope so." Ethan placed his satchel on the counter and held out his hand. "I'm Ethan."

"Margaret Simon." She shook Ethan's hand, and he felt every bone and vein in her freezing grip.

"Not many libraries would be open the day after

Thanksgiving. I was told you have an internet connection I can use."

"Yes, the two computers there have access." She pointed to the far wall where two large box screens sat, the archaic grayish-brown color of early Apples and Hewlett Packards, with cords thicker than hoses. "Or you can plug in your own computer to the open ports."

"Excellent. Thank you."

Only after he realized he didn't have an Ethernet cable did he force himself to try the massive paperweight already in place. The mouse was like a clunky butter dish with a gray button in the center. But thankfully, the internet window wasn't much different than what he expected. Just insanely slow.

A few minutes later, he hadn't found any Mackineer newspaper articles. He couldn't even find the Mackineer local paper's website. Surely they had a local paper. Every town had one.

The squeak of the shelving cart rolled behind Ethan and he heard the librarian's "tsk" behind him.

"If you're looking for newspaper articles from around here," her brittle voice said, "you have to do it the old-fashioned way."

He swung around on the rolly-chair. "What do you mean?"

"You young'uns." She shook her head. "By opening a book. Archived newspaper articles are held in those cabinets there." She motioned to the back wall and waited for him to follow. "They are sorted by year. What timeframe are you looking for?"

"Um, about ten years ago."

He almost bumped into her when she stopped and looked at him, her piercing stare waiting for something.

"What's the purpose of your research?"

"I'm a writer."

Better to keep things as general as possible. Ethan learned a long time ago not to give too much detail when he researched a story, otherwise people wouldn't be willing to help him if they learned the truth. On the few instances he needed help.

For a split second, her eyes narrowed but she continued to the right cabinet and pulled open the drawer. Long, brown books, that looked more like artist portfolios were each labeled with volume numbers and dates. The oldest in the drawer looked to be from 1990.

"This drawer holds 1995 to 2005. Please be very delicate with these. They are the only archives in the town. If you need to make copies of anything, please let me know and I'll take care of it for you."

"You keep newspaper articles in cabinets? Why not online?"

"Because I choose not to spend the time scanning them in." Her peacock-like face peering over spectacles gave him the uncanny feeling of being scolded by one of his high school teachers. "This is the system we have. The 1970s or earlier is considerably more fragile, so if you need any of those, please ask me and I'll bring them out."

When she strolled away and continued filing books, Ethan pulled out the 2002 album and perused the carefully preserved pages. The Mackineer Eagle newspaper headlines peered out through plastic sleeves, at which Ethan groaned inwardly. Knowing this was going to take a lot longer than he anticipated, he shrugged out of his coat and relocated to an open table on the other side of the stacks, along with the album.

Searching front page headlines seemed the best idea. Some event, or possible murder, in this tiny town had to make the main headline. Perusing obituaries would've been fruitless, since he didn't know the name of the deceased.

Thirty minutes and the 2003 album later, desperate for more coffee or something to quench his dry throat, he found it. If he wasn't shocked by the image, he would've started drooling.

On the front page of November 29th, 2003, the headline read "MACKINEER QB DAVIS DEAD AFTER CAR CRASH." The large photo underneath depicted a mangled mess of metal that used to be an old car surrounded by police tape. Ethan's gut wrenched at the though of a human being inside the twisted heap grimly portrayed on the front page. Next to it was a portrait, a pretty boy with wavy hair smiling out from the black and white ink. The subtext read: "Jackson Davis school photo, courtesy Mackineer High School."

The article followed underneath:

Mackineer High School quarterback, Jackson Davis, was found dead late Friday night, at the scene of an accident on FM-158. In addition, senior Audrey Biddinger was discovered severely injured. Police suspect the driver lost control of the vehicle and rolled several times, causing both individuals to be ejected over thirty feet from the wreckage. It is unclear who was driving at the time of the incident and police have not indicated what caused the driver to lose control. Biddinger was taken to a hospital in Tyler and is currently in critical condition. The Davis and Biddinger families have declined to comment.

Jackson Davis and the Mackineer Eagles football

team had just won their last playoff game on Friday, November 25th, a few hours before the accident. They are due to play the Temple Tigers in the State Championship on Saturday, December 3rd. Davis had planned to join the military upon graduation, and held aspirations to serve in public office. He is the only child of Carl and Claire Davis. His memorial is set for December 2nd at Mackineer Funeral Home.

Ethan leaned back in the small plastic chair, fighting between a grin and grief. He knew this is what he wanted to find, this was the story to start off the rest of his life. Move to the next step and make it to the high rollers of journalism. But a growing part inside of him suddenly regretted what he found.

She was in a car accident that killed someone. That was the news any politician would try to keep covered up. The kind of news that kept many politicians from winning elections. Or even trying.

But this wasn't enough. There had to something else to this. A reason to warrant a brick through a window, even after all this time. Why people treated her so unwelcomingly, especially her brother.

He leaned forward and flipped more pages, carefully surveying every article. The next day's paper made his heart jump.

More Investigation Into Mackineer QB Death

Police continue their rigorous ongoing investigation into the death of Jackson Davis, who was involved in a car accident on Friday night with girlfriend, Audrey Biddinger. Officials have determined the vehicle was speeding at the time of the accident, although it is unclear what caused them to lose control. Police believe Audrey Biddinger was driving at the time of the accident, although that has not been confirmed. Audrey Biddinger is in fair condition at Tyler Memorial Hospital, upgraded from critical, but has been unable to answer police questions.

Quarterback Jackson Davis suffered a shoulder injury during Friday night's playoff game with Rockwall High School, which led police to believe he was not driving the vehicle at the time of the accident, combined with forensic evidence. Davis was pronounced dead at the scene on Friday night. A coroner's report scheduled for Tuesday will determine the exact cause of death.

Davis' memorial will be held on Friday at 5 p.m. at Mackineer Funeral Home.

Bingo. Not only did someone die, but she was driving. He could almost hear the nail in the coffin of Audrey Allen's political career.

As he read more and more throughout the rest of the week's papers, tidbits here and there arose of more details surrounding the accident. But the most important article crushing any doubts were on that Saturday's column.

No Justice for QB Jackson Davis

Jackson Davis, beloved quarterback of the Mackineer Eagles, was laid to rest yesterday, surrounded by his family, friends, and teammates. However, justice for his stolen life will not be delivered now that police announced his death as an accident and will not press charges against Audrey Biddinger for manslaughter.

Police suspect Biddinger was driving the vehicle at the time of the accident, although conclusive evidence has not been determined. Police have described

Biddinger's interviews as uncooperative, at best. Both families involved in this tragedy have refused to comment to the media.

Although friends described Davis as the quintessential All-American boy destined for glory and larger-than-life aspirations, no one understood his attraction to girlfriend Audrey Biddinger, characterized as an outsider, combative, and suspected of at least half a dozen pranks on school property.

The Mackineer football team is scheduled to play Temple High School for the state championships tonight, and players will wear Davis' jersey number taped to their helmets in tribute of their lost leader.

"That whole mess was a mountain of shame."

The librarian's dejected voice carried softly over his shoulder. He turned and saw her glancing at the album, sympathy filling every wrinkle and carefully placed hair.

"You remember this story?"

"Of course. Biggest thing to happen around here since the New London school explosion in the 1930's."

"Wow."

"I knew you were lookin' for this when you said ten years."

"Then why'd you make me take the time to search?"

"'Cuz you boys need to learn how to look for things the right way."

"You boys?"

"Reporters."

Another one. The whole town has a serious aversion. Maybe something in the water.

"The first reporter there caused a whole lot of

unnecessary ruckus and pain. All because he didn't look hard enough for the right stuff, and only stopped at the surface."

"Common practice around here, from what I've seen."

Ms. Simon looked at him curiously. "You're a peculiar one, Ethan. You seem to pay attention more than your brethren."

My brethren? "Have there been other reporters in here?"

"Not for a long time."

The air whooshed out of his lungs, although he tried to hide his relief. Another journalist digging his claws into this story would have crushed him.

Ms. Simon took the seat beside him and moved forward a few pages in the album, carefully turning the preserved articles between her bony fingers.

"The rest of this story happened weeks after the accident. All starting with the loss of the State Championship game." She stopped at the following Sunday's front page headline:

Mackineer Eagles Lose State Championship to Tyler: 36 – 0

Underneath the headline was the entire front line of the football team pictured walking off the field with ripped pants and mud-covered jerseys. Their dismal faces portrayed all the physical and emotional anguish of a team unexpected of such defeat.

"A lot of dreams were crushed that day," the librarian continued, almost solemnly. "When they lost that game, most of them lost their scholarship aspirations for college. Only a few even continued to university, while the coach resigned and moved away."

"What about the rest of the players who didn't go to university?"

"Some moved away, but most are still right here. Working the rigs or other jobs. Broke a lot of girls' hearts too. Expecting to leave on parade floats with their boyfriends. But none more broken than that poor Audrey Biddinger."

Ethan swiveled in his chair and crossed his arms. The recorder in his pocket burned against his jeans and he itched to bring it out and catch the rest of this for his article.

"How long was she in the hospital?"

"Several weeks. But that was only the beginning. That journalist painted her as the murderer of the town's golden boy. And he hounded her and her family for months afterwards trying to prove it. Went after the Davises, too."

"Is the journalist still around, so I can talk to him?"

"No, he died a few years back of liver disease. But by the time the girl had left the hospital, he'd turned the whole town against her. It was easy for people to blame her, since she was already so different than everyone."

"How do you mean?"

"Audrey came here a lot. She loved to read. I remember putting back so many Renaissance era books and artist biographies after she came in. But of course, like most artists, she had a rebellious side. Never ran with the main crowd. In fact, the only people I ever saw her with were her brother and the Davis boy. Most folks didn't approve of that matchup. Didn't understand what he saw in her. But I suppose it was inevitable."

"Opposites attract? Good ol' boy and the town deviant?"

"Not at all. The three were inseparable throughout childhood, the two Biddingers and Davis. Spent so much time together and knew each other better than anyone, it was bound to grow into something more."

"What did his parents think about her?"

Ms. Simon paused and stared at him. But she didn't answer.

"Are they still here?" He pressed more.

"Don't try digging up that stone. That family was traumatized enough. And I won't be the one leading another prowling journalist to their front door."

This woman really was a pistol, but for some reason Ethan liked her. Reminded him of a pushy grandmother set in her ways, but did everything out of love, even overzealous protective instincts. He watched as she pushed the book cart along, chin high and tough heels. Even though she refused to say more, Ethan couldn't thank her enough for all of the information. Nor could his boss.

For the forty-five minutes he sat there, his boss had called at least six times. But he wasn't going to pull the vibrating cell from his pocket and interrupt the granny from giving him more background on the dirt he needed. He'd buzz him back when he wasn't around curious ears.

He flipped through more pages and found another photograph of Jackson's grave, from the funeral no doubt. A black marble marker just below a large oak tree. More than likely he had to be buried in the graveyard they passed on the way here. Ethan glanced at his wristwatch, thinking a half mile trek down the road wouldn't take him more than fifteen minutes. A picture of this kid's grave would definitely get a response from Audrey, especially since her spine stiffened when they passed the cemetery. She tried to hide it, but Ethan sensed her fear.

The brick through the window set his nerves on edge. And that scorching kiss fried them even more. But Audrey was tougher than he originally thought. Tough, yet still wounded. And the fear she felt while passing the graveyard had to be the source of it all.

He'd started to read her emotions better than he could with anyone else. All she had to do was walk into a room and he could feel her, without looking up. Audrey was like a sweet magnet. But when he showed her the photo, her magnetism might morph into a vicious electrical storm. In the end, she'd be forced to tell the rest of the story and then try to persuade him not to publish it.

He'd heard similar pleading before from the county commissioner's admin/mistress after she'd spilled the beans of his gambling problems and the banking information she kept hidden for him. Any red-blooded man could hardly deny her sultry advances after he'd met her at a bar and pushed a few buttons. It wasn't hard fueling her already-flaming desires, and by the time they were finished, she'd spilled the beans on her boss without Ethan having to ask many questions.

He could see why the commissioner wouldn't let that creative woman go, but he really didn't have good taste in choosing confidential employees.

Audrey didn't seem like the type to beg for his silence, but she definitely aroused him more than the commissioner's admin. Even if he wasn't shoveling for something on her, he certainly wanted to dig around in the covers with her.

Restrain yourself, man. Now's not the time for fantasy. Quite the opposite. This was where real life met the hard sting of regret.

After marking each article with a slip of paper, he took it back to Ms. Simon and asked for a copy of each. She reluctantly agreed.

"Ms. Simon, do you mind my asking who you plan to vote for in the upcoming runoff Senate election?"

Without looking up, she hit the "Start" button and answered. "I don't believe that's any of your business, young man. But I've always loved Renaissance art."

She handed him the copies and adjusted her glasses, all trace of a smile gone. "Good luck, Ethan. Happy Thanksgiving."

Shortly after Ethan had his precious copies in hand, he walked along the side of the road away from the library and toward the cemetery. The gravel crunched underneath his feet as the chill from the morning wind barely started to subside and let the air warm up. After he grabbed a snapshot of the headstone, he'd have to find the Davises' address and try to speak with them. More than likely, they didn't have that great an opinion of Audrey, if they were anything like the rest of this town.

That would probably be the last trumpet sounded for her campaign hopes. And the last time he'd ever feel those delicious lips against his or see those dark ocean eyes look at him with respect. He tripped over a stone, but kept walking.

Chapter Eighteen

The sun finally graced the air with its warmth when the clouds dissipated, but a slight chill nipped at Audrey's face as she sat against the oak tree overlooking the pond.

Glimmers chased each other across the water's surface as each rustle of wind blew more bright leaves from the branches and landed with soft ripples. Fresh woodsy scent drifted in the air and the only thing missing to finish Audrey's perfect moment of peace was her sketchpad and pencil.

Ten years. Ten years ago today Audrey's life had changed, in more ways than one. The course that her life was on wasn't meant to be, but she wished so many people's dreams hadn't been destroyed along with her mistake.

Jack deserved better. His life was meant to go somewhere, so much farther than her original modest plan of art school. She'd told him a hundred times that her eccentricities and outward thinking wasn't good for him, but he wouldn't listen. And before the end, it was hard to let him go. She'd loved him. Her first and only, to this day. He was the only one who truly understood her and didn't judge her differences. Even before the accident, her own brother had started to distance himself from her.

Which inevitably led everyone to believe the worst.

By the time she was able to leave the hospital, everyone had pointed fingers and condemning stares without ever listening. So she retreated to the only mindset she knew: not caring what they thought. No one else mattered but Jack. And since he no longer lived to see his dreams a reality, she'd make them happen for him. Granted, it was extremely hard to accomplish when she didn't have her family's support, but in the end it gave her the hard shove she needed to get the dreams in motion. Her depression would have burned out her struggling flame of life in her parent's house in the tiny, small-minded town.

Now the Crisis Center was weeks away from reality and in a few days she could be a senator. Jack's life could live on in spirit. She owed him that much.

"This is your hot date?"

The world froze as she jerked her head to the graveyard and saw Ethan standing just in front of Jack's headstone. No arrogant smile, no judging look, just serious eyes and a frown. And his phone.

"What are you doing here?"

"I should ask the senate candidate the same question. But then again, I already know."

Audrey pushed against the oak tree to get to her feet and pulled her jacket tight against her torso. The air was suddenly frigid.

Ethan glanced down at the headstone and his jaw clenched. Somehow he didn't look happy to find the dirt Audrey had hoped he wouldn't find. Instead, his forehead crinkled and he looked like he downed a shot of tequila. "Jackson *Allen* Davis."

A lump climbed its way into Audrey's throat and tears touched the edge of her eyes. She didn't want to cry in front of him. Not to the one man she knew was nothing but trouble, yet couldn't resist.

"Why didn't you take his last name, instead?"

She swallowed the lump and blinked away the first tear. "I didn't have his parents' permission. It felt…disrespectful."

"But his middle name was fair game?" His biting tone hurt more than she expected.

"Why are you angry?"

He stared at her. "I'm not."

"You're a bad liar."

"So are you."

"I never lied."

He waited a long time before he said anything. Audrey just kept watching him, holding her breath for his next move. Exposure couldn't be rawer than this moment.

Ethan slowly lifted his phone and positioned it over Jack's grave.

"Don't you have any respect for the dead?" She fought to keep from crying out.

"It's just a piece of rock."

"It's a hell of a lot more than that, and you know it."

"Were you driving the car that night?" His fierce gaze pinned her to the ground. It was a familiar feeling, but not from him. Normally his gazes had melted her insides, but this was a completely different Ethan. Not the journalist, not the playboy charmer, but an angry man. She swallowed on the lump that wouldn't budge, letting her silence fill the space between them.

He grimaced at her lack of response. "You're right. It's a piece of rock and the scandal you've been trying to hide to protect your career."

"I don't give a shit about my career."

That got his attention. He looked at her like he'd never seen her before and lowered his phone.

"You are the perfect politician. You spit out that lie like you actually meant it."

The hatred in his eyes almost ripped through her skin. Why did he keep looking at her like this? For a journalist who'd just found his massive bone, she thought he'd be drooling. But he was furious. And there was no way he'd hear anything she had to say. There was no point defending herself. So she used the only weapon she had left. "I do mean it. Leave his family with whatever dignity they have left, and keep your promise."

"What promise?"

A deep breath helped keep her tears in check. "Leave the Davises out of the article. They've suffered enough."

As she trudged her heavy feet down the hill back to her car, she heard the click of a camera behind her. Her heart wept, realizing she'd betrayed her own mind and trusted a newsman, even if only for a moment. And had been bitten by it once again.

An hour later, after they'd dropped off her father's lunch at his natural gas rig, to which he thanked them with a grumble, they pulled into her parents' driveway. The air was just as chilled as this morning, as was the silence in the car during the drive. She hated the silence. But worse, she hated what he planned to do with her promise: to crush it.

Chapter Nineteen

"I've hit the jackpot," Ethan almost growled into the phone, safe in the guest room. "Audrey's campaign will be over by the time I'm done."

By the time they had reached the house, Bose had called another dozen times. But instead of crawling in his seat to answer the phone in anticipation for one of the greatest phone calls in his career, he'd never been more upset in his life.

Even more upset than when his father called during his mother's funeral to offer him a banking job, knowing the devastation he suffered mixed with his desire to go to graduate school. He'd smashed his laptop on the ground after that phone call, and drowned himself in two bottles of whiskey.

"I'm drooling, Ethan. Whatcha got?" Bose's voice jumped through the phone. At least someone in the media was excited over the ghosts he uncovered in Audrey's closet.

"She killed someone." Ethan grimaced as he said the words. They tasted horrible.

Dead silence on the other side.

"Not intentionally," Ethan continued, quashing the heartburn rising in his chest. "But her high school sweetheart died in a car accident, and she was driving."

"You're better than good." Bose managed to mutter through his excitement. "You're the messiah of tabloid heaven."

"That's what you aspire to be? A tabloid junkie?"

Nothing felt right anymore. His insides squirmed at everything around him. And the part that scared him the most, the only thing he wanted to do was curl up with Audrey on a couch, or bed, and hold her like she'd never been held before. To protect and defend her, the way she should have been treated ten years ago. To feel those luscious lips against his again. But he was the last person she wanted to see right now. He was sure of that much.

"When can I have the article? Tonight?"

"No, I told you, tomorrow. I have a few sources I need to talk with first."

"Make sure every angle is covered. I don't want to have to retract anything right before the election. In the end, it's Allen who goes down. Not us."

Ethan felt the bile rising in his throat. So much that he couldn't answer.

"What's wrong with you?" Bose barked at him.

"Nothing," he squeaked out.

"Don't you dare grow a conscience on me."

"I gotta go," Ethan grumbled.

"One story, and it's New York for you," Bose blurted before Ethan shut his phone.

He darted to the bathroom and chugged a cup of water. Sweat collected at his temples and the back of his neck. The nausea finally receded and he strolled back into the bedroom. He laid all of the article copies across the bed and stared at each one, immersing himself in each image like a toddler in the deep end.

The article with Jackson's senior portrait lay on top, the kid's grin growing more mocking with each second. He was pretty boy and he knew it. Ethan grabbed the paper and hid it beneath another one.

Jealousy was a brand new feeling for him and he didn't like it. Flat out hated it. It was worse than irrational. The kid was dead, and ten years ago to boot. But he was clearly Audrey's high school sweetheart. More than likely her first love. And those were hard to live up to. Worse, the kid had died, with her in the car, and everyone romanticized the dead. Especially this town.

Ethan pulled out the recorder in his pocket and dragged a chair in front of the mattress, straddling it for his brainstorming routine. With a click of the red button, he began. "Audrey Biddinger is the high school misfit, dating the town hero. Something specific about this one kid that everyone loved. They get into an accident where he dies. Damn, can this town hold a grudge." He picked up the article where Audrey's senior photo was pictured, her crazy hairstyle and crossed eyes mocking his process. "The reporter and police sway things against her, but don't have enough to charge her. She changes her name to Allen to escape the ridicule, taking her boyfriend's middle name— sentimental touch." He growled back the tinge of jealousy. "Audrey claims taking his last name would be disrespectful." He scoffed. "Up until this point, Audrey is described as an outsider and prankster, who wouldn't seem like the type who cares about respect. Then the accident and she does a 180 in life. But then goes into politics? The one profession where a troublesome and quirky artist would feel the most uncomfortable in front of cameras and the media, whom Audrey absolutely hates. Doesn't add up. Something's missing..."

He grabbed Audrey's campaign photo, the sapphire irises smiling politely, but hiding something painful. He'd never seen it the first fifty times he looked in her photo, but now that he'd seen her school pictures, there was a big difference, as clear as cellophane. And just as fragile.

How many bricks were thrown through her window to shatter that light in her eyes?

"She's not the least bit interested in defending herself against the accusations. Never even flinched when she was called a murderer. Why would she run for such a public office and expose the trauma?"

"Because she's heartless," a gruff and heated voice answered.

The bedroom door swung open and Adam's fierce glare darkened the room. *Privacy is impossible in this house.*

Ethan stood, still holding the recorder in his hand, and faced him.

"Hard thing to say about your sister."

Adam's eyes shifted about the room, absorbing every inch of Ethan's presence with a grimace. "This used to be my room."

The simple factual statement held the unmistakable undercurrent of a warning. But Ethan wouldn't let the bulk of a man intimidate him. So he waited, looking right back at him as Adam slowly walked in and perused all the articles scattered across the comforter. Picking up each photo one by one, he dropped them back on the bed like flicking a bug off his hand. He paused at the newspaper article with Jackson Davis' photo smiling up at them.

"This is the story you all danced around." Ethan

needed to get this guy talking. Maybe he held the missing pieces to what pushed Audrey into this disaster. Would he spill the beans on this fiasco, or did he care enough about his sister to at least try and protect her career?

Instead he shook his head and dropped the paper on the bed with a bitter scowl.

"So you're pissed off at your sister for allegedly killing the quarterback. That's a lot of anger to grip onto for a decade."

One death look could ice over hell from Adam's stern five o'clock shadow. The same vehemence every soldier showed toward the ultimate enemy. Where was Sally's calming influence over him when he needed it?

"A decade ago—today," he seethed. Another long moment passed before he continued. "What would you know of losing a best friend? People like you collect sources, not friends."

"Is that why she came home? For...an anniversary?"

"More like to rub it in."

"From everything I've read, it was just an accident. And grudges are what this town does best." Ethan paused as Adam's nostrils flared, watching for any sign of a fist. "But I don't understand why her brother who spent his life side by side with her seems to have the largest amount of hatred."

"She was a tag-along. Never got along with anyone, so hung around Jack and I for years. One day, Jack was different. I could hear every time she snuck out her bedroom at night. Or when he snuck up into hers. He and I were supposed to go to West Point together, but she changed his mind. She ruined everything."

Controlling anger was clearly not one of Adam's fortes. His hands trembled into fists at his sides and every heartbeat pulsed through the vein at his temple.

"So this is more than just losing a bid for sheriff," Ethan summarized, keeping his face as calm as possible with a beast ready to slaughter at any second.

Which lasted only two seconds. Adam's hands shot out like bullets and grabbed Ethan's shirt, dragging him forward so their noses were only inches apart. His fists shook with adrenaline as Ethan fought to keep his balance on his toes. "She destroyed my life! No state championship, which turned the whole town against me and the rest of my family for her recklessness! Enlisting was the only option I had left, and I had to do it alone. Without Jack. When I got out, the only job I could get was in the sheriff's department who was hurtin' for men with experience. My father has lost over fifty contracts because of the shame she caused, which means they can't afford Addy's college. It's all her fault!"

The pounding in Ethan's ears rushed through his body, and it was harder than he expected to keep his voice low with Adam on the verge of exploding. Despite the threat in his face, he couldn't hit a cop.

"Do you really want to go here? You're a deputy."

Adam never blinked. He just kept clenching Ethan's shirt, but his hands slowly stopped shaking.

"She almost died," Ethan barely spoke above a whisper. "And then everyone turned their back on her. Put yourself in her hospital bed. How do you think she felt?"

He blinked. The anger in Adam's face morphed

into a troubled daze and he finally released Ethan's shirt. But more surprising was Ethan hearing his own words. Was he really defending Audrey Allen? The goal was to uncover her ghosts and use them against her for his own advancement. But this didn't sound like the Ethan Tanner he knew. *What's wrong with me?*

Heaving and stepping back toward the door, Adam glanced back at the bed covered with newspaper clippings. "Put those away, right now." He pointed at them, resuming his less shaky voice. "I don't want my mother reliving that. You have no idea what this has done to my family."

"Clearly not as much as it's done to you."

Both men swung around and saw Myrna, Audrey, and Adelaide hovering at the door. Myrna's admonishment matched her furious glare, hands at her hips and blocking the doorway like Atilla the Hun, with reading glasses.

"This is how you treat a guest in my house? Shame on you, Adam."

The wrinkles in his shirt felt like nothing compared to the rumpled thoughts bouncing around his head. His first instinct was to study Audrey's reaction behind her mother, but then a close second was to hide the evidence lying on the bed. Like being caught butt naked covered in mud. But for some reason his feet wouldn't move. The dark blue eyes of The Peacemaker raged a war between him and Adam, freezing him to the floor, while the only prolific thing about her was how tight her lips pursed. And for the first time, an enraged woman's face hurt him to the core. The fuming look she learned from her mother's mastered expression.

Audrey smoothed her way past her mother and

silently collected the articles on the bed, neatly piling them together and leaving Jackson's photo on top. She paused, staring at his image with a distant pain emerging on her face, before she handed them back to Ethan. She refused to look him in the eye.

"I'm sorry you think I destroyed your life, Adam." Her serious voice was so low, Ethan strained to hear more. "You think I've stayed away all these years because I *wanted* to? Kept myself from my family because I'm heartless?"

The Irish twins' battle of wits stifled the air with tension, and their mother's face twisted with guilt as she and Adelaide watched. But Adam never moved his hateful gaze from Audrey, nor opened his lips to answer.

"My goal was never to hurt Jack or anyone else, least of all you. And everything I've done since then has been to make up for it." Audrey swallowed hard and fought to control her breathing. "I've done everything I can to make you love me again, including leaving you alone. As you wanted. Now I know my hoping for your forgiveness is useless. I'll leave tonight."

Tonight? Panic spiraled through Ethan's nerves as he absorbed what Audrey said. *We can't leave tonight. I still have more questions. More people to interview. I can't leave with only half a story.* Ethan glanced back and forth between Audrey's determined frown and Myrna's hesitant posture, but still no one said anything.

Until Adelaide pushed through. "No!" Adelaide blocked the doorway so Audrey couldn't escape, and pointed her finger into Adam's face when he rolled his eyes. "You two have been doing this for years, and I'm sick of it! You're both going to stay right here and duke it out, because you're family."

Ethan stood shocked at the beauty queen, who proved she didn't only rule on pageant stages, but also rivaled the commanding voice of legendary tyrants.

"I have *two* siblings," she continued. "Despite what anyone else in this town says, and I'm proud of both of you. Who gives a shit what anyone else thinks?"

"Addy!" her mother gasped.

"Don't worry about me. I can take care of myself," Adelaide continued without acknowledging her mother. "But the one thing I can't stand is constantly being told to 'hush up' whenever I ask what happened. The whole town knows more about it than me! In what universe is that fair?"

The only movement in the room was Audrey, who pinched the bridge of her nose and clenched her eyes shut.

"You're supposed to be adults, so start acting like it!"

"Addy, that's enough," Myrna choked. "Go clean your room before you meet with your friends. And if you want any clean clothes for school next week, you best start your own laundry. You've got a pile of dirty wash that will take all weekend."

That's not all that's dirty in her room. Ethan couldn't help but feel a tinge of sorrow for the clueless mother. He always thought parents pretended ignorance with their teens' sex lives. But she really had no idea how 'adult' her youngest acted.

"Ethan, dear," she continued in a much softer tone. "Please forgive this whole mess, including Adam's brief mental lapse." Her eyes threw daggers at her son.

"As soon as he and Audrey are done with their chat, I'm sure he'll be right down to apologize himself. Won't you, son?"

Adam's grumble was as welcoming as jaguar's growl over a piece of meat.

"In the meantime, there's plenty of food downstairs for lunch if you're hungry."

"That sounds great," Ethan pounced on her excuse faster than the sound wave. Whatever took place in this room next was bound to be much more painful. He grabbed his bag and followed Myrna out of the room. As he maneuvered down the hallway, he switched off the recorder in his pocket.

This story grew juicier by the minute, but the sweetness had faded to a bitter crunch. The more he learned of Audrey's tragedy, the more respect he started to feel. The worst part was that he broke his promise to Bose, and himself: he'd started to grow a conscience. And it hurt like a straight razor to the neck.

Chapter Twenty

The stench in the room must have been too great to bear, because Adam wouldn't budge from the window, the cold air seeping into the room. He'd pulled the piece of cardboard away and shook his head at the broken remnants.

Anytime Audrey moved from her spot, he seemed intent on moving away from her, to be in the farthest spot from her as possible.

"You can't keep dancing around me like I've got Ebola."

"Watch me."

"Why couldn't you have said any of that to me? Instead you spill your guts to an investigative journalist?"

Adam stared hard out the window, pretending not to have heard. He was just like their father. A brick wall that sometimes needed a sledgehammer to the head.

"You never knew I could hear every time you crawled out this window." Adam's voice lowered, full of anger.

Heat filled her face, suddenly embarrassed like she was fifteen all over again. *No, I didn't know that.*

"All of a sudden, Jack didn't want to go hunting anymore," he continued. "Fishing wasn't good enough for him. All he wanted to do was play football and hang out with you."

Audrey kept her tongue in check. She knew exactly where this was going. Jack had talked to her a hundred times about his change of plans. To go straight into public service instead of West Point with Adam. He didn't want to tell Adam and ruin their friendship. She couldn't tell her brother then because it would have broken his heart. And then blamed her. It didn't really matter, because both her fears came true anyway. Along with an entire library of other fears.

"He never even asked me if I was okay that you were dating. But I kept my mouth shut. I tried to give you two space." Adam finally turned to look at her, but without any ounce of compassion or sympathy. "But you made it so damn hard every time you mouthed off to people. I spent so much time taking heat for my sister's behavior, that my senior year became an inferno of judgment. For things I never did."

"Now you have a glimpse into what I felt." He really had no idea. He barely scratched the surface into the pain she felt. But this was the most he'd said to her in a decade. She had things to say, too.

"Don't give me that crap. You didn't care that everything you did came back on me tenfold." Adam scraped his short fingernails through his hair. "I took the heat for your fertilizer stunt on the football field. Everyone knew you were the one who wrote 'Dumb Jocks' in manure across the fifty-yard line, but the guys blamed me for desecrating their field. Criticized me for not keeping my sister in check."

Audrey forced the slight smile to remain hidden as she bit back a laugh. It was one of her more brilliant pranks when she younger, creative, and naïve. Despite pulling the stunt in late winter, it was almost two months later when the town was able to view the message written in the fertilized, bright green grass against the more dull, brown turf.

"But worse than that," Adam continued, anger rising with every syllable as he glared into Audrey's face. "All the players blamed you for every bad play, weak throw, or half-assed run that Jack gave. You were a distraction for the quarterback. The quarterback that they all depended on to get them to state, and eventually college. You fucked it all up for them. And guess who my teammates took it out on?"

"That's nonsense," Audrey seethed.

"All those bruises and cut lips I came home with weren't from practice."

The years of pent up anger and humiliation shadowed in his eyes, suddenly creating dark circles and fatigued wrinkles on his face. Sympathy overshadowed her defensive nature, but not for too long. As much pain and suffering her brother had gone through, it was next to nothing compared to her own.

"As a cop, you know everyone is responsible for their own actions." Audrey spoke low and slowly, trying to keep her anger in check. To keep her brother from escalating to an already-dangerous level. But she never blinked. "I didn't know you were treated that way, but I had nothing to do with their violence. Regardless, I took responsibility for my mistakes ten years ago. I've been able to let go of my anger and go on with life. Something I'm sorry to see that you haven't done."

Adam's posture sank with her last few words. As if all hope dissolved on a deep sigh, and whatever remaining light shone in his eyes was gone. "That's exactly what I mean."

Audrey stared at him, waiting.

"You moved on with your life as if nothing happened. As if you weren't responsible for Jack's death, for our family's humiliation, or the pain you caused the people of this town. You just...left. Now you've thrown yourself in front of TV cameras, reporters, and have your photo plastered all over the state. Seeking power that no one here believes you deserve, and you expect us to eat out of your hands like ignorant cattle."

The silence in the room stifled the air, and Audrey couldn't stop the building resentment as she clenched her jaw and shook her head. "You don't get it."

Her footsteps banged on the wood floor as she crossed the room to sit on her bed. But when she reached the mattress, she stopped and turned to him, letting go of her reserve and carefully-practiced patience and unleashed the rage she'd buried for years. "I'm doing this for the young women who need the help I never got!"

Shock and mild disdain flooded Adam's face, but she didn't give in. For the first time, he may actually be listening to her, albeit reluctantly, but dammit, she'd let him have it.

"I opened my eyes in that hospital room after the most tragic moment in my life, hanging on by a thread, to see that everyone had vilified me. Not only did the one I love die right next to me, and whatever little friends I had turn against me, but even my family turned their backs." Drops of wet tears tinged the edges of her eyes and her voice quivered as she continued, but she never paused. "I lost *everything* that was important to me. And instead of relying on the support of my family, I was told to leave. *Ordered* to leave. Depression crippled me for years, and when I finally find a cause that's worth the effort, to help save other lives, you condemn me."

Adam's disdain was gone. Shock and dismay replaced it, along with continued silence.

A single tear trailed down her cheek as her voice quivered more. "You were my best friend, the one I was closest to our entire childhood. When I needed you the most, you turned away. I still remember the disgust on your face when I came home from the hospital that day."

Her heart sank when Adam looked away, staring out the window again, covered in shame. Shame of his sister, his anger, their relationship, Audrey couldn't tell which. She swallowed her tears and forced air into her lungs with a deep breath. Forcing the politician back into her mind.

"I didn't come here for your vote. I knew that would have been as pointless as asking for your forgiveness. I came, foolishly, hoping for your love." She swallowed again, the lump in her throat expanding with every breath. She stomped to her bedroom door and yanked it open, even though Adam clearly knew the way out. "Something I won't ever dare ask of you again."

A cold wind fluttered into the room, rustling the drapes against Adam's arm. As cold as the expression on his face. He paused, staring hard into Audrey's face and finally, slowly, tromped out of the bedroom, slamming the door behind him.

Chapter Twenty-One

Audrey's father stewed over his beer glass, judging eyes tossed at Ethan every few minutes. Ethan traced a finger on the rim of his coffee, wishing it were a beer. The bar was crowded for the Friday night after Thanksgiving. Granted, it was the only bar in town, and most of the men in the dark and smoke-filled atmosphere either had no family, or had had enough of theirs for one day.

Ethan gathered that Paul fit into the latter category. The man clearly had a lot to say, but maybe didn't know how to phrase it. Paul would lean forward as if about to lay into Ethan like a father to a teenage son who'd trashed the family truck, but then think his way out of it, sip his beer, and lean back in his chair once again, and instead watch the football game on the TV behind Ethan's head.

Ethan knew what was coming. As he'd strolled out of Audrey's room to let the two siblings argue over a long grudge, Paul had walked in and caught Ethan with the pile of articles in his hand. One glance at his wife and youngest daughter, and Paul realized which kind of manure had stunk up his house.

Without a second thought, he'd tossed his lunch pail in the kitchen and opened the front door, waiting for Ethan to lead him out with a glare. His one order was as foreboding as his tone: "Let's get a beer."

They sat in the creaky chairs pretending to watch the football game, and pretending they'd already had the serious discussion that had to yet to happen. Ethan had to keep his professional hat on. This was his job, and no matter how painful the oncoming talk was going to be, this was the story of his career.

He'd lost count of how many targets had begged him not to publish the dirt he found, and each plea had been more pathetic than the last. The angry ones were always the most interesting. It was kind of a thrill, wondering if he'd need a restraining order after a particular article graced the headlines. He'd been skilled enough not to need one to this point, or maybe just lucky. But the death threats, either in person or by email, were standard for his business.

Not that he expected anything like that from Audrey's father, although he wouldn't blame him if he did. For some reason, this story felt different. Maybe this was guilt. Or shame. Sorrow of some kind. He didn't like the feeling.

"You a Baptist?"

Ethan stared at Paul, the simple question too soft and unrelated to what Ethan expected. Where was he going with this?

"No," he replied curiously.

"Mormon?"

Ethan's eyebrows drew together.

"It's the second time you've refused a drink from me," Paul commented. "Gotta be religious."

Ethan smirked. "Let's just say I'm too big a fan of alcohol. I've learned my lesson…the hard way."

"Fair enough." Paul nodded, as if he understood more than the simple words conveyed.

Ethan had also lost count of how many times the other patrons glanced at them. Specifically at Paul. Not acknowledging them seemed the best decision at this point, merely following Paul's example, but Ethan had rubbed his nose or ran his hand through his hair a few times. The more it happened, the more uncomfortable Ethan became in his seat. There was no way Audrey's father missed it, but he just continued to ignore them.

Finally, after one particular lanky and grungy man with a backwards baseball cap and bloodshot eyes across the bar had stared viciously at them for at least fifteen minutes, Ethan couldn't ignore it anymore.

"What's Thin-Man's problem over there?"

Paul's eyes shifted to the man across the bar mid-sip, and returned to Ethan just as casually. He waited before he responded, savoring the beer in his mouth.

"That's Ashe. He's my motor man on the rig. Along with several others in here."

"He's a ray of sunshine, isn't he?"

Paul shrugged and sipped his beer again. "I don't care if he spouts sonnets or dances on the roof, so long as he does his job right and minds his own drink. And other…issues."

Ashe cracked a joke to the guy next to him and snickered, glancing back at them gripping his beer with jittery hands. An audience must be a common practice for Paul. Or maybe it was the unfamiliar, flashy journalist in tow. Not that Ethan wore flashy clothes, but his slacks and buttoned shirt didn't fit the profile of the roughnecks around them.

But the red-eyed Thin Man in the corner was the only one with clear symptoms of crack addiction oozing from every shaky nerve ending, unlike most roughnecks. His skin hung loose on a bony frame and he flicked his fingers like a cigarette, one at a time in rapid fire.

"Reporters aren't Audrey's strong suit," Paul started uncomfortably drawing Ethan's attention from the pissy stickman.

The perfect cue-in to find Audrey's weaknesses, and get more dirt for his story. The next question out of Ethan's mouth should have been "why not?" But instead, he heard himself respond: "What is?"

Paul studied his beer bottle, pausing as he battled through his thoughts. Then sighed, almost a grumble. But he never got the chance to answer.

"Lying," an edgy voice shouted for him, followed by an unguarded belch. Thin Man clunked his beer bottle on the bar and slid off the stool, jerking up his worn jeans over his exposed tightie-whities.

The noise in the whole bar quieted so suddenly, Ethan thought he'd gone deaf, if not for the soft cheers from the football game on TV. No one bothered hiding their stares at Paul anymore, except for the few who stared blatantly at Ashe. Waiting. Including Ethan.

"Lying is Audrey Biddinger's strong suit. Real fitting trait for a politician, don't you think?"

Ashe's eyes grew more menacing by the second, keeping his glare on Paul's neck, who still refused to acknowledge him. But the grief behind the man's face was unmistakable.

"What's she doin' back in town, Paul? Campaignin' for more votes?" Ashe leaned back to the bar and grabbed his beer, taking another swig and then let it dangle at his thigh. "Does that murderer really expect to get a vote from this town? Amazing they even let someone like her run. Should be a law against it."

"Amazed you even know there's an election goin' on, Ashe. Since when do you care about politics?" Paul finally replied, roughly and without looking at him.

Ashe kept on as if he hadn't heard. But instead stepped toward Ethan. "You lookin' for a story, big city reporter? I'll give you a story."

Still twitchy and uncoordinated, Ashe flipped his middle finger at him, a playful smirk on his lips and hate in his eyes. "You see this finger? This finger should have a state championship ring on it. But there ain't, is there?"

The putrid smell of beer and gingivitis wafted under Ethan's nose. The grime on his yellowed teeth was almost as bad as the dirt covering Ashe's hand, including underneath his fingernail, which he still held in front of Ethan's face. The need for personal hygiene was the least of this guy's problems.

"News flash. They don't give state champ rings in peewee football," Ethan replied dryly. He tried to turn away and focus on his coffee, but the snickers throughout the bar infuriated Ashe more. Ethan should have known his smart-ass mouth would get him in trouble again, but he just couldn't help it. Thin Man needed to lose the ego. Instead, strong, jittery fingers yanked on his shirt and lifted him from his chair, dragging him to his feet.

How in the hell was this scrawny drunk strong enough to haul me out of my seat? The redneck's eyes flared only inches away from Ethan's face, ready for a fight and giving him a whiff of hot, putrid breath. Ethan doubted Ashe was coordinated enough to actually throw and connect a punch, but his overall disgust could have a seasoned vet throwing up his hands for mercy. He was lucky Ethan stopped drinking. Otherwise, Thin Man would end up knocked cold on the floor while Ethan wondered why his knuckles were bloodied and bruised the next morning. *Hell, the insult wasn't that good anyway.* Witty banter wasn't fun with a staggering drunk.

"Funny guy, huh? Suppose that's all you got…words. Lousy reporter and all."

"Let go of my shirt, before you lose your teeth," Ethan warned, low and deep. "Or what's left of them."

The two men battled each other with their eyes, waiting for the other to blink, flinch, or breath.

"Ashe, that's enough," Paul growled.

Slowly, Ashe released Ethan's shirt and stepped back. Ethan straightened his shirt, feeling a hint of disappointment at being denied his fight, but grateful for the returned ability to breath fresh air.

"Of course you wouldn't be interested in this gripping story. That thief probably has her claws into you, too. Two dozen guys in this town were robbed of that state champ ring, and a ticket out of here—all because of her. Should be the headline for…*Wall Street Journal* or something."

"You read the *Wall Street Journal* often?" Ethan took his seat and sipped his coffee to hide the snickering. "Don't recall it having a comics section or personal ads." Laughter bubbled up Ethan's throat. He couldn't stop it. From the glare on Ashe's face, it was the wrong reaction, but a few other giggles around the bar proved Ethan wasn't the only one amused by the lanky man's ignorance.

"Knock it off, both of you." Paul threw a reproving

glare at Ethan. "Ashe, finish your beer and go home. You've had enough for one night."

"You're not my father," Ashe barked back. "Hell, if you were any kind of father at all, you'd tell your daughter to skip town or check into the nearest jail cell."

The chuckles around the room stopped instantly. Not because of Ashe's insult, but because Paul finally stood out of his chair. Even Ethan's heart raced when Paul reached out and fisted Thin-Man's shirt in his hand, yanking him forward faster than his jaw twitched. At full height, he easily towered over Ashe by half a foot. The kid's frail shoulders and skinny arms were twigs compared to the massive trunk of Paul's stature.

"If you want a job tomorrow, along with your jaw intact," he gnashed. "Go home. Now."

Ashe's glower matched his boss's, but he didn't say anything back. That was the first smart thing he'd done all night. When Paul released him, Ashe took a final swig of his beer and slowly turned to the bar. Fishing a few bills out of his pocket, he tossed them on the counter.

"Better tell that reporter to watch his back," Ashe threw over his shoulder as he trudged to the exit, tripping over a barstool leg. "Or he'll be the next sorry sucker to end up dead."

The words were drunkenly shouted as the door closed behind him. The bar was still silent. Paul still stood, braced for a fight. "Anyone else got somethin' they wanna say?"

No one moved.

With a final twitch of his jaw, Paul finally took his seat again. "He's a mean drunk," he murmured.

"Hard to believe Thin Man was a footballer."

Paul grunted. "A kicker. And shoddy, at that."

Everyone in the bar turned back to their own conversations, watched the game, or pretended to ignore them. Ethan slowly twirled his coffee cup on the table, letting the heat penetrate his fingertips. The heat from the cup had simmered to dull warmth. "What am I missing?"

Paul lifted his eyes to Ethan's, but didn't answer.

"From what I've read, it was just a car accident. So, she wasn't liked much beforehand, and when the QB was killed, it gave the players an excuse to dislike her more. But then why the whole town? What am I missing?"

A long moment passed with the two staring at each other. Whatever he was missing, this was the big part of the story. The crucial piece that pulled everything together. But damn, this man was hard to crack.

"Just now is the only ounce of defense you've shown for her. Not when Adam attacked her, not when everyone else is throwing insults at her. And you haven't told Addy what happened either, that's clear. Which means you think Audrey's responsible for his death, too."

Paul clenched his jaw again, but the anger in his eyes drifted into regret.

"You think it's her fault, too. Along with everyone else in this town. Why?" Ethan nudged further. He had to get something out of him. When Paul continued to stare at the table, instead of answering, it was time for Ethan to change his tactics.

"Your daughter was dating the quarterback, the glory boy of this town. She was making good grades and ready for college. Why wouldn't you be proud of that? What's the *whole* story?"

Paul leaned his elbows on the table. "You never quit, do you?"

Never.

"That night..." Paul began, refusing to meet Ethan's face. A myriad of emotions flickered across his face in that pause. As if he relived the last decade of events in the space of a few seconds. "There are some things fathers are never prepared to hear. Especially about their daughters. In the South, it's impossible to overcome stigmas. Family shames. But now Audrey is making something of herself. I don't want to see that destroyed because of town folk here who can't get over a decade-old grudge."

Whether Paul kept his voice low to avoid being heard by others, or couldn't stand discussing what weighed so heavily on his heart, Ethan didn't know. But ten years was too long to let a wound like this fester. Ten years was too long to be rejected by your father. Ethan knew that better than anyone.

"It's best she doesn't come back here," Paul continued, guilt dripping with every word. "People are cruel. You've seen 'em. She should stay where she can really shine. Make a difference."

"So you're keeping her out of your life—at a mile's reach—for *her* benefit? To keep her from coming back?"

The words hung between them, cruel realization hitting Paul in the face, and defensive anger filling Ethan's. This whole time, the dejected aversion to comforting his daughter was his twisted way of protecting her. But he didn't see that his behavior was far worse than anything any neighbors or strangers had done to his daughter.

"I've only known your daughter personally for a few days. Even I can see how wonderful she is. No matter what she was like in high school, I see the determined, confident, and strong woman she is now. And she *is* making a difference. The number of bills she's helped pass, the people she's supporting, just the amount of voters she has believing in her... Have you even *heard* her in a debate? She's fucking brilliant."

The shock on Paul's face was nothing compared to Ethan's as he realized the words that just came out of his mouth.

"Aren't you the one trying to exploit her?"

Yes I am. But I'm no competition against the people she calls family.

"If you could see her at what she does best, you'd see that she doesn't need you to protect her like that. She's more than capable of protecting herself. But she needs your love. Your support. All children want approval from their parents, whether they're five or fifty. Believe me, I know."

"Are you saying you're not going to write your article?"

When did I become a cheerleader for Audrey Allen? Ethan's mind went blank, and all he could see was Audrey. Her infectious smile, the long dark hair, her long lashes, those deep sapphire eyes boring into his heart. And the familiar urge she'd inspired in him several times the last twenty-four hours. When had he lost track of his career? This was supposed to be about his chance in New York. His chance at sticking it to his father. When had he grown this massive splinter of concern and defensive nature for Audrey?

"Admit it, boy." Paul's southern drawl broke through Ethan's flusters. "You've been T-boned. Hurts, don't it?"

"What?"

"Caring."

Chapter Twenty-Two

Audrey slammed her car door shut and stood by the trunk. A freezing wind blew against her cheeks as she stared at the door of the only bar in town, knowing her father and Ethan were inside, more than likely on their third or fourth beer. Judging by the number of trucks and beat-up cars in the parking lot, they were being watched by half the men of Mackineer. Tears stung the edges of her eyes, which she blamed fully on the wind chill.

Coming home was a mistake, she thought as she stared at the neon OPEN sign buzzing in the dilapidated window. Not just because Ethan was fishing for dirt for his article and feeling proud of himself for blackballing another politician's career. But because all of the agonizing memories had resurfaced the minute she walked in the front door, along with the crippling anger and self-doubt. Adam's hatred only fueled the flames of that pain. It had been years since she let anger fill her gut this much. And years longer before she had the confidence in herself to go after her newfound dreams. Without Jack. Without her family.

Every minute she stayed in this town only let the resentment take a firmer hold on her patience. Chipping away at her confidence, one insult and cold glare at a time. Tomorrow wasn't soon enough to get back to her life—to her career, as damaged as it may be.

All she had to do was suffer through one last confrontation: walking in the bar, past the forty eyes of the ones who hated her most, to get Ethan and drive away. If he wasn't ready to leave, he'd have to walk home. All 115 miles.

Stick to your gut, Audrey. Leave now.

She shoved her hands in her coat pockets and stamped into the bar, head held high and eyes fixed straight ahead. The bell over the door rang as it closed behind her. Her steps were quick and even as she strode through the bar to her father's usual table, and ignored the silence and cold glares around her. Even the TV seemed to mute itself upon her entrance, every heartbeat thumping against her rib cage to the pace of her steps.

The hushed murmurs around the bar infiltrated into her brain.

"What the hell is she *doing here?"*

"Salvaging her campaign... typical politician."

"Hasn't she done enough here?

"Heartless killer needs to go home."

But she refused to acknowledge them. When she opened her mouth to announce it was time to go, Ethan's eyes lifted to meet hers. The words crumbled on her tongue, along with every thought, as he looked at her. She'd never seen that tortured grimace on his face, vulnerable eyes staring back at her with…pity?

No. Ethan Tanner wasn't capable of pity. This had to be something else. The awkward look on her father's face as he watched her, then Ethan, then back to Audrey, was…anticipation. *For what? A fight?*

The light in Ethan's eyes shifted, watching her with some feeling she couldn't identify. A warm touch grazed her palm, and she saw his fingers trying to interlace with hers. Her heart skipped. She didn't realize she'd taken her hand out of her pocket.

Wrapping her fingers around his hand felt instinctual, a reflex. As if their skin were meant to connect and electrify their senses. His fresh, woodsy aftershave blended with the strong coffee under her nose, and it hit her.

He's not drinking. Who comes to a bar to drink coffee?

Audrey pulled her hand out of Ethan's fingers and shoved it back in her pocket.

Someone who wants to remain sober when he investigates his target.

"It's time to go," she said sharply.

"Now?" Ethan asked, his eyebrows raised an inch while the muscles on his face contracted from the rejection.

"Damn right," another murmur, less hushed than before. Audrey ignored it.

"Surely the great Ethan Tanner has the info for his article by now. I want to hit the road before it gets dark."

"You and your brother have your little chat?" her father asked, holding his beer a hair from his lips.

Audrey glanced at him and bit the inside of her cheek. "We…understand each other perfectly. Which is why we need to go."

Ethan stood, but didn't grab his jacket from the back of the chair. Instead, he leaned into Audrey's ear and his warm breath sent ripples of goose bumps down her neck.

"I really think we should stay a little longer."

"Why, so you can dig up more dirt? If you want to stay, fine. Walk home."

"Come on. Order a drink and sit with us. Tell me what Adam said."

"Like you care what happened between me and my brother." She glared at him. She wouldn't fall for the concern in his eyes or the gentle hold he had on her elbow. Ethan Tanner would do anything to get the info for his article. He didn't really care about her. That toe-curling kiss in her bedroom last night was a ploy, she was sure of it. Just to soften her up to get the dirt he wanted. The ache filled her heart more as he continued to look at her with tenderness. Because she knew he didn't mean it.

"I can tell you need it. Just one. Bartender?" He raised his hand, simultaneously pulling out the chair in front of Audrey. "One merlot, please."

He knows my choice of wine. After one drink.

"Sorry, city boy," the bartender replied gruffly, arms crossed and leaning against the back counter. "All out."

"What about the Kendall Jackson bottle behind you?"

The bartender sighed and stared straight through him. "Won't serve her."

Audrey cringed inside. *Would this humiliation ever end?*

"What?" Ethan stopped, just as the rest of the bar silenced once again.

"You heard me."

Ethan squeezed Audrey's elbow, another moment of support from the one she expected it the least.

"*I'm* asking for the wine, pal." Ethan spoke

quicker, voice tinged with irritation.

The bartender grunted. "I doubt even a city boy like you drinks red wine. Sorry."

"Ethan, forget it. I'm driving anyway." Audrey took a deep breath and pulled her keys from her pocket. "You coming?"

"Can't even order a drink in her home town." Ethan bit between gritted teeth. He kept his fingers glued to Audrey's elbow, refusing to let her go as he glared at Paul. "No wonder she left."

Her father hung his shoulders over the table, the wrinkles on his face deepening, as he gripped his beer. Shame. Silent shame. He finally raised his eyes enough to see Audrey's heart crack in two. Again.

He took a slow, deliberate sip on the bottle and glanced back at the bartender.

"Just one glass, Barnes. Let me have a drink with my daughter."

"Have it at home," he replied.

Nothing changes, Audrey thought as she fought back a tear that she couldn't blame on wind chill. *He suffers a similar disgrace, only lives with it daily.* Before Audrey could turn and march out of the bar, pretending not to notice everyone's fury-filled eyes or the humiliation crawling up her spine, the bell over the door rang.

The air in the room seemed to suck in at once, oxygen levels fell and it became impossible to breathe. Audrey's heart ceased to exist as even the pulse between her ears stopped.

A tall, less-than-brawny man with foggy glasses stepped through the door and ran his gloves through his short chestnut colored hair. Water droplets fell from the silver tinges above his ears as he pulled off his gloves and removed his glasses.

Audrey couldn't inhale. An older image of Jack lifted his head and peered into her face.

Carl Davis.

If Audrey were the fainting type, this would have been the moment to lose all consciousness. Had Jack lived, she was sure he would have looked just like his father, staring back at her with those dark almond eyes, strong angled chin and gently sloping jaw line. Like Frank Sinatra with sparkling baby brown irises.

When Carl smiled, directly at her, Audrey's knees buckled.

Chapter Twenty-Three

Had Ethan not been holding her elbow, Audrey would have fallen to her knees. Right in front of Jack's father. She quickly recovered her balance, but held onto the back of the chair just in case her legs betrayed her again.

She hadn't seen Jack's parents since just after the accident. And not while she was entirely lucid. They'd visited her in the hospital while she recovered and she had been on strong pain medication. When Mrs. Davis stepped into the room, carrying a bouquet of roses, Audrey wanted to be dead and instantly healed simultaneously. The pain of knowing her only son was gone consumed her, but the urge to show her respect by standing and hugging her battled against it.

But she couldn't. For days, Audrey thought she'd hallucinated when Jack's mother hugged her in the hospital room, either woman unable to speak.

Now those feelings flooded over her once again, looking into Jack's father's face. Carl slowly moved to the back table, a slight limp in his left leg, but the smile firmly implanted on his cheeks. "I heard you were back in town, Audrey," he started, a joyful ring in his voice. He turned to her father and held out his hand. "Paul, good to see you."

Somehow her father had made it to his feet and she hadn't noticed. Probably when she almost collapsed on the floor. Her father shook Carl's hand wearing a sympathetic smile.

"Same to you. How's your back treatin' you in retirement?"

"Cold days like this don't help, but I'm chuggin' along. I'm looking forward to Tuesday. Claire and I are excited to vote for you, Audrey. How's the campaign goin'?"

Audrey blinked. She must have hallucinated. *Mr. Davis intends to vote for me?*

This was the point where her Peacemaker hat should have been firmly shoved back on her head, thanking him for his vote and schmoozing for more support, but the words didn't make its way past her tongue.

Judging from the baffled half-smile on Ethan's face, he was just as surprised. But the open jaws around the room unsettled her stomach more.

"Thank you," she managed to stammer out. "It's…been a rough one with Wyatt Williams, but…"

"But that's politics," Carl finished for her. "Well, Claire and I are real proud of you. You must be her boyfriend." He stuck out his hand, waiting for Ethan to shake it. "Carl Davis. Nice to meet you."

"Ethan Tanner." He shook his hand.

"You've got a good woman here. Be good to her."

"Carl," Audrey's father interrupted. "He's not her boyfriend. He's a journalist for the *Dallas Mornin' Journal*. Writin' an article on Audrey's campaign."

"Oh." The man released Ethan's hand. "Well, then that should be a piece of writing that truly glows about her."

From the corner of her eye, Audrey saw Ethan

throw a look at her father. Carl stepped forward and pulled her into a loose hug and kissed her on the cheek.

"Don't be a stranger, darlin'," Jack's father smiled again. "Come see us when you're free. Claire would love to catch up."

Ethan couldn't believe his ears. Carl Davis, the father of the boy that died right next to Audrey, pledged his vote for her. As a journalist, he should have wanted some other reaction, something negative, uncomfortable, possibly violent. Something readers would sit on the edge of their seats with. But another side of him filled with warmth. Is that pride?

What he wouldn't give for an interview with this man. The real thoughts and feelings of the victim's family. The perfect full-circle for his article.

"Actually, we're free now if you're available." Ethan couldn't help himself. If this was the lead-in for his questions, he'd do whatever it took. Audrey's stunned face couldn't keep him from it.

"Wonderful," Carl replied, eyes alight with joy.

"Actually…" Paul dropped his hand on Ethan's shoulder. "I'll be taking this man back to the house so he can pack. Audrey, why don't you follow Mr. Davis back to their house, and we'll see you home in a bit."

Shit. Ethan tried to keep his smile intact, but the disappointment raged through his mind. *How am I supposed to get the information I need if I'm not there?* Bose was going to wring his neck if he didn't get this interview. But not just that.

He *had* to know what this man thought of Audrey. A town full of people who clearly hated her, and the one person with the only legitimate reason to despise her, instead showered her with praises.

And he was right. In the brief seconds in which Ethan locked eyes with Audrey, the full truth slammed him in the gut. Had there not been any question over Audrey's past or lack of attention to family, this brilliant woman would be winning the election by a volcanic explosion. Had Audrey Allen been a male candidate, there would have been no need for a runoff election. She would have been voted the next Texas state senator, lovingly embraced by her district, and all of the other senators as well.

But life was a bitch. A bitch with double standards. Ethan knew that better than anyone. And it was just as brutal to Audrey as it had been to him. Maybe more so to her.

But *we're not responsible for the bitchiness of life, only for reporting it.* His boss's words echoed in his thoughts. He used to repeat it to himself during every story and pushed on with his career, but now it sounded more hollow than a marble mausoleum.

"You sure you don't want me to come with you?" Ethan asked Audrey softly, brushing his fingers against her palm. Although he couldn't tell who was more stunned by his tender consolation: her or himself.

The confusion in her eyes was unmistakable, clearly wary of his intentions. Which agenda was Ethan after: his story or her wellbeing? If only Ethan knew himself.

"I'm fine," she breathed wearing a cautious smile. She slowly curled her own fingers into his, and squeezed with a feather's strength. "I'll see you back at the house."

When she turned to leave, his grip tightened on her hand and pulled her back. He couldn't explain where the urge came from, or why he felt if he didn't he'd be losing something precious. But he wrapped his arm around her shoulders and watched her eyes widen as he pressed her close. A heartbeat later, he tucked his head in and kissed her cheek, so close to the corner of her mouth that the warmth of her lips and breath danced across his.

Though it might have been a gasp. Her blueberry eyes deepened into something he couldn't identify. Paul and Mr. Davis looked more surprised than her, standing there and waiting for a punch line. Or just a punch.

Ethan's eyes lingered on the pair as he watched Audrey and Mr. Davis stroll out of the bar, the ache in his chest stronger than ever. The emotional blitz of Audrey's life was just ahead, and Ethan could hardly bear standing on the sidelines and let her struggle through it alone.

Turning back to Paul made him stop and hold his breath. The tight jaw and lowered stare gave the impression of a bull ready to charge. Instead, he slipped his hand into his coat and flipped a few bills on the table.

"They're gonna be a while, city boy."

Ethan shrugged on his jacket, staring into the empty coffee cup on the table. Would he be there for Audrey when they were finished? Would she need a lap to cry on, an ear to vent into, or a heart to connect with?

Knock it off, Ethan. There's no way in hell she'd pick you. You're the enemy to her. He'd be as useless as the empty cup.

Clunking his feet across the wooden planks and watching every hostile pair of eyes follow him out the door felt like an old Western showdown. To think he was a bigger enemy to Audrey Allen than these vicious folks throwing daggers with their eyes. It nearly crippled him inside. He didn't want to be compared to these heartless cretins.

Then you chose the wrong line of work, his father's voice answered his thoughts. The last words he'd ever heard from him, to which he'd slammed the phone against the wall and swore he'd never talk to him again.

Ethan climbed into Paul's truck and slammed the door behind him. He pretended not to notice the old man toss him a glare.

"Can we make a quick stop at the store? I need to pick up a wireless card for my laptop."

Paul gave a slight nod and turned the ignition. Ethan continued to fume his hatred through the foggy window.

Screw you, Dad. I made it this far without you, and I'll finish this the same way.

Chapter Twenty-Four

The words flew from Ethan's brain and onto the keyboard faster than his fingers could manage. The aluminum laptop could have been flimsy plastic from the anger with which he punched every key.

When he and Paul had arrived back to their house, Ethan marched upstairs without greeting Myrna and closed the bedroom door. He'd ignored the half-dozen voicemail messages on his phone. No doubt from Bose, chomping at the bullhorn for his article.

The suitcase sat open on the floor by the window, empty. The rage pouring through Ethan's veins erupted and he yanked his clothes from the hangers in the adjacent closet and tossed them in the suitcase. When the fire still raged inside, he knew the only thing left was to write.

He grabbed the wireless card he'd bought on the way home and yanked open the plastic, tossing the remnants on the floor. He shoved the card in the slot and waited for his computer to hum to life.

Get the story down. Use the energy to imbed passion into the words and finish what he came here to do. Write the story and seal his career.

It didn't matter that with every angry punch of the RETURN button, he'd envisioned his father's face bruised and battered underneath it.

"Take the job offer, Ethan. You're wasting your

life with that tabloid crap. God knows your mother put that ridiculous shit in your head," his father chastised over the phone.

"I don't want the job," Ethan roared back, his maroon graduation gown still clinging on his sleeve. "This 'tabloid shit' is what I want to do. And Mom knew writing is what I loved. You would know that if you hadn't left us in that one-room shack without a dollar in Mom's pocket."

"If you want something from me, boy, this is it. The opportunity of a lifetime that could change your life for the better."

"Don't call me 'boy.' And I have changed my life for the better. You're not in it."

"Then you chose the wrong line of work."

Ethan crushed the phone closed, along with the banking "opportunity" and any claim he had to his father's life.

No matter how many times Ethan pounded the Delete or Return button, his father's face still sneered back at him.

Less than an hour later the writing was done. His anger spent and fingers cramped, he hovered over the Send button on his email. The mouse cursor blinked at him, daring him to push it and give Bose the article he wanted. The article of his career, and the death warrant on Audrey Allen's election.

All it would take was one little push. And New York would be in his grasp.

Then Audrey would hate him forever.

Suddenly, Ethan couldn't breath. Couldn't swallow. Guilt gripped him by the throat and an emptiness deeper than the Mariana Trench split him in two.

He didn't deserve her. Why did he cling to this unfathomable hope of a life with a woman of impeccable reputation? Greener pastures, maybe.

Which is exactly why she was better off without him. He'd never be satisfied. In the end, he'd behave just like his father and leave the perfect woman in ruin.

But Audrey was strong. She could bounce back from this. She was the queen—no, the empress—of overcoming adversity. She had the ideas for a brighter future, and the support to pull it off. Audrey would make a difference. Unlike Ethan.

So hit the Send button and move on.

Ethan clamped his eyes shut and clicked the button. Audrey's sparkling eyes, plush lips and truffle hair drifted into his mind, a desolate tear gracing her alabaster cheek.

Chapter Twenty-Five

Jack's pictures littered the Davises' small living room, his charming adolescent eyes and Sinatra smile surrounded Audrey with the past she was condemned with. But was it the reminder of Jack in every corner, or his mother's tired and worn face smiling at her from the couch that hurt more?

All of the moisture had been drawn from her mouth and relocated to her eyes. No matter how many times she blinked them away, the water always refilled her tear ducts. *Keep it together, Audrey.*

She had turned countless tough rooms in her career, each audience more brutal than the next. Each issue more important and daunting than before. But all of her finesse and tough-as-diamonds arguments couldn't help her now.

"We've been watching you on the news," Claire started after a sip from her powder blue coffee mug. "It's wonderful to see how far you've come, Audrey."

"Thank you, Mrs. Davis." Audrey gripped the handle of her mug, willing herself not to cry. Though Jack was the carbon copy of his father, the smile belonged to his mother. Thin upper lip slightly overlapping a fuller bottom lip, rosy and always set in a smile.

"Please, call me Claire. And this Crisis Center you keep mentioning...how long has it been running?"

"Actually…" Audrey cleared her throat. "We just received the funding for it this week, so it should open by Christmas. Hopefully."

"Where is this?" Carl interjected, stepping into the room carrying his own mug of tea and sitting in the brown leather armchair next to Audrey.

"East Dallas."

"What kinds of services will it provide?" Claire asked, the genuine interest in her voice sounding so similar to Jack, it nearly caught Audrey's breath.

"It's geared to help single mothers without an income, battered women, and homeless women." Morphing into her pre-written elevator sales pitch was second nature. She'd said it so often over the last six months it had become part of her subconscious. "Relocation assistance including their children, therapy, and job placement services. Eventually we'll offer classes on interviewing skills, computer programs, and parenting instruction. Daycare service while they're in school or on interviews. It will be the largest all-in-one assistance location for pregnant teens or runaways who are on their own." Audrey stopped. This wasn't a campaign speech or selling point. And by the sympathetic frowns on both Davises' faces, she'd struck a nerve. Both theirs and hers.

Audrey stared into the swirling steam of her coffee, suddenly engulfed by Jack's presence.

"The kind of help you didn't get."

The words were spoken so softly, Audrey couldn't tell who had said them. Lifting her chin to answer was harder than she could admit.

"The kind I didn't deserve."

A cold drop of something landed on her thumb.

When she glanced down, she realized it was a tear. Hers.

Hold it back, Audrey.

Forcing a deep breath into her lungs, she looked back into Claire's face, whose smile had finally broken. "Sweetheart, that wasn't your fault," the older woman nearly broke into a sob herself as she held her chest.

"No. It was," Audrey whispered. Setting her coffee on the table in front of her, she swallowed back more sobs. She knew she was going to lose it. What she had fought so hard against the last hour. The last two days. The last ten years. "If I hadn't been out with him that night, he would have been at home. Not out on the road to crash into a telephone pole. He'd be sitting…right…" Tears streamed down her face. "Right where I am."

Carl's warm palms covered her hands. *When had he moved next to me?*

"I'm so sorry," Audrey wept. "You have every right to hate me."

"Shh, Audrey," Carl whispered in her ear.

"Jack would have done so many great things; he deserved better than me." She didn't bother trying to hold back her tears now. It was useless. Finally facing the true judge and jury of her mistakes was as hard as she expected. Only the room didn't feel full of judgment. Instead, it cradled her. "I've been trying so hard ever since to make up for it. To make the difference he had wanted."

"Audrey, please look at me," Claire's soft and strangled voice asked. Jack's mother knelt in front of her, her wrinkly and pale hands resting on Audrey's knees. "We never blamed you, Audrey. We just really missed him." She pulled a hanky from her pocket and wiped Audrey's cheeks. "You didn't deserve any of that backlash from the newspaper or the town. And my regret is not doing enough to stop it when it was happening. We were so caught up in our grief, I didn't see the damage it was doing to you. To your family."

A new wave of tears escaped, along with a flood from her nose. She blew her nose into the tissues that Claire offered. But her throat was too swollen to answer.

"Contrary to whatever rumors you heard, we loved you and thought you and Jack were a beautiful young couple. The way he spoke of you with such love and respect, and how bright and talented you were, we were so proud to have you a part of his life. And just as proud that you took his middle name as your own."

The tears slowed as Carl wrapped his arm around her shoulder, supporting her against his side with a firm yet gentle grip.

"We have something to show you." Claire's voice seemed to smile through tears as she spoke. "Will you come upstairs with me?"

Audrey wiped her eyes once more and slowly followed Claire's ginger steps upstairs. Carl followed a short distance behind, just as Jack always did. Giving her plenty of space, but never more than an arm's length away.

The short hallway was illuminated with soft lamps and bright carpeting. Her footsteps didn't sound or feel empty as she moved along the plush fabric beneath her feet. It was four more steps to Jack's old bedroom, the second door on the left. Now three…two…

When Claire swung open the door, Jack's spirit

didn't burst from the room as Audrey half expected. No icy blast of air, ghostly howl, or faint chills up her spine. Instead, just a warm light.

Sunlight filled the room between the wispy curtains. The cherry-wood furniture from Jack's childhood was gone, along with the army posters and football trophies. Scattered across the salmon textured walls were landscape portraits and framed paintings matched perfectly to the floral bedspread on the light maple-wood four-poster.

The décor was the exact opposite of Jack's room. Whereas she remembered a darker hunting and military theme typical for teenage boys in East Texas, the room was now a soft, country efflorescent feeling.

"What do you think?"

Audrey stumbled over the words that were slow to form in her mind from Claire's question.

"This is gorgeous...and completely different." *She wanted to show me their guest room?*

A deep chuckle rose from behind her.

"She doesn't get it, honey," Carl noted. "Audrey, look at the walls. Notice anything familiar?"

A closer look made Audrey's jaw fall to her chest. She recognized the paintings. Every single one.

They were hers.

The landscapes she'd painted or sketched for Jack while in high school. Some that she didn't even know Jack knew of. The largest one framed in an ornate gold frame of a large pond glittering in the sunset—her senior class art project. One that, if she remembered correctly, she gave to her art teacher as a gift.

"We found these among Jack's things after he passed," Claire continued. "We fell in love with them and thought they'd be wonderful up in this room. You combine the colors so seamlessly."

Carl swept into the room and motioned to her senior class project. "This one we found at a teacher's garage sale and recognized your work immediately. Paid over fifty dollars for it."

"But…" Audrey's eyes moved from painting to painting. Her fingers twitched remembering every brush stroke, every sharpening of her pencil with each one. "Why?"

"Because they're incredible," Claire replied.

"The way you've captured Mackineer's twilight, right by the pond…amazing skill," Carl continued, still focusing on each painting. "And only a *teenager*."

Looking at each piece after all this time filled Audrey's heart with the same joy she experienced when she made them. The light in the room was perfect and brought out each one's unique details.

"I'm glad you found use for them," Audrey muttered.

"You had such promise. But life blitzes people sometimes." Carl caught her attention with serious eyes. "One minute you're on one path, the next second you're throwing a Hail Mary pass fighting just to stay on your feet."

Audrey's heart ached with his words, though she couldn't stop the smirk from the football analogies.

"Your plans for art school were fumbled. But you've made an incredible comeback and we're so proud of you." Claire cradled Audrey's hands in her own. "If this election is what you really want, we're more than happy to support you. But as long as it's *your* dream. We want you to live *your* life, not Jack's."

The denials came to her brain, but Audrey's couldn't speak. She couldn't refute Claire's concerns, because deep down she couldn't schmooze her way out of this. Facing the hardest question to the ones who knew her answer better than anyone had to be the truth. No matter how long she'd buried that truth inside.

"One more thing." Claire patted her hand as she pulled away and moved to the armoire by the window. A moment later, she returned with a small blue velvet box. "Jack wanted you to have this."

Audrey stared at it, holding the soft cube in her fingers like the lost Grail. She opened it slowly, and stared at the simple gold band with a solitary pear-shaped diamond. Nothing flashy or extravagant. Jack knew her so well.

"The EMTs found this in Jack's pocket that night," Claire murmured. "He was so excited before he left...and nervous. He'd been planning it for several weeks."

All Audrey could do was nod. There were no words, no other gesture to express her bitter happiness staring at the ring Jack had picked for her.

"It was meant for you, so it belongs nowhere else," Carl spoke softly. "You don't have to keep it, but it's your choice. No matter what, you're still a daughter to us."

Audrey closed the box and let the renewed tears fall. She took one step and wrapped her arms around Carl, who hugged her back tightly.

"Please do what makes you happy," he whispered. "That's all we and Jack ever wanted for you."

Chapter Twenty-Six

The frigid breeze nipped at her legs as Audrey trudged the hill full of headstones. Even through her jeans, the wind was unforgiving. But the bulge in her jacket pocket warmed her palm, radiating up her arm and into her chest.

The black headstone blended well into the sunset shadows created by the swaying willow tree branches. But she didn't have to see it to find the beacon of his grave. Audrey knelt and wiped the dead leaves from the top of his name, keeping hold of the top of his marker.

"No more apologies, Jack. You've heard them all over the last ten years, anyway."

She pulled the box from her pocket and opened it once more, letting the diamond catch a few rays of light. She wasn't a writer. But she let the feelings wash over her, leaving only the words that mattered, and then settle in her mind.

"You know I would have said yes. I'd be a completely different person. But I've tried to make you proud."

She set the box on his headstone and grabbed a nearby stick. A few moments later, she'd bored a small hole in the ground, just above where she thought Jack's heart would have been. With a kiss on the velvet fabric, she set the box into the hole and covered it with the loose dirt.

"Now I have to let you go. And I promise to live my own life."

Once back on her feet, she shoved her freezing hands back in her pocket. The residual warmth from the box inside her jacket faded.

"Good bye, Jack."

****

I'm the scum of the Earth, Ethan thought as he drove Myrna's Civic through the black, winding roads of Mackineer. After he'd come downstairs from writing, he had to get out. He had to find her. Just one look on his face, and Myrna offered her car without question.

The anger and bitterness of his words in the article were directed more at his father. And he'd taken it out on Audrey. On her campaign, on her family, and the town itself. But the worst part was that he'd sent the article to Bose anyway.

He'd submitted the most damaging article to Audrey's political career, and in the same breath realized all he wanted was her. Whatever that meant. He didn't care about his New York position anymore, or his career as an investigative journalist. All he cared about was her. How horrible she'd feel when she read the article Sunday morning, the betrayal of a lifetime, and hence the hatred of a generation. And it was all his fault.

Why in the hell would he think he deserved Audrey's love? Certainly not her admiration or loyalty. Given Ethan's track record, people would assume he didn't know the meaning of those words.

Each turn of the steering wheel brought him closer into town. He had to find her. He wasn't sure where the

Davises lived, but he'd search for her car in every parking lot if he had to. Mackineer wasn't that big anyway. Besides, he'd wasted so much of his time on insignificant things and this was the first one that felt important. Critical. Finding Audrey.

The powder blue Acura wasn't in the Piggly Wiggly parking lot, and there was no surprise it wasn't in the bar's lot either. That would have been the last place she'd visit.

Ethan wound his way down the streets, not seeing her car in any driveway he passed. The only things left down this lane were the motel and library. And the cemetery.

The cemetery.

Just as the thought crossed his mind, the road curved and the familiar powder blue SUV appeared, parked on the side of the road by the entrance to the graveyard, underneath a large oak that sprinkled the hood with bright red and orange leaves.

He pulled Myrna's civic next to Audrey's car and shoved the gear into Park. Audrey's full silhouette was easily visible in the darkened air just after sunset, leaning against the large willow tree gazing across the pond. Her espresso-colored hair blew around her shoulders in the crisp breeze, draping down her back. The only angle at which Ethan had a decent view from sitting in the car. God, she was beautiful. She could have been a model. Not one of those skinny runway twigs, but the wholesome women in vacation ads or toothpaste commercials. The ones depicting the dream wife, safe, worthy, girl-next-door turned woman-worth-living-for.

Where the hell did that come from?

219

Drawing a deep breath, he climbed out and moved along the hill, preparing himself for the groveling of a lifetime. And a slap across the face.

The climb only took a minute, and if she heard him she never turned to face him. When he reached her side, the look in her eyes as she stared across the pond made him wish he were telepathic. No tears, no red-rimmed eyes or splotchy face.

Just peace.

What he wouldn't give to feel the same.

A flock of ducks skirted across the pond, then dunked their heads in the water. Despite the chilly air, they seemed comfortable, safe. At home.

Damn, this place is beautiful, too. Audrey sure can pick the inspirational places.

This spot gave multiple perspectives. One view gave this incredible Thomas Kinkaid setting, no doubt the muse for several paintings or country songs, and only a mere turn gave the scene of a country graveyard, simple yet well tended.

Another glance at Audrey's profile proved this place was both her muse and her crutch. The previous conversation with the Davises must have caused her so much pain, wondering if any of them had a real chance to grieve.

But with the tranquility he saw in her eyes, he realized it went better than he expected. Better than she expected.

Ethan put his arm around her and pulled her in for a sideways hug. Whether on instinct or just a reflex, she laid her head against his shoulder and wrapped her arm around his waist, both still focused on the pond. The gesture was so simple, yet comfortable and undemanding.

The fresh scent of her perfume, or maybe that was soap, clean and flowery, calmed his troubled mind. Her warmth infiltrated his coat, spreading through his limbs. How wonderfully she fit into his side. The thought would normally have unnerved him, but he didn't let the negative thoughts linger.

This felt right. This felt safe. Even if only for a moment.

Her body shivered.

"Are you cold?" he asked.

"Not anymore."

"Do you want to head home?"

"Do you have what you need?"

Her question was plain, unassuming and without accusation. He squeezed her shoulder tightly and responded without a thought. "Right here."

They both looked at each other, the confusion in her eyes slowly melting away to an unmistakable wanting. Yearning. And for the first time in Ethan's life, tingles of fear consumed his heart, because he had no agenda. No ulterior motive other than to be right in front of her, full of need to see Audrey looking at him the way she was right now.

Tilting his head forward, he kissed her forehead, so soft it was almost just a breath.

"Are you okay?" he whispered, barely able to speak with the flood of emotion gripping his chest.

He felt her nod underneath his chin and she wrapped her other arm around his waist, holding just as tightly. Did she feel the same fear? Could she sense his hands trembling as he held her, unwilling to let go?

This is terrifying. For the first time since his

mother died, he felt he had something to lose. Something so precious and valuable, yet which was never his to begin with. But damn if he didn't want this to be in his life constantly. This feeling of being needed, *wanted*. Not just the physical, lustful want he'd had with meaningless women before, but this feeling of completion.

"Audrey," Ethan said softly, trying to find the words to explain himself. But they wouldn't come. A writer without words—ironic. "You deserve so much better than—"

"It's okay," she interrupted him. Pulling out of his embrace, she grabbed his hand and led him to the bench a few feet away. The leaves crunched under the feet as the breeze slowly relented and stopped.

They sat on the bench, her thigh pressed against his.

"No one has ever had the full story," she started confidently. "The first reporter never even interviewed me, and drew conclusions from the little details he had, which everyone took as fact. Ever since, I've never held much respect for reporters."

Biting back the shame flooding through him, Ethan waited for her to continue. She looked directly in his eyes and her sincerity held him captive on the bench.

"I can't explain what this is between us, Ethan. My rational side is telling me to push you away. But you feel something for me, I know it. I can see it. And contrary to what others may have told you, I don't run from things. Not from things that matter."

Ethan's throat squeezed in on itself. *I matter to her. This matters. If only I were worthy.*

"So you need to know," she sighed, clutching his

hand. "Do with it what you will, but I'm not telling this to the journalist. I'm telling this to *you*."

Ethan opened his mouth to speak, but she pressed her finger to his lips.

"Please...let me get this out."

With a resigned stare, he kissed her knuckles and waited.

"That night was very much like this one. Cold, but warm at the same time. I was my typical self, stubborn and relentless. I knew he was tired, but I wanted to be alone with him..."

Chapter Twenty-Seven

"Did you see it? That pass was epic," Jack raved *from the driver's seat, winding his way through the back roads one-handed. "The way it just slipped into Adam's fingertips like that. State champs, here we come, baby."*

Audrey grinned at Jack from the passenger seat. She loved the goofy smile he had whenever he talked about football. His dirty blonde hair was longer than she liked tonight, but she wouldn't fuss over his silly superstition during playoffs. "What did the doc say about your shoulder?"

"Just ice and rest."

"That was a really hard plow, Jack. You sure you should start the playoff game tomorrow?"

"I'll be fine. Just a good night's sleep, maybe cut tonight short a bit. But I'm starving. Hand me a burger?"

Audrey reached down and pulled a burger from the paper sack at her feet. Jack opened it with his free hand and scarfed it down. Audrey held his napkin, twisting the end around her finger.

This was horrible timing. She knew it. But playoffs could last for three more weeks, and there'd be no "good timing" for this news anyway.

"You're quiet," Jack said after he'd swallowed the last bite. "What's wrong?"

"Nothing." She handed him the napkin to wipe his mouth. *"Let's just get there."*

His piercing brown eyes caught hers and her breath caught. Damn, he was good at that. All fuzzy inside with just one look.

"Nervous or something?"

Audrey scoffed. "Me?"

He smiled again, that gorgeous Sinatra grin. "Never been anxious like this the dozen times before. I think we're kinda good at it by now."

"A little too good," Audrey murmured.

"What do you mean?" He flipped on the wipers for the slow drizzle that just started.

Shit. Well, you've come this far, Audrey. Time to finish it.

"Audrey?"

"I'm pregnant."

She couldn't look at him. This was it. This was when even the most perfect of guys completely flipped out and became jerks. Things never ended up great for the girl.

A long, silent moment passed and she couldn't bear it. She looked at him.

Stunned. Typical. And gawking at her. "Seriously?" he finally said.

Audrey squirmed in her seat. "Yeah."

Jack kept glancing between the road, Audrey's face, and her stomach. "How far along?"

"Ten weeks."

She couldn't breath. Jack kept staring at her, mouth open, eyes wide.

"That's..." She watched him do the math in his head. "What, two and half months?"

225

"Yeah. And don't you dare *start with that 'it's-not-yours, I-must-be-cheating' crap." The defensive side kicked in. Her combative nature was her default emotion whenever Jack wasn't around. Being the town outcast warranted it. "You're the only one I've been with and you know it."*

Being with the town's black sheep never bothered Jack. It was one of the things she loved most about him. He didn't mind that she was different than everyone. Instead, he loved her for it.

But why he wouldn't say anything now was killing her. She was used to the strange looks from everyone else, like she was a rebellious alien bound to destroy her family's good name, but not from him.

Then, finally, he laughed. The glorious smile burst onto his face, and she felt her own eyes light up. "That's incredible!"

"Really?"

"Well, its several years early, but that was the plan for us anyway, right?"

"Um...I guess."

"Aud..." He reached across the center console to grab her hand, wincing slightly as his shoulder stretched. "This is wonderful!" He kissed her palm and then each of her fingers, sending hot sparks up her arm. "I love you so much."

Audrey unbuckled her seatbelt and leaned across the seat, covering his cheek and neck with kisses.

Thank God! *Jack really was one in a trillion. The whole idea of a baby at eighteen still scared her out of her boots, but at least he'd be at her side. He wasn't like the other jerks she saw on TV.*

For the first time in several weeks, life was

beautiful. This could work. They'd both graduate high school and find a place somewhere close to college. She'd go to art school while he went for his Political Science degree. It would be hard, but together they could do it.

"This is just perfect," Jack said as Audrey sat back in her seat. "The timing…I was gonna wait until we got there, but…"

Jack reached into his pocket, using his injured arm to steer the car for a moment. But his seatbelt was in the way. He un-clicked it and reached again.

The rest of the images in her mind blended together in one flash of a collage, but spread out like an old reel-to-reel film. In slow motion, like a piano solo of "The Descent" by Michele McLaughlin, the headlights veered to the right, and the black and white spots of a cow beamed back at them brighter than the sun. The tires squealed, the high-pitched scream of the brakes mixed with the moo of the cow, and she slammed against her door, the window shattering against her forehead.

Her body lifted out of the seat and her head hit the roof, followed by the sack of food that was originally at her feet. Her body tossed around the car like a ping-pong ball, every jab and scrape more painful than before, and she opened her eyes just in time to see Jack's body eject through the windshield, followed by a massive pole careen through the back seat, ripping the car in shreds. Audrey's body diverted sharply to the right, and a stabbing pain unlike any words could describe spread through her torso and chest.

A few seconds, or hours later, a numbing cold destroyed every nerve in her body.

****

Ethan's hands rested on her thigh and knee, two warming cores against the bitter cold her body still remembered.

"I didn't remember the details for several months," Audrey finished, holding on to one of his hands. "But one day I woke up and remembered everything. And it has replayed in my mind every night since then.

"I miscarried after the accident. And any chance for a piece of Jack to live on was gone. No one else knew I was pregnant. Then, even though I was eighteen, the doctor still told my mother. Probably because I'd need help to recover. I assume she told my father, because he never looked at me the same after that. Neither of them did."

Ethan squeezed her fingers and rested his hand on the small of her back. "Did Jack's parents ever know? Did you tell them tonight?"

Audrey looked into his eyes, sorrow interlaced with every word, but no tears. "No. That would have only reopened the wound for them. What's done is done."

"That's why you reacted so hard to Addy and Brace." She could see him put the pieces together in his mind. "You knew better than anyone what kind of tightrope she was walking."

Audrey nodded. "By the time I remembered the details, that reporter had already painted me as this rebellious murderer, and the truth didn't matter. I had to finish high school from home—not just because of my injuries, but because of the gossip and threats running rampant."

"Because the team lost the state champ game,"

Ethan finished for her. Audrey nodded and pursed her lips. Her grip tightened around Ethan's hand.

"Adam didn't speak to me for months…didn't even acknowledge my existence."

"I'm so sorry, Aud."

The shame and disgust on her brother's face was still clear in her mind. She swallowed against the guilt. "Not a week after I received my diploma in the mail, my parents sent me away to start school at UT Arlington. My father's friend was an aid in Congressman Mason Nichols' office, so I got a job as an intern. He had it all set up before I even left."

Audrey closed her eyes as she remembered her father's last words the day she went away. *"Be useful, for once."* The pain didn't consume her as much anymore.

"I spent the next several years of my life in utter depression as I studied and worked. I didn't have the heart for art school anymore, so I changed my degree to Political Science, along with my name. Used the school's counselors for the little therapy they offered and…that's how the Peacemaker Audrey Allen got her start in politics."

Reading Ethan's face became harder when she finished. The wrinkles on his forehead and his unfamiliar frown hid either his sympathy, empathy, or guilt. But the strangest thing was that he would no longer look her in the eye.

"I've spent the last ten years trying to make up for everything. I promised myself—and Jack—that I would live his dream. I'm now in a position that could make my family proud, as well as Jack's, and as I sit here looking over this pond…" The waters rippled and shards of starlight beamed off the surface, even in the darkness. "My favorite spot in the world," she whispered. "All I want to do now is sketch."

"Sketch?" Ethan asked, now staring in her eyes with amusement and disbelief.

Audrey nodded. "I have at least a dozen drawings of this place. I could easily add another fifty. I had planned to visit every art museum in the Northern Hemisphere. Sell my work on the street in every place I went, to help me get the money to visit the next one."

"You still could," he smiled.

Audrey laughed, quick but deep and hearty. The light in Ethan's eyes matched his genuine smile. The one that grew on her, softened her, more and more every minute.

"No, really. If it's something you really want, why not? You're still young."

"Be realistic, Ethan. The election is only a few days away, and the Women's Crisis Center is just getting off the ground."

"You could do it." He cut her off. "If anyone could do it, it's you. You have more passion and determination than anyone I've ever met. And you really care about people. Congress could use more people like you, but I don't think they deserve you."

The truth in his eyes and sincere words made her stomach flutter. No one had made her feel like this since Jack. The irrational sense of safety and excitement all jumbled at once. He believed in her, and it was as scary as it was fulfilling.

"Is this from Ethan Tanner the journalist, or—"

"It's from me. No reporter hat, writer scarf, or commentator gloves—just me."

He'd never looked sexier to her before. His full lips were uncharacteristic for most men, but they only made it more impossible to look away when he spoke. She remembered his lips against hers and what amazed her most were his eyes, the blue specks in his gray irises sparking with fire.

She didn't have to wait to see that spark again. Her breath stopped as he moved his hands to hold her face, each thumb lightly tracing against her earrings. He held her cheeks strongly, yet tenderly.

His lips cushioned against hers, consuming and thorough, yet immeasurably patient. His soft mouth moved against hers, and she opened for him, lightly skimming her tongue along his teeth. He was hot, a minty taste mixed with a touch of coffee and sugar. He moved against her again, now more forceful and urging, and slid his hands down her neck to her back, pulling her into him.

Audrey waited for her gut to kick in and tell her this was wrong. The wrenching feeling zooming straight to her brain to urge her to disconnect, and regret. But it never came. Only soft morsels of desire growing deeper and stronger within, pushing her to explore and let go. Let go with Ethan Tanner. The writer? The playboy? No. The *man.* Just as she wasn't Audrey Allen, the politician right now. She was just Audrey. A woman. A woman who deserved to be craved, needed…to melt without fear.

She felt the moan deep from Ethan's throat, muffled by their fused lips, as he pushed his frame against hers and skimmed his hand down to cup her bottom.

She needed to melt. Melt into the strong arms of

one who matched her desire. He ached for her, and that knowledge rocketed sparks through her body. Sparks that she dreaded she'd never feel again.

When his other hand drifted below her shoulder and hovered over the side of her breast, her heart leapt. "Wait," she pulled back breathlessly. "Not here."

"Why not?" he whispered and nuzzled her ear.

"For one, it's too cold…"

"I'll keep you warm." His voice vibrated against her neck, sending lightning down her spine. Amazing how she felt him smile against her skin.

"Mmm…wait, stop." She pushed against his shoulders and shot out of the bench. "Come on." In one fluid motion, she gripped his hand and yanked him up, taking off down the hill toward the road.

"In your car? Wow, that's high school." He laughed.

"Not what I had in mind. Can you wait a few hours?"

Ethan almost gagged and whirled her around, leaning her against the passenger door. "Hours? I can't wait a few *minutes*. God, I want you, Audrey. Please don't make me wait hours."

"Well, it can't be at my parents' house. You want a repeat of Addy and Brace?"

"No, I want a repeat of you. Over and over." He nuzzled her neck again, lightly skimming his tongue along her chin. "We're adults, Audrey."

"Yes we are. Which is why you can keep a wrinkle in it until we get back to my condo." When Ethan groaned, she cupped his face hard between her fingers. "I promise I'll speed all the way home."

Chapter Twenty-Eight

Ethan had never gone this crazy over a woman before. Actually agreeing to wait *hours* for her while he stood at full mast since that mouth-watering kiss on the bench. *This is crazy!*

Ethan smothered his face in the hand towel pushing his back against the guest bathroom door. On the other side of this wall Audrey was packing her things, in a frenzied rush, he hoped. He raked the towel through his hair, even though it was bone dry. Anything to relieve the madness that paralyzed his judgment.

This is Audrey Allen, your target. The one you've obliterated into political Siberia. Wouldn't be long before she'd realize it.

Ethan glared at himself in the mirror, focusing on the slight crook in his nose. "You don't deserve her," he told himself. "But, God almighty, if he exists, you've never wanted someone more. So make it right."

How? How in the hell? Cuz if you don't, that's exactly where you're going.

Ethan yanked his phone from his pocket and held down the speed dial.

It rang.

And rang.

"This is Bose McGavin. I'm busy running a newspaper, so..." His voicemail continued with the usual crap.

"Shit! Bose, the *one* time you don't answer your phone!"

Ethan squeezed his fist on the counter, waiting for Bose's voicemail to end. *Finally, the beep.*

"Bose, it's me." Forcing his voice to slow down wasn't possible. Not when he was this desperate to fix things. "Listen, ignore my email. Just delete it. If you've already read it, *don't* run the article. I'll have a better one for you in the morning. Trust me. For once, *don't run it.*"

He clamped his phone shut and tried to inhale. Shaky and shallow. *Holy shit, I'm a goner. One chance with her and I'm a fucking basset hound.*

Hopefully she'd never have to know what he had previously written. The only piece of his work he was truly ashamed of, God willing, would never see the light of day.

Or this shot with Audrey—*shit, is this love?*—would never see the light of day instead.

****

"What do you mean, 'there *might* be a problem,' Audrey?" Miranda hissed through the phone. "Five days before a runoff election and you're canoodling with a writer who's dug up a manslaughter case on you from ten years ago?"

"You're the one who suggested I bring him home for Thanksgiving," Audrey shot back, trying to keep her voice low.

"You were supposed to have a clean slate. An open book, Audrey. You never told me any of this."

"Mandy, it was a car accident when I was eighteen that almost killed me as well. No charges, no civil suits. No one knew about it but the people in this tiny town, but it also started my passion for politics."

"This isn't what I had in mind for playing the family card in this election."

"It's not what I planned either, but...actually, I don't think he's gonna write the nasty exposé we dreaded." Audrey noticed her cheeks were still flushed as she stared into her childhood mirror. Foreplay with Ethan by the pond left her lips slightly swollen as well, ready and willing for more. "I told him the truth, Mandy. All about the accident, what I'd worked for over the last decade, and then he gave me..."

"Gave you what?"

"A *compliment*—from Ethan Tanner."

"Of course. He's throwing you off your guard to tell him more."

"No, really. The things he said, and the *way* he said it...that Congress didn't deserve me. That I care about people and have more passion. The most determination than anyone he's met."

Please don't shred this. Don't take this away from me.

A deep breath on the other side of the phone made Audrey wish she could express her hopes better. She wasn't used to long-shot-hoping like this.

"All right, Audrey. I trust you on this, but it sounds too much like the Titanic here. The first sign of an iceberg, you *have* to let me know. Press releases and commentary after the crash are only deck music 'til the boat sinks."

"Mandy, take off your campaign manager hat for a second."

The sigh lingered on the phone, and her voice softened even before she spoke.

"If it's real, I'm happy for you. *You,* of all people, deserve it. Ethan is smart, sure knows how to talk to women, and, let's face it—is sexier than sex itself."

Audrey laughed. "Sex isn't sexy."

"You could roast marshmallows off his ass, he's that smokin'."

"Great job not objectifying him. Isn't that what women fight so hard against?"

"Equal treatment is a bitch. But that's why you love me. When are you comin' back?"

Audrey shook her head. "In a few hours."

"Well, between your several likely orgasms, call Canyon and go over a few speech items for tomorrow night's fundraiser."

"I won't be calling anybody between those, girl," Audrey laughed.

"Yeah, yeah. Live it up, girl, cuz tomorrow we have a busy day. No time for Mr. Sex-In-A-Cup until after you're voted Senator Allen."

The line ended, and Audrey continued to stare at herself in the mirror.

Senator Allen.

Is this what she really wanted? It was the first time she'd ever questioned it. But Ethan had a point—she could still sketch and paint, too. Maybe even sell her artwork to raise more money for the Crisis Center. Throw in a few museum visits here and there between congress sessions.

Closing her eyes, images of the Met, the Louvre, even the Guggenheim, walking through galleries as her mind filled with inspiration from history's greatest masters and flawless pieces, hand in hand with Ethan.

Her eyes flared open. *Seriously? Would he even*

consider it? A long-term relationship. Could she handle it? Did she even want that?

Yes…yes I do.

"And I want it with *him*," she said to the face in the mirror.

Energy surged through her veins and she quickly packed her bag, ignoring any folding or organizing. She shoved her folders back in her suitcase and grabbed her toiletry kit. A refresh of her perfume and lip gloss, and next was deodorant. But when she lifted her shirt and saw the horrid array of scars down her side and under her arm, she stopped.

Each white, jagged line still rough under her soft fingers. The puffy evidence of her mistake spread to her back and disappeared under her pant line, where a small chunk of her hip was carved out and only more scars remained.

But would he want me? After he sees this…

The scars had always bothered her, but once the stabbing pain and tender aches had ebbed, she'd learned to accept them after a decade. Part of the price she paid for Jack's death. It hadn't stopped her from pursuing her goals. But it had stopped her from pursuing the few relationships that could have blossomed. A classmate in college, a fellow intern, even an investor early on in her political career.

Nothing came of them, not even a lingering kiss, because she wouldn't let it get there. Self-consciousness ran deeper than her scars, leaving her lover count at one. Who'd never lived to see the scars form.

Could she take that risk with Ethan? He'd seemed to dismiss her "murderer" allegations without a second thought, unlike her hometown, but could he handle the scars? Her deformed silhouette?

Audrey forced herself to breathe and then reapplied her deodorant. A few minutes later she stared into Ethan's glittering eyes at the bottom of the stairs. Her pulse skipped. *God, please keep that look in your eyes. Don't let it fade when you see me.*

****

"How'd it go with the Davises?" Myrna asked as she stepped in from the kitchen. Paul approached from the back hallway and leaned against the wall, crossing his arms as he waited.

Ethan couldn't take his eyes off of her. Her skin glowed and hair haloed like an angel from the ceiling light behind her. But what kept him the most entranced were her eyes. Hungry, determined, and yet tinged with dark blue tension. A woman with that many emotions running through her was bound to erupt with passion in a way he'd never thought possible.

But she'd just been through hell not three hours before. And he was anxious to know her response just as much as her parents.

Audrey set her bags next to the staircase and brushed her hair back with her hand. "They said exactly what I needed to hear." She smiled. "The truth."

Without a word, Myrna stepped forward and hugged her daughter, not wiping her tears until she stepped back. But Audrey's father continued to stand in the hallway, fidgeting with an awkward grimace.

"I'll help take your bags to the car," he broke in, gripping the luggage handles and pushing through the door.

"If you can make the drive," Audrey redirected to her mother. "Please come to the fundraiser. It would mean a lot."

"Oh sweetie," she sighed, squeezing her daughter's hand. "I'm sure it's gonna be lovely. But your father has to work and you know him. He'll crash in front of the football game when he gets home. But I'll be thinkin' about you."

Audrey kissed her mother on the cheek with a half smile and stepped out.

"Don't wait too long to come home again, hon," Myrna called from the porch.

Paul shut the trunk and faced Ethan, scowl firmly in place once again. "Ethan, good to meet you. Safe drive back."

The curt words were said along with a tight grip, his eyes holding Ethan's for an additional second. The stare serious as a jail sentence: *Hurt my daughter, and I've got an entire box of ammo with your name on it.*

Ethan nodded. "See you soon."

Really? Wow…first time I've said that to a woman's father.

"Hope not," Paul replied dryly.

Ethan walked around the car, and opened the passenger door. He tried to pretend he didn't hear Paul's words to Audrey, but he stopped anyway, watching him through the rear window.

"You've…done really well, Audrey. Better than I thought you would." His voice broke, which he covered with a cough and shoved his hands in his pockets. "You need to stay where you're appreciated. Keep away from here as long as you can."

Hard ass with no heart, Ethan growled to himself. True, it was his version of keeping his child safe, but all Audrey wanted was some sign of affection from her father. After everything she'd been through, he still couldn't give her that much.

Though he couldn't see Audrey's face, he hoped she wasn't crying. That kind of rejection would have made any adult blubber like a toddler. Audrey leaned forward, kissed her father's cheek and gave him a one-armed hug.

Finally, Paul hugged her back with one quick squeeze and stepped back, clearing his throat as he looked away.

A minute later, Audrey steered through the back roads of Mackineer and accelerated when she hit the highway. She'd only looked in the rearview mirror once as they pulled out of the driveway, and the corner of her mouth lifted into a cute smile. Like an inside joke. Or the confirmation she needed to feel loved.

This woman deserved a lot more than that to feel loved. *I'm going to make sure she feels it. I'll make that small half smile the size of the Atlantic, and move her just as deeply.*

The road sign for Dallas zoomed past his window, ninety-nine miles.

He stared hard at Audrey's profile, the smooth skin, adorable freckles along her nose, and long, dark lashes, and he tried to control the heat filtering into his groin. *I'll pay every speeding ticket wearing a huge ass smile in my birthday suit if she gets us there in less than an hour.*

Chapter Twenty-Nine

Fifty-five minutes later, Audrey closed her front door behind Ethan and set her bags down on the wood floor. Before she could verify the time on the kitchen clock, Ethan dropped his duffel bag and moved to her, smoothly pushing her against the wall and covering her mouth with his own.

He tasted like toothpaste, the fresh, sweet kind. Like the flavor she could eat straight from the tube when she was a kid. But it was his warm cologne that flooded over her most, like a drug that relieved every pain in her body and replaced it with the warmest ache fuzzier than any blanket fresh from the dryer. His soft lips were hungry on hers, demanding and giving simultaneously. His hands moved in tandem along her neck and into her hair, burying his fist at her nape. He massaged her neck and moved along her shoulders, down her arms and to her waist, squeezing every ample mound of flesh.

Her own hands savored each muscle he flexed. She loved how they twitched at her touch, anticipating her fingers and what they'd do next. Grabbing the bottom of his shirt, she yanked it up over his head. He flung the fabric over his shoulder.

Wide shoulders.

The groan from her diaphragm trickled up her throat. The light curls of his chest hair didn't detract from the smoothness of his skin as she spread her fingers across them and along his collarbone. Further down was his flat stomach, all the way to his "innie" belly button, just above the hem of his briefs. The abs weren't defined on the surface, but as she traced her hands across them, she felt them flex and quiver, strong and tight.

Their lips parted and his breath was shallow and hard, quickening at the touch of her hands.

The rock-hard length of him pressed against her waist. Were there no clothes between them she was sure she could feel it pulse with heat. Their lips joined again, feverish and plunging. In the next moment, he'd unzipped her jeans and slid them down her thighs, letting his hands linger over her lace thong. Audrey kicked off her shoes and stepped out of her jeans, moving her lips along his jaw.

A second later, he'd stripped off her sweater and devoured her neck in wet kisses.

Her pulse raced. *Suffocation by passion was a good way to go,* she managed to think, until Ethan held her breasts, kneading and strong, and all thought vanished. His mouth took the place of his fingers over her brown lace bra and Audrey watched him love on her nipples through the fabric.

Everything ached. The best kind of ache. And the white fire spread to her legs until she ground against him. *Let this last...*

His hands froze as Audrey heard him gasp. "Good God, Audrey...is this from the accident?"

Her eyes opened wide and saw the trauma in the lines of his forehead. *Oh God...this is it. Where he runs away in disgust. Refuses to touch me thinking he'll contract a disease.* Fear strangled her words, so she nodded.

Shock morphed into sympathy in one breath and his fingers traced over the white spider web of scars. Tender, barely any pressure—like feeling the texture of a Monet he wasn't supposed to touch.

"Does it hurt?" he asked softer.

Audrey shook her head.

Breathe, Audrey. The first time anyone saw her scars in full, aside from the doctor and her mother. And that was ten years. Not like this. Not like a display waiting for someone to decide if they were attracted, were willing to pretend they didn't exist. She knew how deformed they made her look, how beautiful she would have been had the serrated wounds not destroyed the canvas of her skin.

The lack of control scared her witless. Almost as much as that night.

Trust...just trust.

Ethan cupped her hips within his hands and leaned into her, pressing his lips to her skin. Slowly, he fluttered kisses along every inch of the jagged lines up her waist, side and shoulder. Shivers ran up her spine as he moved down her arm and back to her hip, placing another longer kiss to the largest scar, the chunk missing from her upper thigh.

When he stood, he held out her hands and grazed his eyes over her whole frame, taking in every curve, freckle and heartbeat, along with every flaw. But the sympathy was gone. The look people give to injured puppies or lost children that she expected to see. Instead, his eyes were full of...thirst.

"You're fucking beautiful," he said just above a

whisper.

Heat tinged her cheeks and she smiled. *Please keep looking at me like this. Don't run away.*

"Promise me they don't hurt?"

"Not a bit. Why—umph!"

Ethan yanked her to his body and crushed their lips together. In another fluid motion he cupped her bottom and lifted her like she were a basket of feathers, never releasing her mouth from his own hungry urges. She wrapped her legs around his waist, astonished by the strength in his skinny waist.

"Because I'm not gonna hold anything back." The words almost growled from his chest. "Bedroom?" He mumbled into a deeper kiss.

"Behind you," she panted.

Thank you...

Everything around her faded into fuzzy bubbles, a weightlessness that consumed her soul. The only thing existing in her world was Ethan with his sturdy arms and teasing hands. And the bed.

Somehow he'd slipped off her lace lingerie without removing his mouth from her body. A heartbeat later, he'd stripped his briefs and knelt over her, full glory. The first *man* she'd ever seen completely naked. Forget movies or media. Nothing like up close and private. And glorious. Thick and ready for her.

But more glorious were his eyes. Dark, almost all pupils as the lust dripped from every pore on his face, soaking in her bare body. He nestled his knees between her legs, moving his hands up. Thighs, waist, stomach. Further...until she gasped when he reached her breasts, stroking, massaging, and circling the sensitive tips until they peaked into diamonds.

Lowering his head to one, he sucked it between his teeth, laving it with his hot tongue. Flicking, suckling, while he mimicked with his fingers on the other tip. She wanted to cry out, but bit her lip and groaned.

He switched nipples, giving each the same attention and pleasant torture. When he realized the first made her breathe heavier, he moved back to her other breast and repeated again. Enveloping faster, gyrating, and white hot.

Shit, I'm not gonna last long. Is it him? Or merely the ten years of inattention?

Steadily, his hand moved down her body as he continued, and reached the juncture at her thighs. He slipped a finger between the slick folds and she nearly exploded right then.

"Ethan," she cried as electric shocks sparked in every muscle.

"Don't hold back," he breathed, relentlessly caressing the delicate nub.

"You... asked...for it."

Audrey clamped her thighs around his waist and shoved hard against his shoulders. Like a tidal wave, she flipped him on his back and straddled him. Lips swollen and red, he gazed back with shimmering, playful eyes.

"You've been in the driver's seat all weekend. Don't I get a chance to call the shots?"

"Something tells me you've done that your whole life." She smiled. "And you've had plenty of head-coach moments this weekend. Don't kid yourself."

"Fair enough." He laughed. "There's a condom in my wallet. Right pant pocket."

As Audrey reached across the bed to grab his pants

from the floor, she couldn't hold back a smirk. "Pretty sure of yourself, huh?"

"Just hopeful. Always prepared."

She handed him the gold packet and let him slip it on, watching his skilled hands work like it was second nature. But she kept her doubting questions shoved firmly in the back of her mind. It didn't matter she wasn't as experienced or if he'd played the main role in *Animal House*; she'd match him stroke for stroke, pump for pump.

She glided her hands across his abdomen as he finished putting it on, marveling in the smooth skin, and then he grasped her fingers. He brought her palm to his lips and kissed the cut from the glass shard, light and gentle. Their bodies sank into each other, igniting another tidal wave. Staggering and all-consuming. She moved through it, rising and falling, pressing his hands to her hips and watching the dancing flecks in his eyes with each rippling push.

Everything dissolved around her. The election, the fundraiser, the speeches, interviews, the blaming glares, painful words, and inadequate feelings. Gone. For a good three minutes.

Then another twenty.

Two hours later, they lay on her comforter spread across the floor beside her bed, flat on their backs, panting at the ceiling.

"Now I know why you never wore short skirts or sleeveless shirts on the campaign trail."

My scars. Pitiful time to spotlight my flaws. Audrey wrapped her arm across her chest, gripping her shoulder and let the sweat permeate through her skin.

"You're too hot for your own good," he breathed.

"Your platforms wouldn't have stood a chance against shots of that hourglass you have."

Women's lib enthusiasts would campaign against her to ensure her loss for loving his comment. How could she be irritated when he kept making her smile?

"Skin I can lick like ice cream." He laughed and curled himself on top of her, skimming his fingers up her side. "Hugh Hefner can eat his heart out; you're mine!"

Each nipple received a wet kiss from his lips before he pulled her head onto his shoulder.

"Hefner doesn't stand a chance. I have a brain. And robes are a turn-off for me."

"How about bunny slippers?"

Audrey laughed and sat up, letting her long hair tumble about her shoulders in a glorious morning-after feeling. Though it was only one in the morning.

"Want a drink?"

"I just did," he smirked.

"Cute. I think I've got a beer in the back of my fridge with your name on it."

"I don't drink anymore. Water's fine."

Chapter Thirty

The words came out of his mouth before he could stop them. One minute he was engorged on Audrey's delectable skin, the next he started to spill his intimate side with just a simple question. Not that it was a secret, but Ethan didn't like to talk about his history with alcohol. Not a flattering picture.

"Now there's a story, Mr. Journalist." Audrey returned from the kitchen holding two glasses of water, wearing a short purple bathrobe. Ethan had already pitched the last condom and cleaned himself up, now trying to find his briefs among their heap of clothes scattered across the floor. He took a glass from Audrey and gulped it down, planning his escape from the conversation. Interesting that he wasn't planning his escape from her apartment, like he normally would with other women. Somehow, the way Audrey relaxed across the covers on her bed, thigh revealed in the opening of her robe while she cradled a cup in her hands, so open, casual, comfortable—made him want to stay. An hour. A night. Or maybe…

He set the glass down and continued to fish for his clothes. "Did you hide my underwear?"

Audrey laughed. "Right. 'Cuz I long to cuddle up against your dirty drawers at night and think of you."

The sound of her laugh, hearty, full and easy, filled his brain with…something. Like the froth off the top of a freshly poured beer. The kind that tickles your nose on the first sweet sip.

He pulled on his briefs, which he found hiding underneath Audrey's jeans. Then he climbed under the covers with her, leaning against the headboard studying her inquisitive face. So trusting, with flawless freckles scattered across the bridge of her nose.

"I thought a qualification for all writers was a drinking problem," she smirked and took a sip of water.

"Ha! I don't think there's enough liquor in the world to satisfy all writers, in addition to the drunken frat parties."

"Why don't you drink anymore?"

Ethan shrugged and took a sip of his own water. *Change the subject, pal. You're gonna regret this.*

"Nuh-uh, playboy. We're turning the investigative inquiry on you. Spill."

"Just didn't like the way I felt afterwards. I'm not twenty-two anymore and I've abused my liver enough."

"Dad mentioned you kept refusing drinks." Audrey kept her tone light, and unobtrusive. Ethan noticed. Her sapphire eyes in the dim light pulled at his heart. God, she was beautiful. Why did she have to make this personal?

"You were right. Your family has a big heart. Underneath everything, they're very good people."

Audrey blanched and stared at him. "Nice to know Ethan Tanner approves."

"No, really. I can see where all your determination comes from."

"And yours?"

"What?"

"Your determination to get the story at any

cost…where does that come from?"

Ethan scoffed. "My father, I guess."

"You say that like it's a bad thing."

"Not a quality I'm fond of."

"But that's what makes you a good journalist, right?

Ethan shrugged.

"What does he do in Chicago?"

Holy shit. How in the hell did we get here? Ethan fidgeted under the covers and took another sip of water. He should put the rest of his clothes on and run. He asked the questions, not the other way around. But why won't his heart let him stand up and walk out?

"He's a banker," he bit out. Even he noticed the bitterness in his voice.

"Your mom?"

"Why are you doing this?"

"Doing what?"

"Asking about my family. It doesn't matter."

"We've spent the whole weekend talking about me and my family," Audrey cooed. "You're getting bent out of shape for me wanting to know more about you?"

"I'm not bent out of shape."

"You don't need to get defensive with me, Ethan. I'm not writing an article. I'm not recording this or planning to use anything against you."

You might later, he thought with a grimace.

"How did your mom pass?"

"Cancer." Ethan's throat tightened and no matter how many times he cleared his throat, it wouldn't let go.

"I'm sorry," Audrey whispered as she laid her hand on his arm. Her skin was still warm, glowing. "What did she used to do?"

"Elementary teacher." The edge in his voice faded as he traced her fingers across his skin. "English and reading."

"That's where you get your penchant for writing."

Ethan heard the smile in her voice without looking at her. "When I told her I wanted to be a journalist, she used her savings to buy me a laptop. She was so excited."

Audrey squeezed his hand, a silent gesture of support and to keep him going, he figured. And for the first time, he felt like it.

"When I was accepted to Brown University for my Masters, she cried. Went into her room and brought back an envelope full of cash. She'd sold her wedding ring. Wanted me to use it for tuition." He cleared his throat again, the lump in his esophagus growing larger with every word. "My first semester, she was diagnosed with breast cancer. I wanted to come home and take care of her, but she wouldn't let me. That Christmas was the first time I ever asked my dad for help. It took every ounce of humility I had to pick up the phone. Just something to help cover some of her medical bills or groceries. Instead, he offered me a job as an intern at his banking firm.

"When I refused, he refused. Told me I'd waste my life as a journalist. Wouldn't give my mother a dime. The man has 600 million dollars to his name, and wouldn't spare groceries for the mother of his only child."

Audrey's hand now gripped his fingers, her smile gone as she watched him tell his story. The story he refused to repeat to anyone for years. Feelings that raw needed to be buried. They hurt too much.

"Mom died shortly after. Her church donated most of the funds for her burial. I finished grad school with a mountain of student loans on my neck, but I managed to buy back her wedding ring that she'd pawned for my education. It's the only thing I have left of hers.

"After Mom died, I turned to alcohol as my coping mechanism. Years later, after burying myself in the bottle and countless drunken fights, I woke up one morning to an empty fridge, a trash bin full of empty liquor containers and a cracked jaw. I switched to coffee and haven't touched it since."

"Have you spoken to your dad since then?"

Ethan scowled. "Graduation day from Brown. Announced he wanted to run for Congress and offered me a job on his campaign. I threw it in his face and hung up. Best and worst day of my life."

"Whoa. Congress? After he refused to help your mom?"

Ethan sneered. "Yeah. But he lost the primary. Even his 600 million couldn't help him. Serves the bastard right."

Audrey pursed her lips. "Now I see where you get your thirst for destroying politicians. Hard to argue with that logic."

"Not all politicians," he replied softly. "Not anymore."

Audrey's smile lit up his confidence.

"I've been striving for this job in New York, proving to myself I can make it despite him. And I'm almost there."

"*New York Times*?"

"Yeah."

"Wow, Ethan. That's incredible."

The look in her eyes—pride, amazement, affection—bowled him over. Is this what encouragement felt like? It had been so long since he'd recognized it. "My mom and you are the only ones who've ever said that to me."

"I've read your work, Ethan. Aside from the investigative dirt you dig up, your writing is excellent. You're not afraid to ask the difficult questions."

"Neither are you."

Audrey laughed and picked a piece of lint off her robe. "That's just politics. Not the part I like best."

"No one likes the politics. But *you* get to the heart of every issue, unlike most others in your profession. You've overcome probably the biggest obstacle than anyone I've ever known." Ethan laid his hand on her exposed knee, letting her warmth fill him up. "You keep pushing so hard to make a difference, but you don't see that you already have."

They looked at each other, long and unmoving. Their connection unending and unreserved. It scared the shit out of him. But he wasn't ready for it to end. *I'll be damned. The real thing. I never thought it existed.*

"You're pretty charming when you have your eyes set on something you want."

"You're right." He fixed his gaze on her irises. "And when I'm grateful for something, too."

Ethan leaned forward and touched his lips to hers, slow and tender. When he pulled back, Audrey suckled his bottom lip. He rested his forehead against hers and breathed in everything. Her skin, her breath, her shampoo, even the fabric softener of the comforter. "I'm grateful for you."

Chapter Thirty-One

After another round of showing how grateful he was for Audrey, Ethan watched her even breathing and luscious lips as she slept, tangled amid the comforter and sheet. He wanted to add his own body to the entanglement, envisioning his legs wrapped around her silky calves and nearly-edible feet, but he had one more important thing to do before he felt redeemed.

Rewrite his article.

He'd already tried to call Bose again as soon as Audrey crashed, but since it was close to 2am, he wasn't surprised there was no answer. So now he crept out of the bedroom in the darkened apartment, yet still cozy and comfortable as home. The streetlights a few floors below cast a warm orange glow through the living room blinds as he curled up on the couch.

The flow of words from his mind couldn't keep up with his fingers and he tried to keep his typing quiet. The half-smile reflected in the screen didn't distract him, but only made him grin wider as he wrote. This was an entirely different writing experience.

It was happy. Exhilarating in a self-fulfilling way. There'd be no threats or nasty-grams from readers on this one. Probably the first one in his entire career. But it was no puff-piece, either. Honest, factual, with an undercurrent of hope. Much like Audrey herself.

Bose would claim he'd gone soft, found a

conscience in the little backwoods town, and now was useless as an investigative journalist. But only until he read this.

In less than thirty minutes, his rewrite was done and resubmitted to Bose via email. Which he'd receive when he woke, no doubt. Sunday morning's paper would have one of the highest circulations in the publication's history. Ethan just knew it.

Stretching his muscles, he reached back and his hand hit something on the windowsill.

He set his laptop on the coffee table and looked back. A notebook, larger than a journal with worn leather, dangled off the ledge. Her diary? No. Not left out in the open like this. The binding creaked as he opened it, skimming through the first few pages.

Exquisite. Mostly black and white sketches of faces, quaint street facades and landscapes. A few in color. Particularly several of one he recognized. The pond in Mackineer. Each season depicted in explicit detail, with both spring and fall in full color.

The way she'd spoken about her art before gave him an idea of her passion, but these sketches were breath-stealing. Seeing her work revealed he had no idea the true depths of this woman's capabilities.

If she'd wanted to make a career out of this, Ethan knew at least a dozen people who'd line up for these prints alone. Including himself.

He paused at a gray and black sketching of the graveyard. From the bottom of the hill, Jackson's black marble headstone drew the viewer's eyes to the center, the slightly exaggerated size of the marker made everything else seem faded, and loneliness crept over him.

A true artist. Every feeling visible with each pencil line or brush stroke. Her heart wasn't worn on her sleeve. It lived on every page.

He flipped through the final few sketches and froze. The last one was his face.

Was this a mirror? The close-up of his eyes almost made him turn around to check. Each vein in his irises, the shadows in his pupils, and the varying lengths of his lashes couldn't possibly be this accurate otherwise.

But the emotion throttled him most. Somehow, in the mixture of shades she'd captured the frustration and torment he'd tried to cover beneath determined ambivalence. She *saw* him.

A small inscription on the bottom of the page caught his eye.

The date.

Four days ago. The day he met her.

She saw him this clearly on day one?

Ethan closed the notebook, trying to slow his heartbeat.

Fuck, he was *scared.* Like a boarding school kid, he felt like running into his bunk bed and throwing the covers over his head. *Where did that come from?*

Ethan had lost count of how many women he'd sported with. He used to consider each a little badge on his shoulder. None of them gave him more than a few minutes of indigestion. *Why was this so nerve-wracking?*

If he could punch himself in the face without waking Audrey up, he would. So yanking on his hair was his only comfort in the silent room. He put the notebook back on the windowsill and slipped his laptop bag in his bag.

He moved back into the bedroom, leaning against the doorframe and watched her sleep. Relaxed, secure. He'd give anything to sleep that peacefully.

When she smiled and moved her head on the pillow, still fast asleep, his heart skipped.

Good dreams. How he hoped it was because of him.

Shit. I'm in love with her.

Chapter Thirty-Two

The shrill ring of her cell phone made Audrey want to bury her face deeper in the covers. A squint at the clock from under her pillow showed a bright blue 6:56 a.m.

Audrey groaned.

Then a warm and strong hand slid across her shoulder and wrapped itself around her waist. And squeezed.

Ethan.

He'd stayed all night. With her.

She held her arms around his and the phone stopped.

Even first thing in the mornings he smelled like cologne. Or was that just his natural manly scent? She pushed her hips further back into the spoon their bodies formed and smiled. The rock hard member was at attention. Ready for more.

"Good morning," she murmured through a grin and swayed her hips against him.

A deep moan from his pillow sent prickles across the back of her neck.

"That's a nice wakeup call."

"Yes, you are. But I'm all out of condoms," he replied.

"Aww, shucks," she teased. "You'll have to reel him in yourself. Coffee?"

"Wait." Ethan rose up and pressed on her shoulder, turning her face into his. He pressed his soft lips against hers, slow and gentle. "Mmm, yes please."

Her phone rang again, echoing across the room.

"Someone really wants to talk to you," he mumbled through another kiss.

"Probably Miranda. Go rein in your stallion while I get us some coffee."

Audrey snaked out of the covers and sashayed into the kitchen, grabbing her phone from the dresser as she left.

Yep, Miranda.

She flung it open with a flick of her wrist and yawned. "Can't I have at least one cup of coffee before today's briefing, Lieutenant? At least a bathroom break."

"Shut up and pick up the paper," Mandy bit out.

"Whoa! It's too early for attitude, hon." Audrey pulled a mug down from the cabinet and started filling the coffeemaker with water. "Where's the fire?"

"Spreading across the front page, and it's already ruined us, Aud. Heartbreaker boy hit again."

"It can't be that bad, Mandy." *Not after the night he and I just shared.* "Have you had your Xanax today?"

"Audrey! Pick. Up. The paper."

When she opened the front door, she saw the headline through the plastic wrap sitting on the welcome mat.

HOMETOWN SCANDAL DOOMS ALLEN CAMPAIGN

Her stomach caved as all of the air whooshed out of her lungs, and her legs became brittle and pudding all at once. Holding onto the doorjamb to keep from buckling, she picked up the paper and slid it out of the sleeve, dropping the plastic on the mat.

When unfolded, Jack's high school photo smiled out at her next to a capture of the mangled car wreck. Mandy's voice drowned behind the roaring in Audrey's ears. Just below the photos were four words that gripped her chest:

WRITTEN BY ETHAN TANNER

The pain shot through her arms and down into her belly. The pieces of her heart shattering into every corner of her body.

"I thought you said this was nothing you couldn't handle?" Mandy almost cried into the phone.

"I have to call you back." Her voice sounded hallow, eerie, as if it weren't her own.

"No, Audrey. We have a shit storm of damage control. I've already had a half-dozen phone calls asking for comment."

Audrey closed the phone.

Before her feet would move, a door opened down the hall and an elderly man grabbed the paper in front of his apartment. His slippers shuffled to move back inside, then stopped as he read the headline. His gaze instantly moved to Audrey, still frozen by her door, and his jaw sagged.

Before the neighbor could say anything, Audrey finally darted into her apartment and quietly shut the door. As if she escaped with the least amount of noise, it would cause the least amount of damage to her image. Not that she could run from the crippling words she held in her hand.

The first paragraph set the tone of her dread,

knowing the rest would only get worse. With each sentence, another piece of her heart splintered and withered.

"...ran from her mistakes."

"...wave of pain and resentment in her wake."

"...even her brother pledges not to vote for her."

"...stealing the hometown hero's life and the dreams of dozens."

She couldn't scream. Couldn't cry. Her body wouldn't let what her soul begged for.

Last night was a lie. Everything out of his mouth, his eyes, his body only meant to ensnare her more.

What did you expect from Ethan Tanner? You traded your campaign and respect for one night on a fool's hope.

She cringed through her unguarded heart.

Looking up from the paper, she found herself in the kitchen bracing her arms against the counter. The phone shrilled through the kitchen again, dancing across the counter.

"Good Lord, you're important. Seven a.m. and they're relentless." Ethan's silky voice drifted across the air on his cologne. His wide shoulders leaned against the wall, arms crossed, and he gazed at her the way only a moment ago she would have lost herself in. Like she was a plate full of chocolate soufflé to a starving man.

She wanted to throw up.

"Before your busy campaign schedule today, can you spare an hour for breakfast with me?" She could have slid across the smoothness of his voice like a figure skater on ice. If only it didn't lead her to thinner promises.

"I'm all booked up today," she finally croaked out.

"What's wrong?"

"Really?" She glared into his innocent eyes. "You're gonna play dumb? I didn't think that was in your playbook."

"What are you talking—"

"You, more than anyone else, had the whole story." She cut him off, acid dripping with every word. "I thought you understood…everything you said. No. Forget that. You're just like the rest of them."

"Talk to me," he cooed, placing his hands on her shoulders. But she wiggled out of it.

"I'm *done* talking to you. Get out."

"What?"

Audrey brushed past him, forcing her face to be strong and emotionless, and gathered up his bags in the living room. When she turned around, she strode past him to throw his things out the door, trying to ignore his horrified shock as he read the front page.

"Bose, you son of a—" he murmured under his breath.

"Oh, so it's *not* your fault." She tossed the bags in the hallway. "Place all the blame on someone else. You mean you didn't write that? Those words didn't come out of your mind? You didn't submit that to your press?"

"I swear this isn't what I meant to publish. I had a completely different article—"

"I don't want to hear it." Audrey flung open her front door and waited.

It didn't matter that Ethan played hurt and stunned so well it nearly convinced her. It didn't matter that she started to feel the anguish rip through her heart and up into her throat. It didn't matter that she finally opened herself to another person only to have it exploded back in her face.

"No, Audrey."

What?

"I'm not gonna run from this. Yes, this article is mine, but I wrote it before last night at the pond. When we came home to pack, I called my boss and told him not to run this. I'd have a better one for Sunday. Then after the incredible night we just had, I wrote a different one. One that would ensure your victory, but… I'm so sorry."

Audrey swallowed hard. *Fight the tears… Peacemaker face. Peacemaker…*

"You finished?"

"God, I hope not."

"I don't want your apology, Ethan. But you better call the Davises and give it to them instead. I told you I wasn't concerned about myself. It was his family I wanted to protect."

Peacemaker face had never been so painful in her life. She meant what she said: his family was more important than her own feelings. But this was one thing she couldn't handle.

"Get out," she finished, tearing her watery eyes away from his ashamed face.

"Please, Audrey. How can I fix this?"

You've already ripped out my heart so I can't feel anymore. I'll be immune to everything.

The phone rang again, echoing through the apartment like a firehouse siren. Audrey stood her ground, staring at the wall across from her.

Ethan slowly moved forward, gathered his bags

from the floor at her feet, and stood. Without a word, he leaned in to kiss her cheek, but she pulled back and clamped her jaw shut.

When he stepped through the door, Audrey let a single tear fall down her cheek, the cheek he couldn't see.

"I'll make this right, Audrey."

She slammed the door on the last ring.

Chapter Thirty-Three

Ethan sped through the streets, the adrenaline as rampant in his system as the fuel in his truck. His hand hurt like hell, but the ache in his chest was worse. He couldn't tell if the roaring sound was the diesel engine or the fury pulsing in his ears.

Bose's used-car-salesman grin only infuriated him more. Confronting his boss was useless, but he couldn't stop himself. It wasn't surprising that Bose ran the more damaging article, but it was the first time Ethan had been truly ashamed. Of Bose, his profession, and himself.

But it was his own words that stunned him the most. "I won't keep working like this," he'd yelled.

"What are you talking about?" His boss scoffed at him in his office, the phones ringing like annoying mockingbirds throughout the scattered cubicles. "This is what you've always done, only better. Our volumes have never been higher."

"It was shit, Bose. And you know it."

"Are you saying it wasn't the truth?"

"It wasn't the *whole* truth."

"Then you're fine."

"I'm not trying to save my ass, Bose. I'm trying to do what's right."

"Holy shit," Bose murmured, staring dumbfounded back at Ethan. His slick black hair suddenly looked slimy and unearthly. Just as his eyes. "I warned you, Tanner. You grew a conscience. That backwoods hick town messed with your head."

"No, it didn't. I messed with my own head. I've destroyed her."

"Oh, now I get it. It's Allen, isn't it? You've fallen for her. And now she hates you because of the article."

Ethan stormed forward with shaking fists. Only when his boss stepped back, horrified, did Ethan restrain himself a mere three inches from his face. The snake was right. For all the wrong reasons, but that didn't change the hallow cavity in his chest.

"Fuck you, Bose."

Pacing wasn't going to help, but Ethan did it anyway. Scraping his fist along Bose's desk wouldn't help either. But he did it anyway. Fighting old demons was useless.

"Tanner, take it easy." Bose slipped his fingers through his greasy hair and unknotted his Windsor tie. "Every journalist goes through an ethical crisis at least once. But you've done it. Now you can move on. And as for more good news: New York is expecting you next week."

Ethan's jaw flinched and he stared hard at the desk.

"Didn't you hear me?" Bose leaned forward. "You've got New York."

"I don't give a shit about New York."

"Don't give me that crap, Tanner." Bose ripped off his tie and tossed in on the desk. "For years, you busted my balls for that referral. And now you're throwing it back in my face. Get the hell out of here and come back when you've got your priorities straight."

"I want a retraction."

Bose almost swallowed his tongue. "In a wet dream."

"A retraction and Sunday's front page of the other article. The real one."

"Just so you can get back between the sheets with the salacious slayer, fat chance."

Screw fighting demons.

Ethan swung once and his fist connected with Bose's jaw. His boss swirled and landed in his desk chair, rolling across his office and slamming against the wall.

It was one hell of a resignation notice. Effective. But painful.

Now he raced down the highway to the only person who could help him make this right. If they didn't answer the door with a shotgun.

Chapter Thirty-Four

Ethan didn't have to worry about a shotgun greeting him at the Biddinger's door. His truck didn't even make it a mile into town before an army of parade floats and the high school band stopped him. Trailers covered with tissue paper flowers, streamers, and teenagers sitting on hay bales meandered down the main road at a slug's pace. A Thanksgiving parade... on Saturday. *How quaint.*

Even more podunkesque was a lone deputy guarding the street entrance from traffic. The harsh scowl was easy to identify from a hundred yards.

Adam Biddinger.

The uniform made the gruff man even more intimidating, but Ethan could tell he'd lived most of his life in uniform, one kind or another. The wide stance, squared shoulders: he wore it proudly.

Ethan pulled his truck into the alley behind the Piggly Wiggly, ignoring the *Employees/Vendors Only* sign at the entrance. Locking the doors was pointless because he had no valuables inside and everyone was focused on the parade. Beautiful mornings like this with a chill in the air were perfect for parades. And the potential for getting punched by a cop.

"Adam," Ethan called, crossing the street without looking. Again, pointless.

The man's eyes narrowed like a hawk spotting prey

from a half mile out. "What do you want?"

"We need to talk."

"The hell we do. I'm workin'."

"I need your help."

Adam blanched, but covered it with a grimace. "Are you drunk?"

"I wish."

"Go home, city boy."

"Not until you help me with your sister."

"Yeah, right," Adam scoffed, avoiding Ethan's gaze as he scanned the street. "That's at the top of my priority list."

"It should be."

A flatbed truck rolled up and honked, carrying picnic tables and chairs. Adam moved the barricade to let them through, ignoring Ethan.

"Talk to me, dammit!"

Still no recognition that he existed.

Without Adam, there was no point to his attempted apology to Audrey. He needed the whole family to make this plan work. And starting with the most challenging member was just Ethan's style: suicidal.

That's exactly the method he needed to use.

The nearest thing to him was the garbage can on the street corner. *Isn't that in the wrong spot? Damn, that should be pissing someone off.*

Ethan grabbed the metal can, lifted it over his head and tossed it in the street, spilling trash as it rolled into the barricade.

"What the hell, Tanner?"

Ha! That got his attention. "Destroying public property and littering. Arrest me."

"Did your balls just drop, you juvenile prick?"

"Arrest me."

"I'll do more than that if you don't get your ass out of here, now."

"I'll do whatever it takes to get you to help me."

Following a fierce look, Adam lifted his sunglasses from his shirt pocket and slipped them on. *Damn, the man was trained well.* Nothing battered him when he was focused. Time for something drastic.

Ethan punched the cop in the jaw, with his already sore fist. Adam's sunglasses flew off. The man's face was a brick wall. *Damn, I broke a few knuckles on that shit.* But it worked.

The devil's lair would have frozen over with Adam's glare. Before Ethan could think "Miranda Rights," he was tossed to the ground like a toothpick and handcuffed behind his back. "You're either incredibly stupid or desperate," Adam barked over him.

"Toss up for which one," Ethan huffed, the smell of the blacktop reminding him of his college brawls. He always hated this part, but at least the plan had worked. Adam had to take him to the station himself. Giving Ethan enough time to talk his sanity away with Audrey's brother, uninterrupted. He couldn't run off this time.

The back of the police vehicle was hardly the ideal place for this conversation. Certainly wasn't impressive to prove to the woman's brother that he was worthy of her. But beggars couldn't be picky. At least Adam had given Ethan a little dignity and left the lights and siren off. Or maybe he was too ashamed to admit that he let a man clock him in the middle of the street.

"Whatever you have stuck up your backside about your sister," Ethan started from behind the barred partition. "You have to let it go."

Adam didn't look at him or respond, but Ethan saw the man's jaw line tense.

"She needs your help."

"I thought you were the one that needed the help."

"That's obvious, but I don't care about me." *Damn, these cuffs hurt like hell. I really pissed him off.* "She's about to go through the worst moment in her life, again. All because of me, and she needs you."

Adam shook his head. "Not that I'm any fan of yours…or think she deserves my help, but what did you do?"

"You didn't read the paper this morning, did you?"

"Shit," Adam groaned and pulled the car over. Finally, he looked at Ethan in the rearview mirror. "You slaughtered her in the article, didn't you?"

"Long story, but yeah. Cat's *way* out of the bag on the car accident."

"Which means you dragged the Davises through that hell again, too."

"I'm not proud of myself. Look what I've resorted to: quitting my job, punching a cop, and going to jail just to prove how much I love her."

Ethan swore he could hear every beat of Adam's raging heart in the silence as he stared at him. Adam finally put the car into gear and turned around. Away from the station.

"Where are we going?"

"Pit stop before I book your ass."

"Where?"

"You owe someone an apology."

"Tell them to take a number. I'm making rounds."

The Davises porch was surrounded by flowerpots full of orange and red marigolds. Fresh paint emanated off the porch railing, gleaming white, that matched the hanging chair swing in the corner, where a white-haired lady sat, a book in her lap. *Mrs. Davis.*

The humiliation soared through the roof of the cop car he was cuffed in. *Please God, let this work.*

"Adam Biddinger?" Mrs. Davis called from the porch. "Is everything all right?"

"Mrs. Davis, someone here owes you an apology." He'd rounded the car and opened the back seat, the gravel driveway crunching underneath his feet as he reached inside to pull Ethan out.

By now, the woman had reached the bottom step and pulled her shawl around her shoulders. The drums of the band in the parade carried over the small forest lining the Davises' property line in the distance. The adorable lady hadn't attended the parade with everyone else. *My fault? Yeah, probably.*

"Who is this, Adam?"

"My name's Ethan Tanner, ma'am." *How can I sound more genuine in metal cuffs while held against a police car?* At least he could look the woman in the eye as she realized who he was. Looking into her eyes... recognition dawned on her face. *Yep. She read the article.* But somehow she didn't look as enraged as he'd expected.

"What in the world..." The screen door screeched open and Carl Davis stepped out. "Adam? What's goin' on, son? Is that...Ethan?"

"Yes, sir," Adam answered. "This is the man that wrote an article that dragged you all—"

"Adam," Carl stopped him. "We've not heard a

peep from you in ten years and *this* is how you want to start up a conversation? Bringing a man here in handcuffs?"

"He assaulted an officer."

Both the Davises blanched and looked to Ethan, who wanted to cringe under judgmental eyes, but he kept his chin up.

"You mean he punched you?" Carl deduced.

"It's the only way he'd talk to me," Ethan explained, stretching his wrists in the cuffs. "I have several apologies to make today, and the biggest one to Audrey. I need his help…and yours."

Carl descended the stairs and stood face to face with Adam, the sun gleaming off his spectacles.

"All this because of a silly article? Again?"

"It was disrespectful." Adam squared his jaw, the skin only now reddening after Ethan's punch. "To you, to Jack—"

"Jack's gone, son. Nothing can offend him."

Adam looked down and paused, almost subordinate. And annoyed. This cop was fighting something back. *Maybe the sour taste of being wrong?*

"What are you really here for?" Carl lifted his hand like he was going to hold Adam's shoulder, but stopped short.

"He tried to fight me."

"Just like you and Jack used to."

"This was different."

"How?" Carl caught his eyes.

"Because he's not Jack." Adam's voice rose and eyes flashed.

"No, he's not," Carl checked. "He's not Jack, Adam."

The Biddinger scowl reappeared, with a boiling rage that Ethan wouldn't dare tempt. But Carl had clearly seen it before—he wasn't backing down. *If anyone could reach this guy, maybe...just maybe.*

"If Jack were here, what would you say to him?"

"He's not here. Why does it matter?" Adam's rage trembled into a half-cry.

"Because I don't think anyone has asked you that question, and you need to answer it." Carl finally rested his hand on Adam's shoulder.

The apple of Adam's throat bobbed up and down and he looked away. This volcano was either going to burst red hot lava or a rain cloud so dense it would drown the Sahara.

"What would you say to him, Adam?"

"I'd punch his lights out!" The scream wrenched from Adam's chest, obvious to Ethan's ears. Like the urge had been buried for a decade because he wasn't allowed to say it.

Carl didn't move, nor did his expression change. Adam's admission, however shocking, didn't surprise the old man in the least. He kept on holding Adam's shoulder, with that reassuring empathy. The kind Ethan had always wanted from his own father, but never received.

"Why, son?"

Adam gripped his ears and looked like he would almost rip them off as he fought back the raging emotions—and failed. Red flooded his face as his teeth clenched.

"I know Jack was no saint. That day, I was so mad at him, I really wanted to deck him. The next time I saw him, just drop him to the floor and whale on him.

But…"

"But then you couldn't," Carl finished for him.

Adam turned his back, shaking his head. The radio on the shoulder of his deputy's uniform shook as he fought to control his emotions. The silence between the group would have been perfect timing for one of Ethan Tanner's zingers, but not if he needed to prove his worth. *And he was worth it, dammit.* The more Audrey's family pissed him off, the more he couldn't stay away. The more he had to gain their approval. This was worth it. For her.

"It was Jack's choice," Carl continued. "But living your life angry at a dead man isn't living." Mrs. Davis finally stepped off the porch and reached her husband's side, holding a handkerchief. "And redirecting your anger on Ethan…or Audrey, can't change what happened."

Mrs. Davis reached around Adam's arm and gave him the handkerchief. He'd stopped shaking and turned to look at her, his expression as if he'd been soundly beaten.

"Alienating your sister the way you have…" Her words were soft and tender. Ethan could feel the pain from twenty feet away. "Has that made you feel any better?" The woman's quiet question was perfectly clear in the chilly breeze.

It took a long time for Adam to respond, but he finally shook his head. Not only could the man listen, but the depth of sincerity was ocean deep. This man's need for self-preservation had ruined him for the last decade. *Thank God for the Davises. Why hadn't they done this years ago?*

By now, the cuffs were cutting into Ethan's wrists.

But the guilt of knowing the pain he caused these families with the wrong article was worse. What would they think of him if they read the real article? The one he wanted the paper to publish. Would they help him then?

It still wouldn't be enough. You need something more drastic to prove you're worthy.

The little voice of conscience grew more annoying every day, and Ethan wasn't used to demanding more of himself to please others.

"Adam," his voice croaked as he shifted his weight. The trio turned to look at him, though Adam's glare still made his feet itch. "The fundraiser for Audrey's Crisis Center is tonight. To get this thing off the ground, she needs to rock the house. She could use every ounce of support from her family."

The gravel crunched with every determined step Adam took toward Ethan. He stopped a foot away and bore a hole into Ethan. He removed his sunglasses from his pocket, the best frames impossible to wear.

"You broke my sunglasses."

"I'll buy you a new pair."

They stared each other down. Ethan refused to even blink, let alone look away. If this was the price of winning Audrey back, he'd take it. A night in jail, a criminal record, a pair of sunglasses and braving her brother's fury. *Could be a credit card ad.*

Ten agonizing seconds later, Adam pulled the keys from his belt and un-cuffed Ethan, who gripped his wrists in relief. But he never got a chance to say "thanks."

Adam clocked him in the face.

"We're even."

Chapter Thirty-Five

Audrey Allen was a walking hypocrisy.

Ten minutes before the Crisis Center Fundraiser, she sat in a back office of the hotel's ballroom letting the words of her speech blend into the white note cards. Canyon, her speech writer, argued with Miranda over a few semantics behind her, but their words also faded over her head.

Tonight was supposed to be about hope. Optimism and a fresh start for her life's dream and hundreds of women who desperately needed help.

Ironic when she felt completely dead inside. Hopeless.

The fabric of her black lace evening gown felt like silk under her fingers. The scattered jewels and beads gave the frock a touch of glamour that Miranda loved. They'd sparkle on stage under the bright spotlights, just as she herself was supposed to symbolize as a senator.

The boat neckline was her favorite feature, revealing her collarbone and a touch of cleavage. Reminiscent of fashion pioneer Princess Catherine, Duchess of Cambridge. But also stopping at the edge of her shoulder just before her scars. Not that covering them mattered anymore. The whole world knew of the accident now, thanks to Ethan. No doubt everyone would be staring at her left side waiting for any shift in material to see the atrocity up close.

"Audrey, we've got five minutes," Miranda rushed. "The part on overcoming obstacles that Canyon added will be the most poignant, so you need to be a touch slower there."

"A few places people may clap or cheer, so be prepared to stop. Don't feel like you have to rush through it." Canyon stretched over her shoulder and highlighted the section in yellow. The mid-twenty phenom was one of the best additions to her campaign, and definitely the best dressed. His tux with black on black tie was slightly more formal than his daily crisp suit and perfectly gelled dark hair. She'd hoped to have him with her on future campaigns. But just like herself, he'd be looking for another job after Tuesday's runoff vote, along with Miranda. All thanks to Ethan.

"Canyon." She stopped him. His hazel eyes, lightly emphasized with liner, looked back into hers expectantly, but so full of promise and determination. Just like hers used to be. "Did you always want to be a speech writer?"

He cocked his head and sat in an empty chair. "Yeah," he replied as he crossed his legs. "Brenner always said that I had a gift with words, but I hate the spotlight. So when he asked me to write a few of his conference speeches, I jumped on it. Loved it so much, and he had such a great response, I knew this was my niche."

"How long have you two been together?"

"Since college." He laughed to himself. "I was a fresh-out-of-the-closet freshman still wearing docks and baggy polos when Brenner saw me walking through the commons. I looked so lost, he told me. Hard to believe it's been seven years."

"What will you do after Tuesday?" Her question was honest, concerned, much like she expected her face to mirror.

"Audrey, you can't think like that. It's not over yet."

"Canyon...level with me."

He pursed his thin lips and rested his hand on her knee. "Your campaign has been the most fun I've ever had as a speech writer. Mostly because of you and Miranda. I'd love to stay right by your side, no matter what you do. As long as you'll have me."

She leaned forward, resting her hand over his. "Your talents are too impressive to be lost in tiny campaigns like mine. When this is done, you need to go where yours can make a bigger difference. Like gubernatorial races, or even presidential elections. You're that good."

"You know I love the flattery." He smiled. "But your campaign is only as small as you want it to be. I'm thinking much bigger."

Audrey smiled, then wiped under her eye, careful not to smudge the make-up that Canyon had done for her only an hour before.

"They haven't answered, have they?" he asked softly.

Audrey shook her head and took a deep breath. She'd tried to call the Davises all day, wishing she could have at least softened the blow before they read the article themselves. But it was a constant busy signal on the other end. No doubt they were reliving the torment at this very moment.

"Well, from what you said they told you, this article won't deter them much. Keep your chin up, girl."

Audrey's cell vibrated on the desk. Canyon picked it up for her and read the caller ID. "Damn, that's eight the past hour. That boy doesn't quit, does he?"

Audrey opened the phone and slammed it shut. Two-dozen phone calls to say "I'm sorry" wouldn't fix the damage he'd done to her election. The pain he'd caused Jack's family and her shattered heart would take more than that to heal.

"I'll hold it during the fundraiser," Canyon smiled with sympathy. "You don't need the reminder."

"Thank God for you, Canyon."

"Audrey," Miranda broke in from the open door. "It's time."

He stood and helped her up with both hands. He gripped her fingers and stared into her eyes with a serious smile.

"No, Aud. Thank God for you. Now go kick some ass."

Standing behind the curtains off stage, Audrey heard plates clanking on the tables, the semi-soft hum of gossiping and toasting. It was a packed house. Or supposed to be.

"A few empty chairs, but there's more than double the news cameras we expected." Miranda reported as she peeked through a few folds in the curtain.

"So, you're saying less of the kinda crowd we want, and more of the wrong kind?" Audrey summarized.

"We did the best damage control we could today," she replied with a slightly smaller smile than before. "If anyone can come back from that disaster article, it's you. But it's all up to the voters now."

"Maybe with a little luck," Canyon added. "Wyatt Williams will slip up a bit in his last few speeches."

"Enough," Audrey breathed, focusing on slowing her heartbeat. Every speech or public appearance always made her nervous. Her ritual—of reminding herself she was worth it and could make a difference—wasn't working tonight. "Let's just give these people a good party and make sure this Crisis Center gets off the ground running."

"Couldn't have said it better myself." Miranda gave her arm a squeeze and walked on stage, approaching the podium like Caesar to the Roman Forum.

What Audrey wouldn't give for Miranda's confidence right now. Instead, she fidgeted with the note cards in her hand and prayed for it. A quick pat of her dark hair pulled into a French twist gave no help.

"Good evening, ladies and gentleman," Miranda's energetic voice boomed throughout the room. "Thank you all so much for coming tonight."

The introduction continued as Audrey stared at her hands, waiting for her cue.

Is this what I really want?

Mrs. Davis' words rang through her head—between every applause through the ballroom, with every squeal of the microphone.

That night with Ethan, his honest words made her rethink everything. Or she thought they were honest. For all she knew, it was just his way to feel less guilty about sabotaging her campaign. Get her to think that another dream was possible, build up her hopes, and then run away as fast as his dirty feet could carry him.

But the prick plunged a thorn in her mind. The

glimmer of an idea beyond what she planned for herself. Could she do it?

"Please welcome our hostess for tonight, the woman who put everything in motion, Audrey Allen."

Peacemaker face.

Audrey lifted her chin and walked on stage, smile firmly in place. The spotlights blinded her view to the packed room, and a barrage of camera flashes matched the volume of the crowd's applause.

When she reached the podium, she gave Miranda a quick hug, the anchor she needed to keep from running.

"Make 'em love you, girl," she murmured in her ear, away from the microphone.

A moment later, she stood behind the podium, alone, facing a thousand sets of eyes, and countless more behind the twenty video cameras she counted from the tiny red lights in the back.

"Now *this* is what I call a party." Audrey kept her smile glued in place as cheers and laughter rippled through the room. A quick glance at the podium where her trusty cards rested didn't ease her nerves. Miranda and Canyon's thumbs-up from off stage didn't help either.

"Your support for this Crisis Center means more to these women than simple words can express. Everyone in this room knows, either from someone close or through personal experience, that life throws curveballs. Sometimes nasty ones that smack you in the face, or others that nail you right in the kneecaps. So hard that you need some help getting back on your feet."

Murmurs of approval throughout the crowd should have propelled her forward. Kept them hanging on every word. But she couldn't. The words on the cards in front of her blended together as did every light over her head.

People like you, offering a hand to help them up, make the difference.

The ink made no sense as she read it over and over, feeling the heat rise to her cheeks.

"You never think you're going to be the one who needs the help…"

Was that out loud? Stick to the plan, Audrey. Focus.

But the confidence never came and the emptiness consumed her, staring into the blinding lights.

If only she could breathe.

If only she didn't feel so naked…her scars exposed to the bone.

He thought so little of me. For the briefest moment, he made me feel like anything was possible, and then body-checked me into the mud.

Stop it. Don't crack up, Audrey. Not on stage. Not in front of all these people. Hold it together.

Silence.

More camera flashes. First one, then four, then six.

"Miss Allen, I have a favor to ask you."

The voice came from the darkness beyond the red lights, confident, silky and strong.

And loud.

Only one voice would be that forceful without any hint of respect or humility.

The crowd turned in one tsunami to identify the person as Audrey covered the lights with her hand to find him.

He stepped between the cameras and continued walking—almost strutting—to the side of the ballroom.

Ethan.

In a black tux with platinum tie and vest.

Wearing that half-smug smile and determined stare that she'd love if she didn't hate him so much.

Chapter Thirty-Six

Audrey clamped her jaw together to keep from her mouth falling to the floor. The jerk kept strutting toward her without the slightest hint of regret. This level of anger welling inside her meant only one thing. She loved the prick.

"Ladies and gentlemen, you're looking at the strongest woman in politics. You know that, or you wouldn't be here supporting her."

Audrey's hands were fused to the podium, anything to keep her knees from giving out as this man attempted to destroy her more. She felt Miranda and Canyon step on stage from the wings, but for what purpose? They couldn't stop him. Ask him to leave, sure. But he wouldn't listen.

Maybe to keep me from collapsing.

"But there's one thing you don't know about this woman."

Oh God. What else could he possibly have to spill that he hadn't thrown up in his article?

"Mr. Tanner, if you'd care to take a seat," Miranda interrupted. "The focus for tonight is the Crisis Center."

"Yes it is." He never took his eyes off of Audrey. "And I've brought several people with me who pledge their support for Audrey's dream. As well as their vote."

He motioned to the back doors and Audrey

squinted to see beyond the spotlight.

Holy shit.

Her mouth finally dropped.

"I'd like to introduce Paul and Claire Davis," Ethan continued as the elderly couple moved to the side of the room, hand in hand. Each smiling at Audrey with pride. "For those of you who haven't read the paper this morning, they lost their son in a tragic accident ten years ago. The same accident in which Audrey almost lost her life as well."

Whispers and grumblings around the room made him pause. But not long.

"They're here to show their support for Audrey Allen and this Crisis Center. Along with her family."

Audrey hadn't noticed that right behind the Davises was her mother, teary-eyed and grinning, as well as her father, hands shoved firmly in his suit pockets, the uncomfortable scowl still in place, but his eyes as wide as the room.

Followed by Adam. Slowly escorting a waddling Sally and bubbly Adelaide on his arms.

When she finally absorbed her family's presence, including Adam's humble stare, Ethan had climbed the stage and stood a few feet away from her. A nasty bruise covered the side of his chin. But those eyes. How they looked straight into her, blew open the last remaining shields surrounding her heart and caressed.

All she could do was stare at him as he moved forward and took the microphone off the podium, his hand wrapped in medical tape. Everything about him, his eyes, his gestures, his aura, said *trust me*.

"These two families know devastation." His quasi-preacher style voice rang throughout the room. "They know what it's like to be fast balled in the kneecaps, as Audrey put it. To sacrifice. They know loss and heartache, probably more than anyone else here. Except for Audrey. That's why Crisis Centers like this can make a huge difference. And Audrey's right…" He looked straight at her, right into her eyes down into her heart. "You never think it's going to happen to you. Until that horrible moment where you're lying on a cold, rain-covered road. Alone."

For a second, Ethan's voice broke, studying Audrey's face and his hand over his heart.

"No one should have to face that devastation alone," he softened. "These folks here know that. They spend their lives helping others. They support Audrey. Because they love her. And you all should, too."

Though tearing her eyes away from Ethan's commanding presence was hard, she looked at her family, standing beside the Davises, smiling and ignoring the continuous camera flashes in their faces. Adam had placed his hand over his heart, and the grimace she'd thought he'd permanently etched onto his face was gone. Only replaced with strength, honor. A true military man. Pride.

And the tears slipped out.

"Many of you know there's a small election this Tuesday." Ethan smiled through the chuckles. "Each of these folks here with me tonight pledge their vote for Audrey. And so do I."

Sparse applause scattered among the crowd and Ethan stepped forward, taking Audrey's hand from the podium and holding it like a rare jewel. "I also pledge a donation to the Women's Crisis Center of ten thousand dollars. In Audrey's name."

The applause erupted through the entire room now as she trembled. Whistles and cheers filled the air, but all she could see was Ethan. He set the microphone on the podium and held both her hands.

The arrogance was gone. Only penitence and unending affection glimmered in his eyes. "I love you. I will spend the rest of my life making this up to you. To show how important you are. And how much a difference you've made in my life. Even if you still hate me, I love you."

Through the applause, now a standing ovation, Ethan wrapped his arms around her waist and kissed her. Hesitant at first, waiting for permission. Audrey snaked her hands around his neck and gave in. Releasing her anger with one glide of her tongue along his teeth, the room faded around them in bright lights.

Chapter Thirty-Seven

Adam stood in the back office, shoulders stiff and gray suit stretched along his chest, proud and humble simultaneously. Her parents and the Davises stood just outside chatting with Ethan and mingling with the other donors.

"You look incredible," Adam whispered, having a hard time looking her in the eye.

"Thank you," Audrey smiled, his compliment stunning her to the chair.

"Ethan drove back this morning and we…had a chat."

"Ah," Audrey nodded. "That explains his nasty bruise. And your swollen knuckles."

Adam shrugged and rubbed his palm. "A gentlemen's understanding. He brought Mom and Dad along. The Davises too. Said some things that put stuff into perspective for me." Adam sat in the free chair across from her and leaned his elbows on his knees.

"I owe you an apology. Several, actually." He cleared his throat and looked away.

"Adam, it doesn't matter."

"No. I…" He cleared his throat again. "After your accident, that reporter came around asking for comments while you were still in the hospital. Mom and Dad kicked him off the porch. Then he saw me down at the barn and asked me a whole bunch of

289

questions. I was so angry and hurt that I just started talkin'. That morning, I had found the pregnancy test in the bathroom trash and knew. I was so angry. At both of you. And I lost it. But I had no idea the reporter was gonna twist it the way he did. I'm the one who's responsible."

"Why didn't you say something to me?"

"I could hardly look at you. I was so cooped up in my own resentment."

"For ten years?"

"No, that was more guilt."

"And stubbornness."

"And stubbornness. I was wrong. It's no excuse. What Ethan said…how you were left alone… I didn't understand." Adam wiped a tear from his cheek, then another. "I'm so sorry." And her big brother, the embodiment of strength and protection, cried into his hands.

Audrey stood and hugged him, cradling his head into her shoulder. He gripped her back, letting it come, and as quickly as it started, the tears slowed.

"I love you," she whispered into his hair. "I'm so glad you're here."

"I'm proud of you, Audrey," he said as he held her hands. "Jack would be proud."

Audrey smiled and took a deep breath, letting her brother's praise sink in. "*There's* my brother. It's been a while since I've seen him."

He laughed and wiped his cheek.

"Jack would be proud of you, too."

"Yeah, well…only on some things." Adam grinned. "But one thing hasn't changed."

"What's that?"

"You're still thicker skulled."

"Oh ho! You ain't seen nothin' yet! Let's go back out there and get a drink."

****

Ethan stood on the sidelines nursing a ginger ale as Audrey maneuvered the room, thanking everyone for their support and mingling with the city's do-gooders. Between the hugs, handshakes, and toasts, Ethan watched her chat with every single person. From million-dollar chummies, to those who could only afford the dinner plate. Including a few women from the Crisis Center, in brand new dresses and hairstyles, all on Audrey's dime.

She was the same Audrey with each one of them. Genuine, caring, and one of a kind. This wasn't glad-handing or pandering, like Ethan had seen countless politicians do, including her competitor Wyatt Williams. And his father. *Finally, someone worthy of valuable press.*

Ethan sipped the last of his ginger ale and ordered another. He didn't realize he'd gotten so cynical over the last several years. The anger at his father had festered and left him bitter. And it didn't help that his former boss was the king of cynics and encouraged him into the wrong things. That was Bose's choice, and you couldn't teach an old snake any tricks, let alone new ones.

But Ethan still had time to change. As Audrey accepted another toast with authentic humility, and threw him a wink from across the room, he actually had the desire to change. Or more accurately, stay exactly the same, but redirect his focus to helping the campaigns instead of hindering them and pointing out flaws.

Anyone can point out flaws, he thought as he meandered around the tables toward Audrey's latest crowd, which included the Dallas mayor. But the only people who made real change in life were those that pointed out solutions and focused on the positive aspects. Like the Crisis Center.

In the darkest parts of a woman's life, or a man's, sometimes the smallest glimmer of help can make the difference. Can turn their lives around and create the next Audrey Allen, Tony Robbins, or Ted Turner.

But more promising was that Audrey's family was here to support her. Despite all the suffering, she had her family back, especially her brother. Adam recognized the Hail Mary pass that Carl Davis gave him earlier today, and he caught it. Ten years off the football field and he could still recover downs and save a shitty play. Amazingly, Ethan didn't need trick questions or journalist games. Only the truth. Not to mention a mean right hook and a shit-load of guts.

Ethan reached Audrey's side as the crowd dispersed and pulled her into a sideways hug, kissing the top of her forehead.

"You look like you're having fun," he said.

"Tons, but I'm exhausted."

"You look so incredible, I have to chew on my glass to keep from taking you right here in this room."

"Then I'll be sure to thank Canyon for helping me pick out this dress." She pressed her lips against his, lingering for several seconds. "He could give you a few pointers on your wardrobe, too. Although this suit would be a favorite of his."

"No, thanks. I've lost enough of my man-card

today by begging. Can't afford the loss of my remaining masculinity by asking for style tips."

Audrey laughed. "What begging?"

Ethan held up his bandaged hand. "To get your father to open the door today and put down the shotgun. Myrna and Adelaide forced him to sit and listen to me. Felt like a teenager who stole his daughter."

"He brought out the shotgun, huh? You should know better than to cross the porch of an East Texan who holds a grudge."

"Proof enough that you mean that much to me?"

Audrey chuckled again and kissed his neck.

"Are you ready to go?" Ethan traced his finger along her neckline and across the lace on her shoulder.

"Almost. I need to thank the registration desk ladies."

"Oh my God." His finger stopped when he reached her bra, also lace with more intricate designs. And even thinner.

"What?"

"Is this a teddy?" He groaned. "I'm dying to see this."

Audrey laughed and kissed the tip of his nose. "Soon. Very soon."

"Please tell me Canyon didn't pick that out for you as well."

"You'll never know."

Epilogue

"Audrey, these paintings are phenomenal, but we need the space for when your family gets here."

Ethan collected the unfinished canvases from the dining room and moved them into the bedroom. The table and chairs had become easels over the last few months, the walls were covered with sketches, both in color and back and white, as Audrey poured her creativity and emotions into every piece.

"I have five more I need to finish in time for the auction next week," Audrey called from the kitchen, trimming the ham and shoving it in the oven. "Besides, it's not like they haven't seen my work before."

"You want us to eat with our elbows in paint swatches?"

"How is that any different than the last four months?" Audrey stepped around the corner and leaned against the wall, pulling her hair out of its ponytail and rubbing her fingers against her scalp.

God, she looked incredible. Even paint smudges on her cheeks didn't stop the raging passion he had for this woman. He set down the last canvas and moved to her, wrapping his arms around her lower waist and pulling her into him.

"Because I don't mind washing paint off you with my bare hands and licking your entire body clean."

Their kiss was slow, savory and deep. Ethan's

fingers dove into her hair, twirling the soft curls around his thumbs and lingering over her earlobes. It was only a taste of what was to come.

"We've got a lot things to do before they get here." Audrey gave a quick squeeze to Ethan's butt before turning and finishing up in the kitchen.

"Easter dinner at your apartment was your idea. Lord only knows you wouldn't have time for all of this had you been elected senator."

"Thanks to you," she called back to him.

"You're going to keep hounding my ass on that one, aren't you?"

"But it's such a cute ass."

When she moved to help clean up the dining room, Ethan pulled her back and held her in place with his eyes.

"I'm so sorry."

"Stop apologizing, Ethan."

"I thought the other article that I made Bose publish would help patch things up, but…"

"Ethan, I love you. I'm happy. If I resented you for that article, I wouldn't have asked you to move in. So drop the guilt. It doesn't look good on you."

"At least it was a close election. If you wanted to run again in the future you could. But, Miranda will never forgive me."

"Sure she will." Audrey went back to chopping carrots. "She already warmed up to you after the donation you gave the Crisis Center. Besides, she's too busy keeping Canyon in line with the governor's race next year. A Jewish campaign manager and gay speechwriter on the Republican ticket's staff. I love Texas."

"That's a killer promotion for them."

"Just don't get on her bad side again. I'm only a Peacemaker in politics, and I can't have my best friend and boyfriend at each other's throats."

"You deserved the senate seat."

Audrey took a deep breath and set down the knife. Ethan's disappointed lips would only smile again with another kiss. So she did. But Ethan still wouldn't let it go.

"You could have done so much more than that Wyatt—"

"Just as much as you deserved New York."

Ethan cupped Audrey's face, mesmerized by her unfailing faith. "I realized I wanted something more."

Audrey kissed him again, this one more sweet and endearing. "Greedy."

Two hours later after cleaning, cooking, and a quick romp in the bedroom, Audrey was fresh out of the shower and composed as she opened the door to her parents and Adelaide. Her mother and sister, both smiled, holding foil-covered dishes that filled her entryway with memories of childhood Sunday dinners. Her father's stubborn façade lifted only slightly as he offered a closed smile and one-armed hug before stepping into her apartment with reserved eyes.

"Paul, good to see you." Ethan shook hands with Audrey's father. "Hope the drive was quiet."

Audrey's father grimaced and finished looking around the living room. No doubt looking for any blatant evidence of Ethan's personal possessions. Living with his daughter. Unmarried. "Fat chance with those two."

"Oh hush," Myrna interjected. "You love being

surrounded by women. Audrey, sweetie, where can I set these dishes?"

"Right on the table. The ham should be done in about fifteen minutes. Where's Adam and Sally? I want to see my nephew."

"They'll be along in just a minute. Kid threw a fit in the car." Paul grunted. "Awful lot of ruckus that one makes."

"Poor Adam." Ethan smiled. "Did the baby sleep through it?"

Adelaide laughed as she plopped herself on the couch and started flipping through the magazines on the coffee table. When she realized they were news and political magazines, not *Cosmo* or *US Weekly*, she started perusing the photo albums and frames scattered about the room.

"How long have you been living here, Ethan?"

The two men's eyes locked on one another, and the silent duel filling the space between them caught even Myrna's and Audrey's attention. Even after the heart-to-heart four months ago, the burly guy was still skeptical of Ethan. Not that Ethan could blame him. Neither of them was accustomed to backing down.

"One month," Audrey replied for them, failing to hide a smile.

Paul never took his eyes from Ethan. "New York turned you down?"

"Other way around."

Paul grunted.

"Hey, Addy. Don't I get a hug?" Ethan turned from the awkward tension building between he and Paul, and held out his arms. "I don't get to hug a beauty queen very often. Congrats!"

Adelaide grinned and jumped off the couch and into Ethan's hug. "The judges gave me higher scores for my tumbling routine. Everyone else sang or tap danced."

"She had the whole audience on their feet," Myrna added from the kitchen.

"Was Brace there?" Ethan murmured so only Adelaide could hear.

"No," she smirked. "I kicked him to the wings. He wasn't interested in a hands-off relationship."

"Good for you." Ethan hugged her again. "You're too smart for playboys like that. You can do better."

A knock sounded at the door and in walked Sally, carrying a small and loud bundle in her arms, followed by Adam. To say the new parents looked exhausted with frazzled faces and extra luggage under their eyes was like saying the Middle East had anger management issues.

"This place looks lovely," Sally almost panted as Adam dropped the armful of gear by the door. The poor guy looked like he'd been slugged by a perpetrator. A four month old perp.

"Aud, where's the can?"

"Down the hallway." She held out her arms to take the screaming child from Sally. Adam darted off like his bladder was on a meter that ran out of coins.

"Meet Jackson Davis Biddinger," Sally beamed. Ethan had heard the story of how they decided to change the baby's name after the fundraiser. New name or not, this kid cried a lot.

Good Lord, babies are a lot of work. They needed an entire entourage to manage them. Ethan stepped forward to see the kid, who at first glance looked like nothing but bulges of skin. But as Audrey held him, an oddly peaceful and fulfilling smile on her face, even Ethan warmed to the kid's whimpers.

****

Audrey held her nephew with a tinge of sorrow in the back of her mind. Remembering the baby she almost bore all those years ago was a new feeling, but she let it enter her thoughts and simmer for a moment. And just as quickly, it vanished. Her nephew's face turned lobster red as he continued to scream, no matter how she positioned him. Over the shoulder, tucked like a football in her elbow, or on his tummy. Nothing eased him.

"This colic will be the death of me." Sally plopped on the couch just as Myrna held out a glass of water.

Adam returned, looking a little more composed. "Sorry. I was holding that since we hit Forney." He wrapped an arm around Audrey's shoulder and kissed her forehead, then his son's. "I promise he doesn't cry *all* the time."

"How long does colic last?" Ethan asked.

"A few more months," Sally replied. "Maybe."

"Ethan, good to see you." Adam shook his hand. "Found another paper to scandalize?"

"Nope."

"He runs the Crisis Center's publicity now," Audrey chimed in, still trying to calm her nephew.

"Ethan, be a real man. Hold a baby." Adam grinned. Jackson screamed louder.

"I don't think I'm qualified."

"Nothing to it. Just hold the head like an egg."

Before Ethan had another second to protest, Adam lifted Jackson from his sister's hands and rested the bundle in Ethan's arms. The kid fidgeted and fussed as Ethan balanced the head against the crook of his elbow. And finally the baby stopped crying.

"I broke it." Ethan panicked.

"Wow." Adam stared. "Exactly the opposite."

"What do you mean?"

Jackson's face turned a light pink color as he looked straight up at Ethan with the same dark blueberry eyes as Audrey and stared. Ethan couldn't move. Just stood there watching this kid watch him. Any second, this baby would start screaming again. Somehow Ethan had broken something and it was only a little time before the kid felt it. But he never did. He just kept looking at Ethan.

Sally shot up from the couch and tiptoed over to Ethan. "How did you do that?"

"Do what?"

"Whatever you do, don't stop."

"Stop what? I haven't done anything."

Quiet gasps sounded all around him as Jackson slowly closed his eyes and dozed, safe against Ethan's chest.

"Hallelujah," Adam murmured. "You've got the magic touch, Ethan. Who'da thought?"

Sally placed her hands on Ethan's shoulders and slowly guided him to the couch. "Sit down as softly as you can. Try not to wake him."

As soon as Ethan was settled on the couch, the rest of the adults went into the kitchen to fix a drink and get dinner on the table, leaving the writer alone with the first baby he'd ever held.

Jackson made little sucking noises as his lips twitched. He continued to slumber against Ethan's shirt.

Babies had always seemed daunting to him throughout his life, but he was surprised at how relaxed he felt right now. Once he'd stopped screaming, the kid was actually kinda…adorable.

This wouldn't be so bad, after all.

****

Audrey leaned against the wall for a moment, watching Ethan look into her nephew's face. Something crawled into her gut at how natural he looked. Kissing him right now could wake the baby, so she refrained. But the urge was intense.

Wow. The feeling hit her like a slug to the face. But instead of a painful bruise afterwards, an incredible joy and peace consumed her. *He's it for me.*

"Heavens, Audrey. How much food did you cook?"

Audrey turned back into the kitchen and saw her mother wearing her rooster mitts and pulling the ham out of the oven.

"I wanted to take leftovers to the Crisis Center this afternoon." Audrey beamed as she unrolled the foil away from the ham. Steam filtered in the air and the savory smell swarmed her face. Her first Easter ham. "We've got a mother with three kids staying there this weekend and they could use some home cookin'."

"I'm so proud of you." Myrna kissed her on the cheek. "Not just for this incredible meal, which I'm glad you paid attention back in high school. I could have sworn you were more interested in scribbling in that journal book. But also for that Center. Everyone back home keeps asking about it."

"It's been a great success so far. The application list for therapists and counselors is a foot deep, and donations keep pouring in." Audrey pulled out napkins and silverware and set them on the counter. "Dad, can you set these on the dining room table?"

Without a word Paul complied, never setting down his beer can.

"And thanks to Ethan," Audrey continued. "We have journalists writing pieces about us every week."

"Have the Davises been by to see it yet?" Adam asked, carrying over a bowl of corn to the table.

"No. They're coming in over Memorial Day to see it. Mrs. Davis agreed to speak about handling grief. A perfect topic for the women there. We have so many workshops set up over the next month, I'm so excited. After dinner, I'd like to take you all over for a tour."

"As long as Ethan keeps that baby in his arms, I'm up for anything," Sally laughed.

A short while later with Jackson resting comfortably in his car seat on the floor, everyone sat at the dining room table with the Easter feast in front of their noses. Audrey's dining set only came with five cushioned chairs, so she and Adelaide sat in folding chairs, everyone rubbing elbows.

"A little smaller than Mama's table," Paul commented, placing a napkin in his lap. "But still cozy."

"The pocketbook is still a little tight to look at houses." Audrey filled her glass with wine. "Maybe someday soon."

After they said grace, Ethan held up his glass of sparkling cider for a toast. "To family and full tummies." He glanced at Jackson, sleeping away. "Happy Easter." Everyone clinked glasses.

"Ethan, why don't you carve the ham." Audrey

winked at him from across the table.

"Sure." He stood and walked around the table. But instead of grabbing the knife, he reached into his pocket and pulled out a black velvet box and set it on the table. Right on Audrey's plate.

Silence spread across the room. Audrey caught her breath and looked at the box like it might disappear any second.

Suddenly, Adelaide giggled in quick, soft spasms. "Oh my God. Really? Oh my God!"

"Shh!" Sally hissed and held the girl's hand.

The simple, small box was too pretty to open. If there were earrings or a pearl bracelet inside, Audrey would die of disappointment. She wanted a life with Ethan. *Could he have possibly realized it before me? There's no way I'm this lucky.*

Her mother dabbed at her eyes with a napkin, grinning, while her father had an amused tilt to his lips. *Really? Even Dad is okay with this?*

The thought of his approval, of his pride and acceptance, couldn't have filled her with more joy.

Well, maybe one thing could do more.

She finally braved to look at the man still standing next to her. He had that playful smile that she loved. *Please don't let this be a joke. A gimmick. A practical joke that would crush my heart.*

"Don't look so scared. Open it." He put his hands in his pockets.

A heartbeat and deep breath later, she did. A keychain. With two silver keys attached.

"Please don't tell me these are the keys to your heart. That is way too cliché for a gifted writer like you."

"These are keys to something more practical." He pulled out a folded paper from the same pocket and handed it to her. When she opened it, she gasped. A picture of a house. A gorgeous, but simple, one-story home with navy blue shutters and a glass door.

"The deed is in your name. We're free to move in when your lease is up here."

"How did you—"

"I used the money I saved for New York." He pulled his hand from his other pocket and knelt in front of her. "A house to go with this."

The diamond ring sparkled under her eyes, the silver band polished so thoroughly it was like a mirror.

Adelaide giggled again, only a little more hysterically.

"Addy, hush!" Adam whispered.

Ethan's playful smile was gone, replaced with the same look he gave her when he woke up in the morning. Completely happy and serene.

"This was my mother's ring. The one she sacrificed so I could go to college. That I bought back. It's fitting that this one remaining token of my mother's love resides on your hand. The only other woman I've loved."

A small sob came from Audrey's mother and she covered her mouth. Ethan smiled through it. "Your family gave me their blessing. The idea of a family has grown on me so much ever since I met you, there's no other life I want. A life with you. I want to wake up with you every morning, live your dreams right beside you, and go to sleep every night the same way."

Audrey's eyes misted over until all she could see was Ethan's face and the glittering diamond ring.

"Please marry me, Audrey."

This wasn't a practical joke. This was real. She couldn't stop the giddiness inside of her if she wanted to. It was amazing this man realized the truth before she did.

"Hurry up and answer, hon," her father grinned. "The food is getting cold."

When everyone started laughing, Audrey leaned forward and kissed Ethan. "I will, you greedy man."

A word about the author...

Susan writes contemporary romance, romantic suspense, and women's fiction. After spending six years in the corporate world, her true passion wouldn't let go and she's been writing ever since. She lives and laughs in Texas with her husband and son.

...

Follow Susan Sheehey on her website:
www.susansheehey.com
as well as on Facebook & Twitter.